DOCUMENTS RELATING TO THE SENTIMENTAL AGENTS IN THE VOLYEN EMPIRE

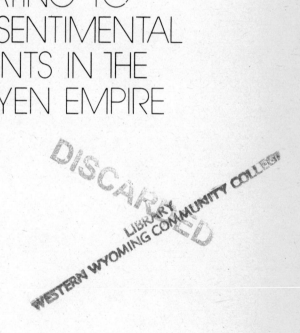

DORIS LESSING

CANOPUS IN ARGOS: ARCHIVES

DOCUMENTS RELATING TO THE SENTIMENTAL AGENTS IN THE VOLYEN EMPIRE

VINTAGE BOOKS

A DIVISION OF RANDOM HOUSE   NEW YORK

First Vintage Books Edition, March 1984

Copyright © 1983 by Doris Lessing

All rights reserved under International and Pan-American
Copyright Conventions. Published in the United States by
Random House, Inc., New York. Originally published by
Alfred A. Knopf, Inc. in 1983.

Library of Congress Cataloging in Publication Data

Lessing, Doris May, 1919–

Documents relating to the sentimental agents in the
Volyen Empire.

(Canopus in Argos—archives)

I. Title.

II. Series: Lessing, Doris, 1919–
Canopus in Argos—archives.

PR6023.E833D59 1984   823'.914   83-40297

ISBN 0-394-72386-4 (pbk.)

Manufactured in the United States of America

This is the fifth in the novel-sequence

CANOPUS IN ARGOS: ARCHIVES.

The first was *Re: Colonised Planet 5, Shikasta.*

The second, *The Marriages Between Zones Three, Four, and Five.*

The third, *The Sirian Experiments.*

The fourth, *The Making of the Representative for Planet 8.*

DOCUMENTS RELATING TO THE SENTIMENTAL AGENTS IN THE VOLYEN EMPIRE

KLORATHY, FROM INDEPENDENT
PLANET VOLYEN, TO
JOHOR ON CANOPUS.

I requested leave from service on Shikasta; I find myself on a planet whose dominant feature is the same as Shikasta's. Very well! I will stick it out for this term of duty. But I hereby give notice, *formally*, that I am applying to be sent, when I'm finished here, to a planet as backward as you like, as challenging as you like, but not one whose populations seem permanently afflicted by self-destructive dementia.

Now for my initial report. I have been here five V-years, and can confirm recent reports that our agent Incent did succumb to an attack of Rhetoric—not, after all, unknown, and not, as I may remind you, always unwelcome if regarded as an inoculation against worse—but unfortunately he did not recover, and suffers still from a stubborn condition of Undulant Rhetoric.

It was ten V-years ago that he fell to the wiles of Shammat, reporting his reactions in a letter which I attach herewith. Please see that it reaches the Archives.

Klorathy, I am taking the liberty of writing to you direct, instead of to the Colonial Office, because of our meeting when I came home to Canopus on leave last year and you said you had been assigned my supervision. I feel that what I want to ask is so important it goes beyond my little personal problems, but on the other hand I have no actual administrative problems as such to report.

To come to the point, I met someone on this planet's second planet, Volyendesta, when I was there because of the riots, which necessitated the withdrawal of Volyen's Imperial Forces. I do not have to tell you that all through my training as Colonial Servant, and during my briefing session, the dangers of Shammat were drummed into me—and everyone else! But imagine my surprise after the most inspiring evening of my whole life when I found that my companion was from Shammat!

When he said he was Krolgul of Shammat I thought he was joking. I was awake all night in torment, Klorathy; I can't remember ever spending such an awful night. Then I met him again by chance in the courts as the rebels were being sentenced, and I saw a man of such compassion, such warmth of heart, such sensitivity to others' sufferings. This was the terrible Shammat! This wonderful being who wept as the rebels were led out to execution! I spent the next weeks with him. I was given a view of, first, Volyen, and then of the Volyen "Empire." I put it in inverted commas as is our Canopean way—but does this not show arrogance on our part? The Volyen Empire, consisting of the two moons, Volyenadna and Volyendesta, and two neighbouring planets, Maken and Slovin in Volyen terminology (the Sirian planets PE 70 and PE 71), hardly stands comparison with our Rule, or that of the Sirian Empire, but from their point of view it is something, an achievement. I was quite ashamed to see Krolgul's ironic but kind smile when I spoke of the Volyen Empire with what I am afraid I now see as something not far from contempt.

And it was not only of Volyen affairs but of Sirius and ourselves as well that I was introduced to a very different view.

So different there was a point when I realized, and with what shock and distress I hardly dare to say, that my attitude was no longer consistent with that of a loyal servant of Canopus.

I am prepared to offer my resignation. What shall I do?

Your always grateful pupil,

Incent.

I did not reply to this, though, of course, had he resigned I would have asked him to reconsider. But he did not. I heard he was sufficiently involved with the rebel forces on Volyendesta, to the point where he was wounded in the arm and had to be hospitalized. Since I was due in the Volyen system, I decided to wait till I had seen him.

Volyen itself seethes with emotions of all kinds, its four colonies no less—to the extent that there is nowhere I could place Incent hoping he would be free from the stimulus of words long enough to recover his balance. No, I had either to send him home to Canopus with the recommendation that he was unfit for Colonial Service, and this I was reluctant to do—as you know, I am always unwilling to waste such experiences in young officials who might be strengthened by them in the long run—or to regard it as a case where we must decide to exercise patience.

Of course we can decide to submit him to the Total Immersion Cure, but that does seem rather a last resort. Meanwhile, he is still in hospital.

THE HISTORY OF THE VOLYEN EMPIRE.
SUMMARY CHAPTER. (EXCERPTS.)

This is the largest planet of a Class 18 Star situated on the remotest verges of the Galaxy, on the outside edge of its outer spiral arm. It is in a very poor position for Harmonic Cosmic Development; and for this reason it has never been part of the Canopean Empire. We did not do more than maintain Basic Surveillance for thirty thousand Canopean years. At the beginning of this period an evolutionary leap had taken the population from Type 11 to Type 4 (that is to say, Galactian Basic), and a predominantly gathering-and-hunting type soon developed agriculture, trade, and the beginnings of metallurgy, and built towns. There was little contact between Volyen and near planets. Then, because of a cosmic disturbance resulting from the violent "soul-searchings" of the neighbouring Sirian Empire, the population increased rapidly, material development accelerated, and a ruling caste came to dominate the entire planet, making slaves of nine-tenths of the population. All the planets in that sector were similarly affected, and there began a period of history during which they have been invading and settling one another, as short-lived and unstable "Empires," for twenty-one C-years.

Volyen has several times been dominant, and several times a subject.

The Sirian Empire, like us, had never made any attempt to absorb Volyen. During Volyen's stable period, Sirius was more or less stable and had made a decision not to expand. When Sirian influences upset the balances of Volyen, it was because of the turmoil, from end to end of the Sirian Empire, attendant upon the conflict between the two parties known as the Conservers and the Questioners, a conflict that split even the governing oligarchy of Sirius, the Five. Some of their outlying planets rebelled, and were instantly punished. Some asked to be permitted to secede and become self-governing. There were reprisals. These energetic, not to say savage, measures caused the Questioners to redouble their protests and demands that Sirius should be studying its own nature and potentialities from points of view not exploitative. For a short period the Conservers were dominant, and the Questioners were also punished. While all this upheaval went on, the fact that Volyen, in a dominant phase again, had developed its armies and sent them out to conquer its two moons, or planet's planets, went virtually unnoticed. When Volyen dubbed itself the Volyen Empire, Sirius, like us, merely noted the fact, as we had done before. But when Volyen expanded beyond its own planets and sent armies into the two other planets of its solar system, Sirius did take notice. For these two planets had been for S-millenniums subjects of sharp debate and disagreement. When the Sirian Empire, long before this time, had made a decision not to expand further, it was these two planets (Maken and Slovin) that had been next on the list for conquest and colonization. Neither we nor Sirius had named these planets; in their system they were designated PE 70 and PE 71 (Possible Expansion). The Questioners volubly, not to say violently, objected to having any attention whatsoever paid to this "Empire," which from their point of view was useless because of its backwardness, but they were overruled. The decision of the Sirian governing body, the Four, to "punish" Volyen, and to claim PE 70 and PE 71, marked the beginning of a renewed Sirian expansion, which was nothing like the planned and controlled developments of Sirian expansion under the Five but was the result of internal convulsions. The Sirian Empire made a wild surge outwards, intensifying its own instability, and leading inevitably to its collapse.

NOTE BY ARCHIVIST. Klorathy arrived in the Volyen "Empire" when its two planets and Sirian PE 70 and PE 71 were in revolt and rebellion against Volyen, and before Sirius invaded.

KLORATHY TO JOHOR, FROM
MOON II OF VOLYEN, VOLYENDESTA.

Apologies. I have been engaged in cultivating Shammat on Volyen's planets, found myself afflicted by brief attack of Shammatis, put myself into Restorative Detention while it lasted, and came out to deal with Incent, as a priority. This because of the key role he is now in with Shammat. I told you Incent was hospitalized for a flesh wound. I had him transferred to the Hospital for Rhetorical Diseases, and went to visit him there.

I positioned this hospital on Volyendesta because of probability forecasts that Volyen itself, as its "Empire" collapses, will be savagely overrun, whereas Volyendesta will be little affected. As indication of the healthy state of Volyendesta: Agent 23 was able to have the hospital built and equipped by the rebellious party that is led by a rather remarkable character, one Ormarin, of whom more later, on whose *comparative* freedom from illusions I am learning to rely. The concept of the hospital, as I explained it to him, amounting to a (for him) completely new outlook on (as he put it, in the current Volyen mode) "the nature of the class struggle"—but we must not expect too much too soon—caused in him a sharp but fortunately short attack of Elation. You will of course have seen that his agreement to build this hospital was partly due to a misunderstanding of our purposes. By the time he had really understood, the place was up and in use. There followed the routine riots and protests. But the effort at attempting to understand this hospital, the discussions and debates, some of them violent: this process itself caused the creation of a new faction, political in expression, which came to support and strengthen Ormarin.

Volyendesta is a watery planet, with a large, rapidly circumgyrating moon afflicting its inhabitants with a vast variety of unstable moods; but the sheer effort needed to cope with these conditions has evolved a breed (partly originating, as you will recall, from the Volyen stock) able to withstand rapid changes of emotional condition while ostensibly succumbing to them. On my first visit to this planet I was disheartened by its inhabitants' violent reactions to everything, but soon came to see that these could be regarded, rather, as surface storms over a comparatively untouched interior. And I saw that a few of the inhabitants had even been able to use this condition of constant stimulation to evolve and strengthen inner calm. Ormarin is one.

I went straight to the Hospital for Rhetorical Diseases. This, on advice from Ormarin which Agent 23 was quick to take, is called by them the Institute for Historical Studies. I was in the guise of a lecturer visiting the place to judge whether I wished to take up an appointment.

The site was chosen after consultation with their geographers to provide the maximum opportunities for natural stimulation. It is on a short and very high peninsula on a stormy coast, where the ocean is permanently in a tumultuous roar, and where its moon has full effect. Immediately behind the peninsula the mainland affords, within achievable limits, extremes of terrain. On one side rise grandiose and gloomy mountains, full of the graves of overambitious mountaineers. On the other reach vast and ancient forests, guaranteed to bring on thoughts of age, the passing of time, inevitable decay. And, extending almost to the hospital itself, a ridge of barren, rocky sand which, if followed, leads to the beginnings of a desert so very hot, cold, bleak, blistering, and hostile; so full of escarpments emphasizing skies sometimes scarlet, sometimes lilac, often a sulphurous yellow, but always changing; so thickly piled with sands, shales, gravels, and dusts incessantly moved from place to place by ever-shifting winds, that reflections on the futility and vanity of all effort are automatically provoked —leading, if the sufferer persists in his stumblings through and over dried bones, bits of stick that were once forest, or the remains of ships (for this desert was once, fortuitously, the bed of an ocean), and rocks in which one may find entombed the imprints of long-dead species, to a most satisfactory and salubrious reaction. This has been named by our Agent 23 as the Law of Instant Reversal, describing what happens when, in the words of the inhabitants themselves, "there is too much of a good thing," causing a stubborn inward strengthening which they express thus: *And so what? One still has to eat!*

I surveyed all this terrain by Space Traveller, comfortably and with enjoyment, and was set down on the ridge of sand far enough from the hospital to enable me to say I had been conducted thither by local means of transport.

Large parts of the building still lie unused. I told Ormarin that the intensifying crisis in the "Empire" would fill them soon enough, and he kept his followers quiet with excuses about faulty planning, unreliable contractors. Who was paying for it? He told them a cock-and-bull story about Sirian spies who were offering money for secret support, and this is close enough to things actually happening for it to be believed. His supposed cleverness in outwitting the Sirians has gone to his credit.

The building does not differ much from others we have devised in similar conditions on several of our colonized planets.

With what dislike I enter these places you know full well: and yes, I have, believe me, understood why I find myself in them so often. I have even mastered myself to the extent of contributing somewhat to the science: I shall shortly come to the Department of Rhetorical Logic which I devised.

I have to report that Incent is in a bad way. I found him in Basic Rhetoric, for he has not progressed beyond it. This ward is at the front of the building, on balconies built over continual crashing, moaning, or murmuring waves. The winds whine and roar all day and all night. To augment this we have arranged background music of the most debilitating kind, largely originating from Shikasta. (See *History of Shikasta, Nineteenth Century Emoters and Complainers: Music*.) Most of the patients—a good many of them our agents, for it will not have escaped your notice how many are succumbing during this phase of heady partisan enthusiasms—have advanced beyond this basic and infantile condition and were in other wards, so poor Incent was by himself. I found him gazing out over the ocean, where a morbid sunset tinted the waves scarlet, his inner condition aptly expressed by a robe of red-and-pink silk, its luxuriousness emphasized and made striking by his soldierly bandaged arm. Tears flooded down his pale and tragic face. You will recall that his choice was for large black soulful eyes, an indication we might have taken more notice of (it comes into my mind for the first time that perhaps *you* did). But it was a bad sign. . . . Yes, large tragic black eyes mourned over the wastes of water—a sentence I might have found in the book that lay open on his knee, again from Shikasta, entitled *The Hero of a Lost Cause*. He was not looking at the screen on which was being projected his medication for the day, which happened to be a programme I am rather proud of: Shikasta again! How invaluable is that poor planet to our Canopean treatment for these conditions! Two vast armies, equipped for killing to the limits of current technology, fight each other for four Shikastan years with the utmost heroism and devotion to duty and in the most vile and brutal conditions, for aims that are to be judged as stupid, self-deluding, and greedy by their own immediate descendants a generation later, urged on by *words* used to inflame violent rival nationalism, each nation convinced, hypnotized by *words* to believe that it is in the right. Millions die, weakening both nations irreparably.

"Incent," said I, "you are not taking your medicine!"

"No," he cried, and he started up and clutched a pillar of the balcony with both hands, gazing with streaming eyes into the crashing and booming waters that flung spray up as high as the hospital windows. "No, I can't stand it. I can't and I won't! I cannot endure the horror of this universe! And as for sitting here hour after hour and watching this record of tragic loss and waste—"

"Well," I remarked, "you are not actually throwing yourself into the sea, are you?"

This was a mistake, Johor. I had underestimated his demoralization, for I was just in time to catch him by the arm as he flung himself over.

"Really," I heard myself scolding him, "how irresponsible can you get? You know quite well you would only have to come back and do it again! You know how much it costs, having to refit you with a new outfit, getting you into the right place at the right time. . . ." I record this little tirade to show you how quickly I was affected by the general atmosphere; are you sure I am really suitable for this work? But he at once collapsed into self-pity and self-accusation, said he was fit for nothing (yes, I have seen the echo here—*thanks!*), not up to it, and unworthy of Canopus. Yes, he was prepared to agree, if I insisted, because he knew I could not be wrong, that Shammat was evil; but it was merely an intellectual assent, his emotions were at odds with his thoughts, he could not believe that he would ever be a whole person again. . . . All this to the accompaniment of Tchaikovsky and Wagner.

I switched on a particularly therapeutic programme illustrated by newsreels of a recent disturbance on a planet situated on the very edge of the Sirian Empire where it borders the Puttioran Empire. Constantly invaded by one or the other of the two Great Powers, sometimes described as Sirian and sometimes as Puttioran, the inhabitants of

Polshi, because of these continual strains and tensions and persecutions, because of the efforts they have always had to make to preserve their planetary identity and their sense of being Polshan, have evolved a dashing, heroic, audacious planetary character for which they have long been famous. Throughout two vast Empires (I do not mention our own) the Polshans are known for this peculiarly dramatic and even self-immolating nature. Their more prudent neighbours criticize them for it, notably those most firmly under the heel of (forgive me) Puttiora or Sirius; but they are admired by other, less pressured, planets, usually in inverse proportion to their distance from centres of power and oppression. Thus, "the Polshan cause" tends to be celebrated most passionately in planets like Volyen, which has not itself been recently invaded.

The wars and massacres that have always afflicted Polshi have recently been absent, long enough for a generation to grow up with no personal experience of anything but the verbal stimulations of Sirian Rhetoric, the ideas generated by Sirian Virtue. And these most admirably brave people announced to Sirius that, by definition, Sirian Virtue and the custodians of it must admire planetary self-determination, justice, freedom, democracy (and so on and so forth). Therefore, Polshi intended forthwith to take control of its own affairs. At the same time, these intrepid ones invited all the neighbouring Sirian colonies to follow the roads of self-determination, democracy, justice, Virtue (and so on and so forth). Sirius (in this case the Conservers) watched all this without surprise, since rebellion is the main thing they study and what they expect, and did nothing whatsoever, refraining from intervention until that moment when the heroes were on the verge of setting up a government that repudiated Sirian Virtue in favour of their own. And then the Sirians moved in. By delaying as they did, they allowed every individual with the potential for Subversion / Self-determination / Heroism / Sedition / Anti-Sirian feelings / Polshan Virtue (and so on and so forth) to expose himself or herself, and were thus enabled to arrest, destroy, isolate, and make harmless the possible opposition. For that generation, at least.

"Klorathy!" demanded Incent, his eyes streaming, "are you saying that tyranny should never be resisted?"

"When have you ever heard me say so?"

"Ah, what nobility! What self-sacrifice! What daring! What reckless heroism! And you stand there dry-eyed, Klorathy! Empires rise and Empires fall, you say, and I remember your cool exposition of the subject in our classes on Canopus. But they fall, surely, because subject peoples rebel?"

"Incent, would you not agree that the outcome of this particular heroic episode was not all that hard to foresee?"

"I don't want to think about it! I can't bear it! I wish I was dead! I don't want to know! Switch that beastly thing off."

"Incent," I said, "you are going to have to take it from me that you are very ill. But you will recover, I assure you."

I withdrew, leaving him sobbing and wringing his hands, then stretching out his arms to the waves as if he needed to embrace the ocean itself.

On consultation with doctors, I discovered that no one before had ever resisted such treatment for so long. I could see they were at a loss. After all, this intense variety of homoeopathic medicine is the best—or worst—we can do. We have never, in short, had a case like Incent's. In every other acute case the stage of "So what!," followed by rapid recovery, has been reached fairly quickly.

The doctors having said they had no suggestions, I reassured them that I would think it all over and take responsibility.

I then briefly visited the Department of Rhetorical Logic, which works on the opposite principle, withdrawal of emotional stimulus.

High in the wing of the building away from the ocean, overlooking the beginnings of the desert, with the mountain peaks on one side and the dark stillness of the forest on the other, we have built rooms of stark white that are kept silent except for the clicking and ticking of the computers, into which are fed by remote control historical propositions such as capitalism = injustice, communism = injustice, a free market = progress, a monarchy is the guarantee of stability, the dictatorship of the proletariat must be followed by the withering away of the state. And so on.

But this ward was empty: its time has not yet come.

I did not take Agent 23 with me to visit Ormarin. He reported unmistakable symptoms of Rhetoric, asked to be put into curative custody, and then showed that the disease had indeed set in seriously by ceasing to see that he was ill and announcing with much emotion that the elevated language of the Constitution of the Volyen "Empire," which promises happiness, freedom, and justice to every one of its citizens as inherent, inalienable rights, seemed to him the "most moving" thing he had ever encountered. He is drying off in Mild Rhetoric and will soon be normal.

Ormarin.

I can most quickly characterize him by saying that he embodies a number of contradictions: his situation is one of high tension, and this is his strength as well as his weakness.

You will recall that when Volyen conquered Volyendesta, the indigenous inhabitants were murdered or enslaved, and their lands was taken from them. You might not remember, because of its basic improbability, that this cruel process was accomplished to the tune of Rhetoric claiming that it was for the benefit of the said natives. The ability to disguise truth by the processes of Rhetoric is of course one in which our Canopean Historical Psychologists are particularly interested in connection with the Sirian Empire, but I feel that they have overlooked the extremities of this pathological condition as exemplified in the Volyen "Empire." At any rate, I am drawing attention to this now because it is of vital importance to what I am finding out as I move (for the most part secretly) about Volyen and its four colonies.

Ormarin has all his life represented "the underdog," though this does not mean the miserable semi-slaves but, rather, the less fortunate of the conquering minority. As an intelligent being he is well aware of the anomaly and, to compensate, is capable, at the slightest stimulus, of providing floods of compassionate and sorrowing words describing their condition. This ability to, as it were, mourn verbally is appreciated by his fellow settlers, who demand from him on ceremonial occasions set pieces of grief on behalf of the exploited, beginning with words such as these: "And now I want to say that the condition of our fellow beings who are workers like ourselves is always in the forefront of my mind. . . ." And so on.

That, then, is the first and worst contradiction in Ormarin.

The next is that, while he represents the worse-off of the settlers, some of whom are indeed deprived, his own way of living can hardly be described as lacking in anything. His tastes are those of the fortunate minority everywhere in the Volyen "Empire"; but he has to conceal this. There was a period when he saw this as hypocrisy and went through some uneasy reversals: making a point of living at one time on the basic wage of the poor, at another on his wage as an employed official; at yet another time making speeches saying that although his position necessitated his living better than the average, this was only to demonstrate what was possible for everyone—and so on. But then there entered another factor—you will have guessed what and who—Shammat, the Father of Lies, in the person of Krolgul. Up and down and around the five units of this "Empire" went Krolgul, as he still does, at his work of making black white, white black.

He is a personable creature, with all the attractions of a robust and unconscious vitality, and he won Ormarin over by his rumbustious enjoyment in putting in clear and unlikable terms the uneasy compromise of which Ormarin's life is composed.

"You've got to face it," said he. "In the times in which we have to live, bad luck for us all, we must go with the tide and adapt ourselves to circumstances."

He evolved for Ormarin a *persona* that would reassure the people who kept him in power, actually an image of themselves, or of how they like to see themselves. Ormarin was taught to present himself as a solid, reliable, affable man—genially tolerant of his own deficiencies with regard to the fleshpots—though these were not allowed to be visible as more than the merest peccadilloes—humorous, slow-speaking, full of common sense.

In fact, in the case of Ormarin the picture is not wildly inaccurate: Ormarin does possess many of these qualities. But Krolgul has been creating these *personae* by the score, all over the "Empire," so that everywhere you go you meet representatives of "the workers" or "the people" who are affable, solid, et cetera, and who all, without exception, smoke a pipe and drink beer and whisky (in moderation, of course), these habits being associated with sound and reliable behaviour.

Ormarin soon stopped pointing out that he loathed pipes and beer, did not care for whisky, and preferred a certain brand of cigarettes captured by space raiders from Sirian cargo ships, along with Sirian (Mother Planet) nectar similarly acquired. He is uneasy about his acquired personality, and apologizes for it if he thinks you are likely to be critical. This, then, is a second strain, or contradiction.

Third, he is of Volyen stock, yet all his life has resisted—verbally— Volyen domination, though he is at the same time a welcome visitor on Volyen, where his children were educated. Volyen drains wealth from its four colonies while presenting itself as their benefactor under such slogans as "Aid to the Unfortunate" and "Development for the Backward." Ormarin, then, is continually involved with schemes to "advance" Volyendesta, originating from Volyen, but he protests continually, in magnificent speeches that draw tears from every eye (even my own if I don't watch myself, and yes, I *am* conscious of the dangers), that these schemes are hypocritical.

Fourth. Sirius. Because Volyen itself is comparatively resistant, with a high morale among the population, who are well fed and well housed and educated, compared with the four colonies, Sirius ignores it (except for infiltrating Volyen with spies) and is putting its pressure first and foremost on the colonies, particularly Volyendesta. Ormarin, hating the "crude imperialism" of Volyen—which is how he, on behalf of his constituents, has always described Volyen, the birthplace of some of his recent forebears—is able more easily than the inhabitants of Volyen itself to be sympathetic to Sirius, whose approaches are always in terms of "aid" or "advice," and of course in interminable and highly developed rhetorical descriptions of the colonial situation of Volyendesta.

Volyendesta, like Volyenadna, like Maken and Slovin, is short of hospitals, physical and emotional, short of every kind of educational institution, lacking in amenities Volyen takes for granted—and these Sirius offers, "without strings."

Sometimes, among the proliferations of Volyen Rhetoric, we find pithy and accurate phrases. One of them is "There is no such thing as a free lunch." Unfortunately Ormarin was not applying this mnemonic to his own situation.

My situation was complicated by the fact that I didn't want him to apply it to me, where it doesn't apply.

I found him on an official occasion: he was standing on a low hillside, with a group of associates, watching a section of road being built by a Sirian contractor. The road, an admirable construction, a double highway, is to stretch from capital to seaport. Sirius flies in continually renewed supplies of labour from her Planets 46 and 51, houses them in adequate compounds, oversees and guards them. These unfortunates are permitted no contact with the locals, on the request of the Volyendestan government. And thus it was that I approached Ormarin in yet another of the ambiguous roles that characterize him: he and his mates could not possibly approve of the use of this slave labour or of how they were treated, and yet they were there to applaud the "gift" of the road. As I approached, all the male officials took out pipes and began to smoke them, and the two females hastily hid some attractive scarves and jewellery of Sirian origin. I was just in time to hear Ormarin's speech, which was being broadcast for the benefit of the workers, their guards, and the Sirian delegation.

"Speaking on behalf of the working men and women of this planet, I have the great pleasure to open this section of the highway and to express gratitude to our generous benefactors the Sirian . . ." et cetera. Ormarin had seen who it was by then.

Ormarin likes me and is always pleased to see me. This is because he knows he does not have to disguise himself from me. Yet he suspects me of being a Sirian spy, or sometimes does; or of being some kind of a spy from somewhere, the central Volyen government perhaps. He jokes sometimes that he "should not be associating with spies," giving me looks that compound the "frank honest modesty" of his public *persona* with the inner uneasiness of his role. Or roles . . .

I joke that at any given time among his associates there is at least one spy from the Volyen central government, one from the Volyendestan central government, probably one each from Volyenadna, PE 70, and PE 71, and several from Sirius. He jokes that if that were true then half of his associates at any given time would be spies. I joke that he surely understands that this is an accurate statement of his position. He puts on the look obligatory at such moments, when one is forced to admit *impossible* truths—that of a wry, worldly-wise regret, tinged with a scepticism that makes it possible to dismiss the necessity of doing anything about it.

He is in fact surrounded by spies of all kinds, some of them his most efficient associates. Spies who have certain talents for, let's say, administration, and who are in administration for the purposes of espionage, often enjoy this secondary occupation and even rise to a high position, at which point they may regret that they didn't start off in a career of simple "public service," as this kind of work is styled, and they suffer private sessions of "Oh, if only I had seen early enough that I was fit for real work, and didn't have to settle for spying." But that is another story.

Ormarin soon ended the official part of the occasion; his colleagues went off; he shed his public self with a small smile of complicity with me; and we sat down together on the hilltop. On the hilltop opposite us the Sirian contingent were heading back to their spacecraft. The several hundred Sirian workers swarmed over and around the road, and we could hear the barks and yelps of the supervisors.

This planet's weather is unstable, but one may enjoy intervals without needing to adjust to unpleasant heat, cold, or assaults of various substances from the skies.

We watched, without comment, one of the men who had just been with us running to join the group of Sirians: a report on me and my arrival.

I was relieved that Ormarin decided against a ritual lament along the lines of "Oh, what a terrible thing it is to have to work with deceivers . . ." and so on. Instead, he said to me, on a questioning note, "That's a very fine road they are making down there?"

"Indeed it is. If there is one thing the Sirians know how to do, it is road-building. This is a first-class, grade I road, for War, Type II, Total Occupation."

This was deliberate: I wanted him to ask at last, But *where* are you from?

"I am sure it could be used for any number of purposes!" said he hastily, and looked about for something neutral to comment on.

"No, no," I said firmly. "When Sirius builds, she builds to an accurately defined purpose. This is for the purposes of Total Occupation, after Type II War."

Was he now going to ask me? No! "Oh, come come, you don't have to look all gift horses in the mouth."

"Yes, you do. Particularly this one."

Alas, I had miscalculated my stimulus, for he assumed a heroic posture, seated as he was on a small rock beside a rather attractive flowering bush, and declaimed: "We shall fight them on the beaches, we shall fight them on the roads, we shall fight them in the air. . . ."

"I don't think you'll get very far, fighting Sirius in the air," I said in a sensible voice, designed to dissolve this declamatory mode into which all of them fall so easily.

A silence. He kept sending me short anxious glances. He didn't know what to ask, though. Rather, he didn't want to ask me the key question, and perhaps it was just as well. The trouble is, "Canopus" has become a concept so dense with mythic association that perhaps he would not have been able to take it in, or not as fast as I needed.

I made it easy for him to think of me as Sirian, at least temporarily. "I've seen this type of road on a dozen planets before a takeover."

A silence.

"Oh, no, no," he said, "I really can't accept it. I mean, we all know that Sirius has quite enough trouble as it is, keeping her outlying planets in subjection; she's not going to add to her troubles . . . and anyway . . . they needn't think they are going to prevail over . . ." There followed a few minutes in the ritual patriotic mode.

After which, since I said nothing, he said, in a different voice, low, appalled: "But I can't face it; I really don't think I would want to live under Sirian occupation."

I recited a portion of the history of Volyendesta, as it appears in our annals.

"Of the fourteen planets of Star P 79 three are inhabited, Planet 3 and its two moons. The central feature of their history is that they have been invading and settling one another for millenniums. The longest stable period was of several thousand millenniums, when Moon II overran and conquered the other two and maintained by a particularly savage despotism—"

He interrupted, as I wanted him to: "Excuse me, Moon II, is that this planet or . . . ?"

"You. Volyenadna is Moon I."

It was wonderful to see the look of satisfied pride, which he was unaware of. "We, Volyendesta, administered all three planets? Volyen was an underdog then?"

"As you so graphically put it, Volyen and your brother planet Volyenadna were underdogs."

He became conscious that his reaction of exulting pride was hardly becoming to an opponent of Empires, adjusted his expression, and said, "There is nothing of that in our history. And besides . . ." The opponent of Empires was struggling for the appropriate words. "The locals here, the natives, they are pretty backward. I mean, it is not their fault"—and here he cast fearful glances right and left, in case he might have been overheard—"there are sound historical reasons for it, but they are just a little, let us say . . ."

"Backward," I said firmly, and he looked relieved.

"As always happens," I went on, "there came a time when the peoples of your two enslaved planets grew strong and self-reliant through overcoming hardships, and they evolved in secret the methods and technologies to overthrow—not you, but your predecessors, who were almost entirely wiped out. A rather unpleasant race, they were. Not much loss, or at least so it was felt by those whom they had subjugated. But one may still see traces of them in these natives here, if one knows how to look."

"Extraordinary," he murmured, his broad and honest face (genuinely honest, on the whole) showing the tensions of historical perspective. "And we know nothing of all that!"

This was my clue to say, "But luckily we do . . ." but I had decided against the subject of Canopus, for the time being. I saw his eyes most shrewdly and thoughtfully at work on my face; he knew a good deal more than he was saying, and more, perhaps, than he was admitting to himself.

"You don't want to know the rest?" I asked.

"It is all a bit of a shock; you must realize that."

"What I am going to say now is in your histories, though certainly very differently from how it appears in ours. I shall continue, then. Moon II—you—and Moon I were occupied for several V-centuries by Volyen. It was not entirely a bad thing. Moon II, this planet, was sunk in barbarism, so thoroughly had your former subjects from Volyen defeated you. Volyen's inhabitants, so recently your slaves, were full of confidence, knew all kinds of skills and techniques, most of them learned from you. You could say that it was they who preserved your inheritance for you, at least partly. These qualities were introduced, reintroduced if you like, and maintained by Volyens—though interbreeding soon made it hard to say what was native and what Volyen in what had become a vigorous new people. And the same process was going on in the more temperate parts of Volyenadna. Even faster there, because the awful hardships of life on that icy planet had always produced strong and enduring people. Very soon Moon I, or Volyenadna, partly threw off, partly absorbed its Volyen invaders, and then conquered Volyen, and settled this planet."

"One of my ancestors," said he, with pride, "was a Westerman from Volyenadna."

"I can see it in you," said I.

He looked modest, while holding out his hands for me to admire. They are very large strong hands, the distinguishing mark of Westermen from Volyenadna.

"Mind you, we gave them a good fight, it wasn't just a walkover," he boasted.

"No, an army of one thousand Volyendestans met them as they landed, and every one of the Volyendestans was killed. You died to a man, all blasted to cinders by the weapons of Moon I."

"That's right. Our Gallant One Thousand. And as for the invaders, nine-tenths of us were killed, even though the Volyendestans had only primitive weapons in comparison."

"What a massacre that was—of both invaders and invaded."

"Yes."

"A glorious chapter in the annals of both sides."

"Yes."

"I was admiring today the two memorials standing side by side in your main town square, commemorating that glorious day, one for the Gallant One Thousand, the Volyendestans, or Moon II, and the other for the Heroic Volyenadnans, or Moon I. Your ancestors, whose blood runs in your veins. Together, of course, with the blood of the Volyens, and many others."

He was regarding me steadily, with a thoughtful expression tinged with bitterness.

"Right, mate," he said. "I know you well enough by now. What is it you are warning me about?"

"Well, what do you think, Ormarin?"

"You really think Sirius will . . . ?"

"You are weak, divided, declining."

"We'll fight them on the—"

"Yes, yes, but don't you think . . ."

"How is it you are so sure of it, if you aren't a Sirian agent, that is? I'm beginning to think—"

"No, I am not, Ormarin. And I am sure that you don't really think anything of the kind. Why should I have to have any special sources of information to enable me to see what is obvious? When a planet is weak, divided, declining, nearly always it is taken over by a stronger planet or group of planets. If not Sirius, then some other power. What makes you think you are immune to this law, Ormarin?"

Down in the valley dark was falling. The hundreds of slave labourers were being pushed into a double file on the new road by the guards who ran and scampered all around them: they were being marched off for the night.

"Poor creatures,", he said suddenly, his voice hot with pity. "And is that going to be our fate?"

I said, "The Sirian Empire is well past its peak. It has been expanding slowly, for— But if I told you how many millenniums, would you be able to take it in? *Your* history covers a few thousand of your years. The Sirian Empire is the greatest *in size* in our galaxy. There have been periods when its growth was checked, periods when it was reduced, because of indecision on the part of the rulers of Sirius. But, looked at overall, it has grown. This last period is one of frenetic and frantic unplanned growth, because of the internal battles going on inside the Sirian ruling classes. It is an interesting fact that the theory governing the Sirian Empire at this time does not include the idea of expansion! Expansion is not on its agenda. They are not stupid, the Sirians, or not all of them: some at least know they are not in control of what they do, and they have just begun to understand that such a thing is possible, that an Empire may control its development according to . . . but that is another story." I was watching his face for a glimmer of understanding, and if he had showed any sign I would have gone on to talk of Canopus, and what governs *us*. But there was nothing there but the strain of trying to follow ideas, if not beyond him, at least too new for easy assimilation. "Recently—talking comparatively, of course—Sirius has conquered several new planets, not as a result of a planned and considered decision, no, but because of some hasty decision made to meet an emergency."

"Hasty," murmured Ormarin, indicating the fine road below us, along which the slave labourers were being marched to their barracks for the night.

"The decision to build this road was made a year ago—a Sirian year. When Volyen conquered the two planets that Sirius considered were part of their Empire."

"You didn't finish that history."

"The Westermen, those unscrupulous conquerors of whose blood you are so proud, created here and on Volyen a highly structured society of multifarious skills." Here I saw him smile wryly down at those formidable Westerman hands. "But, as always has to happen, Moon I and its two colonies lost impetus. . . . This time it was Volyen's turn to rise again and conquer. A quite interesting little Empire it has been, the recent Volyen Empire, with some mild ideas of justice, not indifferent to the welfare of its inhabitants, at least in theory, trying to absorb into its ruling classes the upper echelons of the conquered. . . ."

I saw him begin to feel ashamed, and heard him sigh.

"Well," I said, "you could have chosen to live in the compounds and barracks with the natives, rather than compromise, but you didn't. . . ."

"Oh, believe me," said he, in the hoarse, suffering voice I had almost deliberately invoked, "I have lain awake night after night, hating myself."

"Yes, yes, yes," I said, "but the fact is, you did do what you've done, and as a result your position on this planet is a key one. And when the Sirians invade—"

But I had miscalculated. The stimulus had been too much.

He leaped to his feet on the now dark hill, with the stars coming up bright behind him—one of them Volyen, his present master—and, holding up his right fist, his Westerman or Volyenadnan fist, he orated: "I stand here as a free man, breathing free air, my feet on my own soil! Rather than submit to the tyrannies of alien invaders I will pick up stones from the hillside if need be, and sticks from the forest, and fight until death overcomes me and—"

"Ormarin!" I tried to interrupt. "What have all those fine words got to do with your situation? For one thing, you have efficient modern weapons, you free peoples of the Volyen Empire. . . ." But it was no use.

"Who with real manhood in his veins would choose to live as a slave when he can die on his feet fighting? Which man, woman, or child among you who has known what it is to stand upright . . ."

I am afraid I must report that this was a bad attack. I had to have him confined to the hospital for a few days.

But I have worse to tell you. While there, I went to see how poor Incent was and, finding him comparatively sensible and able to talk about his situation, asked for his permission to administer a test.

It was the simplest possible test, based on the word *history*.

At this word itself, he was able to maintain composure. The word *historical* caused his pulse to quicken, but then it steadied. At *historical processes*, he remained firm. *Perspective of history*—so far so good. *Winds of history*—he showed signs of agitation. These did not decrease. I then decided, wrongly, to increase the dose, trying *logic of history*. At this point I began to realize the hopelessness of it, for his breathing was rapid, his face pale, his pupils dilating. *Inevitability of* . . . *lessons of* . . . *historical tasks* . . .

But it was not until *dustbin of history* that I gave up. He was on his feet, wildly exultant, both arms held up, preparatory to launching himself into declamation, and I said, "Incent, *what* are we going to do with you?"

Which flight of Rhetoric must be excused by the circumstances.

I gave instructions for him to have the best of care.

He has escaped. I did not have to be told where. I am leaving for Volyenadna, where Krolgul is active. I shall report again from there.

KLORATHY TO JOHOR, FROM MOON I OF VOLYEN, VOLYENADNA.

This is not the most attractive of planets. The ice sheets which until recently covered it have retreated to the poles, leaving behind a characteristic landscape. This is harsh and dry, scarred by the violent movements of ice and of wind. The vegetation is meagre and dull. The rivers are savage, still carrying melting snow and ice, hard to navigate, offering little in the way of pleasure and relaxation.

The original inhabitants, evolved from creatures of the ice, were heavy, thick, slow, and strong. The great hands that Ormarin is so proud of built walls of ice blocks and hauled animals from half-frozen water, strangled, hammered, wrenched, broke, tore, made tools from antlers and bones. Invasions of less hardy peoples (unlike Moon II, this planet was conquered and settled more than once by Planets S-PE 70 and S-PE 71) did not weaken the stock, because the conditions continued harsh, and those who did not adapt died.

The history of this planet, then, not so unlike that of Volyendesta, exemplifies the power of the natural environment. This is a dour and melancholy people, slow to move, but with terrible rages and fits of madness, and even now, in the wary turn of a head, the glare of eyes that seem to listen as much as to look, you can see how their ancestors waited for sounds that could never be anything but warnings and threats—the whining howl of the wind, the creak of straining ice, the thud of snow massing on snow.

The latest conquest, by Volyen, has worsened conditions. Because of the planet's abundant minerals, everywhere you look are factories, mines, whole cities that exist only to extract and process minerals for the use of Volyen. The natives who work these mines live in slave conditions, and die young of diseases caused mostly by poverty or dusts and radiations resulting from the processing of the minerals. The ruling class of the planet lives either on Volyen or in the few more favoured areas of this moon supported and maintained by Volyen; its members do their best not to know about the terrible lives of their compatriots.

So extreme are the conditions on Volyenadna that I think it is permissible to call it a slave planet, and this, as I am sure you are not surprised to hear, is how Krolgul apostrophizes it: "O slave planet, how long will you bear your chains?"

I arrived on a grim and grey day near a grim and grey city, walked into the central square and found Krolgul addressing a grey, grim, and silent crowd: "O slave planet, O Volyenadna, how long will you bear your chains?"

There was a long groan from the crowd, but then it fell silent again. Listening.

Krolgul was standing on a plinth that supported an imposing statue of a miner holding up clenched fists and glaring over the heads of the crowd; he was deliberately copying this pose—a famous one, for the statue is used as a symbol for the workers' movements. Near Krolgul, his nervous, agitated stance in sharp contrast to Krolgul's, stood Incent, sometimes smiling, sometimes scowling, for he was not able to find or maintain a satisfactory public pose. Krolgul saw me, as I intended. In this crowd of heavy, slow people, there were three who stood out: me, basic Canopean, but here seen as "Volyen," as anything alien has to be; Incent, so slight and lithe and nervous; and Krolgul, though he does everything to look Volyenadnan.

You may remember Krolgul as a large, not to say fleshy, easygoing, affable goodfellow, all eagerness to please: his adaptation on this planet is quite a triumph of self-discipline, for he has created a dedicated, brooding, heroic *persona*; known to live in a bare room on less than a worker's wage, he has a smile so rare that it has inspired ballads.

> ... *Volyen's minions fired.*
> *Our dead lay on the ground.*
> *Krolgul frowned.*
> *"We shall march," we cried,*
> *In accents stern and wild.*
> *And Krolgul smiled.*

The trouble here is that these people are so slow to move, and Krolgul has been given little occasion for smiling. What he wants them to do is "rise all at once, once and for all" and take over everything.

What is preventing this is the basic common sense of the Volyenadnans, who know from the bitterest experience that the Volyen armies are efficient and ruthless.

So Krolgul started to build up a head of hate, at first directed towards "all Volyen," and then, this proving too general a target to be effective, at Lord Grice, the Volyen Governor, whose name has acquired, like additional titles, epithets such as Greasy, Gross, Greatfat, Greenguts. To such a point that a citizen may be heard saying something like "Lord Grice Greatfat visited so-and-so yesterday," but so much a matter of habit has this become that he himself might not be aware of it. And even Lord Grice, so the rumour has it, was once heard to introduce himself on a ceremonial visit to a local governor, "I'm Grice the Greasy, don't you know. . . ."

As a matter of fact, he is a tall, dry, rather weedy fellow, of a natural melancholy much enhanced by the rigours of this planet, and full of doubts as to his role as Governor.

This genuine representative of Volyen was at a window of the Residency that stands on the square, listening to Krolgul and making no attempt at all to conceal himself.

He was a threat to Krolgul's oratory, because the people in the square had only to turn their heads to see this criminal. . . .

"And what are we to say about that arch-charlatan Grice the Greedy! In one person we see embodied the whole villainy of the Volyen tyranny! Sucking the blood of the . . ." And so on.

The crowd had begun to growl and stir. These lethargic, stolid people were at last showing signs of action.

Krolgul, however, did not want them actually to storm the Residency. He intended to use Grice as a means for a good while yet. Therefore, he skilfully swung them into song. We will march, We will march, We will overthrow . . . and the mass roared into song.

A few youths at the back of the crowd, longing for action, turned towards the Residency, saw in a window on the first floor a solitary figure, swarmed up onto the balcony, and confronted this observer with shouts of "We've come to get him! Don't try to hide him. Where's Grice the Guts?"

"Here," said Grice, coming forward with modest alacrity.

At which the louts spat at him, aimed a kick or two in his direction, and told him to warn Grice-Guts they were "coming to do him." They then jumped back into the crowd and joined in the singing.

The singing was less fervent, however, than Krolgul wanted. The faces I looked at, while entranced by the singing, were still patient, even thoughtful.

I went into a little eating place on the square and watched the crowds disperse.

Down from the plinth came Krolgul, smiling and acknowledging homage (comradely greetings) from the crowd. With him Incent, eyes flashing, aroused, palpitating, but doing his best to present the stern and dedicated seriousness appropriate to the military look he aspired to. Like two soldiers they came towards the café, followed by the usual adoring females and some younger males.

They had seated themselves before Incent saw me. Far from showing guilt, he seemed delighted. He came, first running, and then, remembering his new role, striding across. "Wasn't that just the most moving thing you have ever seen?" he demanded, and sat down opposite me, beaming.

Newspapers were brought in. Headlines: "Inspiring . . . Moving . . . Inspirational . . ." Incent seized one, and although he had for the past several hours been involved in this meeting, sat poring over an account of it.

Krolgul, who had seen me, met my eyes with a sardonic, almost cynical smile, which he instantly abolished in favour of his revolutionary sternness. There he sat, in the corner, positioned so that he could watch through the windows how the crowd dispersed, and at the same time survey the interior of the café. Into which now came a group of the miners' leaders, headed by Calder, who sat down in a corner, having nodded at Krolgul, but no more.

Incent did not notice this. He was gazing at the men with such passionate admiration that Krolgul directed towards him a cold, warning stare.

"They are such marvellous, *wonderful* people," said Incent, trying to attract the attention of Calder, who at last gave him a friendly nod.

"*Incent*," I said.

"Oh, I know, you are going to punish me. You are going to send me back to that dreadful hospital!"

"You seemed to me to be rather enjoying it."

"Ah, but that was different. Now I am in the thick of the real thing."

The café was packed. Everyone in it was a miner; Volyenadnans every one, except for three—me, Incent, Krolgul. All foreigners are assumed to be of the Volyen administration, or spies from either Volyen or—but these suspicions were recent—Sirius. The miners, fifty or so of them, here after the rally to discuss their situation, to feel their plight, were obviously wondering how they came to be represented by Krolgul and by his shadow, Incent.

Krolgul, sensing how people were looking at him, occupied himself in earnest, frowning discussion with a young woman from this town, a native, and in moving papers about, the image of efficiency.

But it was easy to see that Calder was not satisfied. He exchanged a few words with his associates and stood up.

"Krolgul," he said. It was not a large place, and by standing and speaking, he unified it.

Krolgul acknowledged him with a modification of the fist-high salute: he lifted a loose fist from the table to half shoulder height, and opened it and shut it once or twice like a mouth.

"I and the mates here are not altogether happy with the way things are going," Calder said.

"But we concretized the agreed objectives," said Krolgul.

"That is for us to say, isn't it?"

Given this confrontation, for it was one, Krolgul could only agree; but Incent was half up, holding on to his chair, his face dimmed by disappointment. "Oh," he said, "but that was the most *moving* . . . the most . . . the most *moving* . . ."

"Yes, yes," said Calder. "But I don't think it was entirely on the lines we agreed."

"But in our analysis of the situation we decided—" began Krolgul, and was stopped by Calder's, "This one here, is he a friend of yours?"

Meaning, of course, me. Fifty pairs of eyes focused on me—hard, grey, distrustful eyes.

"Well, I think I could say that," said Krolgul, with a heaving of silent laughter that could have been taken various ways, but which Calder took badly.

"Speak for yourself," said he to me.

"No, I am not a friend of Krolgul's," I said.

"Visiting here, perhaps?"

"He's a friend of mine, a friend of mine," shouted Incent, and then wondered if he had done right; with a gasp and a half smile, he subsided back into his seat.

"Yes, I am visiting."

"From Volyen, perhaps?"

"No," I said.

"A friend of this lad here, who is a friend of Krolgul, but not a friend of Krolgul," said someone sardonically, and everyone laughed.

"You are here to write a travel book?" Laughter. "An analysis of our situation?" Laughter. "A report for—"

"For Canopus," I said, knowing that the word would sound to them like an old song, a fable.

Silence.

Krolgul could not hide his shock: he knew then, for the first time, that my being here was serious, that we account his activities at this time serious. It is a strange thing that people engaged in his kind of half-mocking, half-experimental, wholly theatrical intrigues often lose the capacity for seeing themselves and their situation. *Enjoyment* of manipulation, of power, of *watching themselves in a role*, dims judgment.

I looked round slowly from face to face. Strong, grey faces that showed all the exhaustion of their lives. Faces like stones. In their eyes, grey, slow eyes, I saw that they were remembering, trying to remember.

Calder, still on his feet, his great hand on his chair-back, the miners' leader whose desperation had allowed him to become subject to the manipulations of Krolgul, looked hard and long at me and said, "You can tell them, where you come from, that we are very unfortunate people."

And at this there was a long involuntary groan, and then silence.

This, what was happening now, was of a different kind and quality from anything that had happened in the square, or anything that emanated from Krolgul. I was looking at Incent, since, after all, he was the key to the situation, and saw him impressed and silent, even thoughtful.

And Krolgul too knew the moment was crucial. He slowly, deliberately got to his feet. He held out both clenched fists in front of him. And now the eyes of everyone had turned to him.

"Unfortunate!" he said in a low, only just audible voice, so that people had to strain to listen. "Yes, that is a word we may say and say again. . . ." His voice was rising, and slowly his fists were rising too. "Misfortune was the inheritance of your fathers, misfortune is what you eat and drink, and misfortune will be the lot of your children!" He had ended on a shout, and his fists had fallen to his sides. He stood there, appealing to them with the brave set of his body, his pale face, with eyes that actually managed to look sunken and hungry.

But he had miscalculated: he had not taken them with him.

"Yes, I think we are all aware of it," said Calder, and turned to me. "You, from—where did you say it was? but never mind—what do you have to say?" This was a half-jeer, but let us say a hopeful jeer, and now all the eyes had shifted back to me, and they leaned forward, waiting.

"I would say that you could begin by describing your actual situation, as it is."

This chilled them, and Incent's face, turned towards me suddenly, looked as if I had hit him deliberately, meaning to hurt. Johor: it is not going to be easy for Incent. It is the hardest thing in the Galaxy, if you have been the plaything of words, words, words, to become independent of their ability to intoxicate.

"I think we are all able to," said Calder dryly, sitting down again and half turning away from me, back to his mates. But not entirely. He still kept half an eye on me, and so did all the others.

Krolgul was seated again, staring hard at Incent. Incent, feeling this gaze, was shifting about, uneasy and in terrible conflict. I was sensing him as a vacuum from which the powers of Canopus were being drained and sucked out by Krolgul. Incent might be sitting there with me, at my table, my "friend," but he was in the power of Krolgul. Now that Krolgul could see how he had lost the allegiance— though, he hoped, temporarily—of the Volyenadnans, Incent was what he had left. It was like watching blood being emptied from a victim as he gasps and shrinks, but it wasn't blood that Incent fed, is feeding, Krolgul.

Calder was my only hope.

I stood up, so that everyone could see me.

"You're leaving?" asked Calder, and he was disappointed.

But I had hoped for what then happened. Calder said, "Perhaps we could have the benefit of an outside view, an objective opinion?"

"I have a suggestion," I said. "You get together as many of you as you can, and we will meet, with Krolgul here, and talk it all out."

They didn't agree at once, but in the end they did. Krolgul had no alternative, though he hated it.

Of course, we could have done it all where we were, in the café, but I was concerned with Incent.

I did not order him to follow me as I left the café, but he came with me. Physically, he came with me.

I took him to my lodgings in a poor part of the town. A miner's widow, with children to support, let out rooms. Almost the first thing she had said to me was, "We are unfortunate people," and it was with a calm sense and dignity that could be, I hope, what would save them all from Krolgul.

She agreed to give us some supper in my room.

It wasn't much; they are indeed poor people.

Over bread and some fruit, Incent and I sat opposite each other.

"Incent?" I said to him. "What am I going to do with you?" And it was far from rhetorical.

"You're going to punish me, you're going to punish me," he kept groaning, but with the enjoyment he has learned from Krolgul.

"Yes, of course you will be punished. Not by me, not even by Canopus, but by the inherent laws of action and interaction."

"Cruel, cruel," he sobbed, and fell asleep, all his emotional apparatus in disarray, his intellectual machineries in subjection to this disorder. But he is strong enough physically; that is something.

Leaving him asleep, and asking the woman of the house to keep an eye on him, I spent the night in the bars of the town and its suburbs. Everywhere unrest, even a sense of impending upheaval. Hard to determine whether this was mainly because of worsening conditions on the planet, or because of the efforts of Krolgul . . . who, interestingly, was talked of much less than Incent. No wonder Incent is exhausted. He seems to have travelled to all the main centres of Volyenadna, and to most of the smaller ones as well. To extract the essence of what people have found in him: it is that *he is noticed*. He has impressed himself. In city after city he has moved from one meeting place to another: cafés, miners' clubs, women's clubs, and his right to be everywhere has been his conviction that his cause must make him welcome. He brings no credentials. On the rare occasions he is challenged, he impatiently, even contemptuously, rejects the need for it, as if his interlocutors are showing pettiness and worse, and after a few hours of earnest exhortation—which clearly exhaust his hearers, who betray, even after several days' interval, all the signs of nervous strain— he leaves for the next appointment with destiny.

Can I say he is not trusted? It is more interesting than that. . . .

There is a type of revolutionary always to be seen at times when there is potential for change. At first tentative, even timid, then amazed that this burning conviction of his can convince others, he soon becomes filled with contempt for them. He can hardly believe that he, that small unit, and an unworthy one (for, at least at the beginning, he may possess some view of himself as a fallible individual), can be taken seriously by those older than he, more experienced—persons sometimes of worth, who may be representatives of masses of people. Yet he, this torch of righteous conviction, armed with no more than his own qualities, is able to come close to them, persuades, convinces, has them in his power. He asks for trust—that first of all—for money, for the use of their influence. In no time he has nests of people in every place doing his bidding, embroiled with one another, willing to listen. To listen, that's the thing. One may observe him, this burning-eyed, coiled spring of a youth, leaning forward at a café table, in the corner of a house, anywhere, fixing his prey with his eyes in a conviction of shared purpose, of conspiracy, of—always—being united in some small purpose against enormous odds. Yet almost at once this small purpose has burgeoned so remarkably. Finding it so easy to talk in terms of limited ends, the creation of a local institution perhaps, a meeting place, a modest petition, suddenly he—no less than others—is surprised to find that what is being talked about is city-wide, then planetary, even interplanetary movements. "We shall sweep the stars for our support!" Incent cried from a platform in one town, and when someone called out from the body of the hall, "Hold on, lad, let's start with something more modest," the laughter was no more than friendly. Of course! If you have been able to rise so far and so fast from such a humble base—in this case, on this planet, that the people generally are very worn down, tired, drained, and they wish for better —then why not "sweep the stars" and "transform everything"?

"Is not the present moment dynamic?" cried Incent from platform after platform, his whole person radiating dynamism, so that the poor tired people listening to him felt dynamic too; though not for long, for it is odd how they feel even more tired, more drained, when he has moved on to the next place that he has decided to stir into action.

"The new forms of life will become dynamically dramatic," he has shouted, though only a moment before he was dealing with a question from the floor about raising wages by means of a petition to Volyen (through Greasy-guts Grice).

Well, such a person does not, as we know, "sweep the stars," but he does set in motion a great many people who even while under his spell feel uneasy. And yet feel uneasy that they do. How dull they have become! How enfeebled by life! How far they are from the flaming days of their youth, which they see before them again in the shape of this noble, inspirational youth, who seems, when he leans forward to hold their eyes with his own, to gather their whole life and pose it before them in the shape of a question.

"What have you become?" those dramatic, those languishing, those shameless eyes demand. For, of course, this young hero, without even knowing it, will use all the means he has to unlock the various forms of resistance he faces, including sex, maternal and paternal love: Oh, if only my son were like this, this very flame of promise and action, if only I had chosen such a one as a husband.

But uneasy they are. It might be for a good cause, but how they are being manipulated! And how is it possible that not only one's unworthy (of course) self is being played on by this man—this youth, not much more than a child, really—but also one's respected and revered colleagues?

This operator has understood from the first, and by instinct (it is nearly all instinct, this, not calculation: our hero is working on a wavelength of pure guess-and-feel, he has never sat down to say, "How can I get this poor sucker under my thumb?"), that of course one must use one "name" to impress another. "I saw Hadder today," he lets fall confidentially and, as it were, by the way, "and he said to me he would talk to Sev, and when I dropped in on Bolli yesterday she said she knew how to lay her hands on . . ." Some large, almost incredible sum seems to materialize; both the inspired youth and the hypnotized victim contemplate it, in silence. "Ye-e-es . . ." murmurs the victim at last, "I see, yes. . . ." And on both faces there appears fleetingly a small self-conscious smile that acknowledges absurdity.

Alone he does it. It is he who possesses the flair, the spark, the drive, the energy, it is he who can set in motion these people or cadres. *He—who?* Who am I? he may mutter in some moment of panic, seeing puppets twitch and dangle everywhere he looks. But how is it possible . . . ? All these skilled, intelligent, experienced people? Doing his bidding?

He feels as if he were himself twitching over an empty space. Moments of panic recur, are evaded, avoided, fled from. . . . He works harder, faster, runs from place to place, sleeps hardly at all, eats only as part of this process of convincing and manipulating people: "No, only a sandwich please, I don't . . ." "Perhaps a glass of water, I don't . . ." But meanwhile, things are happening. They indubitably are. Not exactly on the scale envisaged at the "sweeping the stars" stage of the game. But certainly not, either, as he imagined in those first timid (cowardly?) moments. No, when he first felt those divine wings of rightness and conviction begin to lift, he thought, "Oh, perhaps I may be able to make them see just a little bit of what . . ." No, he is very far from that. Into real, actual existence—paid-up memberships, funds, brochures, letterheads, meetings—have come organizations. They function. Oddly enough, his name is never there. Why not? Simply because the magnitude of his presence, his demand, his command, cannot be contained in anything so paltry as a letterhead, a list of sponsors. Though perhaps his name might appear in the smallest of type somewhere as an assistant secretary or something of the sort. And besides, there is always something a little fishy about these operations. His contempt for the people he operates, his always growing amazement as he promises and persuades, leads him into statements about sums of money that never existed, statements that so-and-so said something which will turn out to be untrue; behind this real, actual, to-be-felt-and-touched thing, the organization, the meetings, the sponsors, the aims, is a whole mirage of lies.

Lies, lies, lies. Flattery and sycophancy and lies.

At some point or other, and sometimes not till years later, the victims will suddenly find themselves muttering, Yes, that fellow—what's his name?—the fact is, he was crazy, wasn't he?

In the meantime, our hero has probably had a spell of actual madness, of the kind that necessitates doctors, or has gone to live in another planet.

It is as if his part in that flurry and fervour of activity never was. His name is not mentioned, or hardly ever, and this is not only because by now the people he made dance are ashamed and wish they could obliterate their part in it all. It is also because there is something that doesn't fit. Just as it wasn't easy to put that dazzling name on a letter-head, or as the signature to a pamphlet full of facts and figures (written stuff of this kind has on the whole to be more accurate than what is said), simply because that burning presence was out of phase with all the other, more humdrum, individuals, so if one is looking back, it is hard to accommodate him into sober and thoughtful memory. This and that event certainly did happen—perhaps even now a society or party still exists, moribund, all the life fled from it—but do you mean to say that it was brought into being by that *psychopath?*

So it comes about that history does not record the names of these heroes. One may search in vain in records of events one has experienced on a day-to-day basis, knowing exactly what went on, and no-where appear the names of the wonder-workers without whom these events would never have taken place.

Incent, like the others of his sort, will not appear in the history books. Meanwhile, everyone is talking about him.

"Yes, he was here last week. He had us up all night listening to him. He's sincere, isn't he?"

"Oh, yes, you could say that, he's sincere, all right."

"It was the most moving occasion I can remember," someone else may say thoughtfully. "Yes . . ."

When I returned to my lodgings, in the early morning, I found that Incent had already gone out. He had kept the woman of the house up listening to him nearly all night, so that she had a flattened and drained look.

"He is a very feeling young one," she said, or murmured, out of semi-sleep. "Yes. Not like those Sirians. You and he come from the same place, he said. Is that so?"

And that is what I have to contend with.

When he returned at midday he was so intoxicated with himself he did not know me. He had visited Krolgul and Calder, and paid a flying visit to a near town which "is ready for the truth," and when he came striding into the little room at the top of the house where I sat waiting for him, it was with a clenched-fist salute and fixed, glazed eyes.

"With me, against me," he chanted, and went striding about the room, unable to check the momentum which had been carrying him for days.

"Incent," I said, "do sit down."

"Wi' me, 'gainst me!"

"Incent, this is Klorathy."

" 'me, 'nst me."

"*Klorathy!*"

"Oh, Klorathy, greetings, servus, all power to the . . . *Klorathy*, I didn't recognize you there, oh, wonderful, I have to tell you . . ." And he passed out on my bed, smiling.

I then went out. I had arranged with Calder and his friends that our "confrontation" should take place in one of the miners' clubs or meeting places; but on the insinuation of Krolgul, Incent had, not consulting Calder but simply informing him, booked one of the trial rooms of the legislature for the occasion. This is where, usually, the natives are tried and sentenced by Volyens for various minor acts of insubordination. He had distributed all kinds of pamphlets and leaflets everywhere around the town announcing "A Challenge to Tyranny."

I myself went to Calder, and found him with a group of men in his house. He was angry, and formidable.

I said to him that in my view the "confrontation" should be cancelled, and that we—he, I, Incent and Krolgul, and perhaps ten or so of the miners' representatives—should meet informally in his house or in a café.

But since I had seen him, he had been immersed in Rhetoric. Furious that "the powers that be" had "tricked" him by substituting for one of their clubs a venue associated by them with the Volyen hegemony, furious with himself for being swayed by Incent, whom, when he was out of his company, Calder distrusted, angry because of Krolgul, who had sent him a message saying he had nothing to do with Incent's recent manoeuvrings, he now saw me as an accomplice of Incent.

"You and he come from the same place," he said to me, as I sat there faced with a dozen or so steady, cold, angry pairs of Volyenadnan eyes.

"Yes, we do. But that doesn't mean to say I support what he does."

"You are telling us that you and he come from that place, very far away it is too, and you don't see eye to eye with him on what he is doing here?"

"Calder," I said, "I want you to believe me, I have had nothing to do with these new arrangements. I think they are a mistake."

But it was no good: he, they all, had been subjected to burning sincerity from Incent for some hours.

"We'll meet you in that Volyen place. Yes. We'll meet you there, and let truth prevail," shouted Calder, bringing a great fist down on the table in an obvious ritual for putting an end to discussion.

And so that is what is about to happen.

Krolgul is keeping modestly out of sight. Incent is still asleep, but tossing and starting up, smiling and emitting fragmented oratory, and falling back, smiling, to dream of the "confrontation"—which I am afraid is hardly likely to go well.

And this is what happened.

Towards the end of Incent's long sleep, its quality changed and he became inert and heavy. He woke slowly, and was dazed for some minutes. Clearly, he could not remember at once what had happened. Where was the "dynamic," vibrant, passionate conspirator? At last he pulled himself up off the bed and muttered, "Krolgul, I must get to Krolgul."

"Why?"

He looked at me in amazement. "*Why?*"

"Yes, why? There is no need for you ever to have anything to do with Krolgul."

He subsided again on the bed, staring.

"In a few minutes we have to make our way to the Hall of Justice, room number three, in order to talk to Calder and his mates," I said.

He shook his head, as if trying to dislodge buzzing thoughts.

"Arranged by you," I said.

"Klorathy," he asked from his old self, tentative, stubborn, honest, "I have been a bit crazy, I think?"

"Yes, you have. But please try to hold on to what you are now, for we must go to this so-called trial or confrontation."

"What are you going to do with me?" he asked.

"Well, if you can maintain yourself as you are now—nothing. Otherwise, I'm afraid you must undergo Total Immersion."

"But that's terrible, isn't it?"

"Let's hope it doesn't come to that."

The council chamber or judgment room of the Volyen administration is arranged to demonstrate the principles of justice: right and wrong; good and bad; punisher and punished. On one side of the circular chamber, which is panelled with some shiny brown stone so that the movements of the individuals inside the chamber are reflected in the gleams of dull colour, stands the apparatus of judgment itself: an imposing chair or throne, subsidiary but similar thronelike chairs, boxes for the accusers and witnesses—most of them bound to be hostile to the pitiful representatives of the natives on the other side of the court, where a dozen bare benches are ranged.

Two focuses of opinion is what this Volyen court is designed to hold; if *opinion* can possibly be the word for what always ends in the imprisonment and torture or execution of the people on one side of the court, whereas those on the other side go off to their homes to be refreshed and made ready for another day of determining justice.

But we were three focuses of opinion, and instinctively, without need for argument, we made our way to the area where the lowly benches stood, ignoring the pomp of the court itself, and arranged them into a rough triangle. Calder and those with him took their places on one side. Krolgul, though with hesitation that looked rather like an attractive diffidence, sat all by himself on another. As usual, he was wearing clothes assembled to seem like a uniform that summed up a situation: a sober tunic in grey, baggy service trousers, and a grey-green scarf around his neck, of the kind used by everyone here to shield his eyes from the glare that comes off the still-unmelted glaciers and snow fields. He looked the picture of responsible service.

But really he was confused. That was because of his creature Incent, who was tagging along with me in a dulled, exhausted condition that made it seem as if he had been drugged or hypnotized. And that was what not only Krolgul but also the Volyenadnans thought had happened. Calder, in fact, did not at once recognize the glossy and persuasive Incent in this pale, slow youth who slumped beside me on the bench. And it certainly did not suit me either, for it was Incent whom I wanted to put forward a point of view not Krolgul's.

Just as Krolgul had wanted Incent to speak for *him*.

And so there we were, sitting quietly on our benches, and no one spoke.

Nor was this a situation without danger, since the use of this court for such a purpose was of course not allowed. Incent had shouted, entirely on impulse, from some platform in the poor part of the city, "We shall take our cause to the heart of Volyen itself!"

So "Volyen itself" could be expected to show up at any moment, in the shape of the police, if not the army.

At last Calder stood up, though there was no need for anyone to stand: he stood because he had been taught by the Volyens that he must stand in the presence of superiors. A great slab of a man, dense and heavy in texture as the schists and shales and compacted clays he worked with, he looked at Incent and remarked, "Our young hero doesn't seem to have much to say for himself today."

I said, without standing, that Incent, as he and all the Volyens knew, had had plenty to say, in fact had not stopped talking for days, if not weeks, and had keeled over exhausted only a few hours ago. I said this in a low, humorous voice, to match the quiet, almost ironical tones of Calder.

"Well, then?" demanded Calder. I noted with pleasure how he sat down again.

"May I suggest," I said, "that *you* state the position. After all, it is you and your people who would suffer the consequences of any action."

"That's right, that's right," came a chorus from the men behind Calder. And I saw that this was indeed what they had all been saying to one another: "It is all right for him, isn't it, but it is us who'll be going to prison for it."

I had taken a risk, of course, because I did not want Krolgul to stand up and launch himself into oratory. I wanted the tone kept low and sensible. He was lounging there on his bench, watching everything without seeming to, and trying to make Incent meet his eyes so that he could once again get the boy under his influence.

I could feel Incent beside me as a blank, a void. He was not Krolgul's then, nor was he himself; he was not acting as a conduit for the strengths and powers of the planet so that Krolgul could tap them; he was not letting the virtues of Canopus drain away through him. He was nothing. And I hoped I could keep him so until the healing powers of Canopus could begin to work.

Krolgul maintained silence. He was banking on getting Incent back under his will.

Calder, after consulting briefly with his fellows, remarked in a bluff but angry voice: "We are here because you people invited us—Volyen or Sirius or Canopus, it's all the same to us. Our situation has become intolerable, and we'll listen to any suggestion."

"Neither Volyen, nor Sirius, nor Canopus—but Shammat," I said. "Krolgul of Shammat."

I risked a great deal in saying this. For if Canopus was not much more than the reminder of long-ago tales and legends, then Shammat was nothing, no more than curses and expletives whose source they had forgotten.

"Shammat, is it?" said Calder, and he was getting angry. His mechanisms were being overloaded; he could not take it all in. "Well, whoever it is, we are here, to listen. So which of you will start?"

I said softly, "Why not *you*, Calder?"

Calder said angrily, standing up to do so, "Our situation is this, that we all of us work, day and night, for all of our lives, which are short and difficult and painful, and the results of our work go to Volyen. And that's all there is to it."

"And," I prompted, "according to Krolgul of Shammat, you ought to remedy this by rising, though how this 'rising' is to be done is not specified, and by murdering Grice the Governor-General? That's it, isn't it? And your troubles will then be at an end."

When they heard it stated like this, there was a stirring and murmuring among the men around Calder. Who stood up and said, for the benefit of invisible recorders and spies: "I have never said that, or anything like it, nor has any one of us."

"No," I said, "but that has been the theme of certain recent speeches. And I have said that there might be alternative things to do. And I am prepared to put them forward."

And now Krolgul acted. He did no more than, as it were, murmur or remark to himself, "Greasy-guts Grice. Grice the Greedy." And remained seated, hands locked around his knees, smiling as if listening to some secret music.

At this Incent stirred and came to himself. "That's it," he shouted, or half shouted, the smile that goes with his self-hypnosis back on his face, "Grice . . . Grim-guts . . . Greasy . . ." And subsided again.

"Well, our young master has woken up, it seems," remarked Calder.

Meanwhile, I had observed that straight ahead of where I sat, high on the brown wall, was reflected a pale patch where there had been nothing. A glance behind me and up showed a small opening above the throne of judgment, and in it was Grice's face, as pallid, as sick, as suffering as it had been yesterday when he was listening to the oratory in the square.

But so far no one else had noticed it.

I said, loudly and firmly, "I will now make a short summary of what I think you might do—"

But Krolgul was on his feet, in the posture of the worker's emblem, and he was shouting: "Death to the tyrant, death to Grice, death to . . ." And Incent had come to life again, and was standing there beside me smiling. "Death," he was stuttering, but his voice was gathering force, "death to the Volyen bully, death . . ."

Is it possible, Johor, that we sometimes *tend*—I put it no stronger than that—to overestimate the forces of reason? I emphasize here that Calder is a solid, sensible man, whose life is spent in exact assessments, judgments, in *measure*.

And certainly, as Incent stood there, swaying a little, still deadly pale but strengthening fast, Calder was smiling in a half-pitying embarrassment.

I asked, in a low, calm voice, "Calder, am I to have my say?"

"If they will let you," said Calder, with a half-derisive, half-admiring laugh, and nodded at the two, Incent and Krolgul, in their heroic stances, chanting, "Death to . . ."

"Only you can stop them," I remarked.

Calder said, "Let him speak. . . ."

Krolgul at once stopped, with a sardonic, contemptuous shrug, and sat down again in his familiar posture that managed to suggest a modest and unassuming personal worth and at the same time an ineffable superiority.

Incent chanted on, until Calder half stood up and said to him, "Sit down, lad; let the opposition have its say." And Incent, gasping, sat, giving me appalled, apologetic looks, and then Krolgul looks of apology and of complicity.

I said: "What you have to do is diversify your economy."

I knew this would be inflammatory, because of its simplicity and because it was unexpected.

Volyenadna was a mining planet. That was what it was. That was what it had been, for as long as the history allowed by Volyen recorded.

A silence. And then Krolgul allowed himself, first of all a long, silent heave of laughter, and then a burst of laughter. Now laughter from the Volyenadnans. From Incent, a blank, heavy look and a loose jaw. I was particularly concerned for him: after all, if I could not save him, return him to himself again, then . . .

"Let him speak," said Calder, but on his face was a heavy sneer.

I said: "You are a slave planet, as Krolgul says you are. A rich planet, whose wealth goes elsewhere."

"To Greasy-guts," remarked Krolgul, in a low, as it were meditative voice.

"No," I said. "For generations the results of your labours have been taken from you. But it was not always thus. Have you forgotten that before you were the subjects of Volyen, you were the subjects of the planet Maken, and before that of planet Slovin, and both took from you the minerals you mined? But before that you were the conquerors. There was a time when you dominated Volyendesta and Volyen itself—"

"With what?" inquired Krolgul. "Ice and snow?"

"As the ice retreated, and you spread over the tundra, you multiplied, and did not find enough to eat or to keep you warm. You stole spaceships from Slovin, who landed here on a foraging trip, and you used them to travel to Maken and to Volyen, and you made others, and you terrorized four planets and took from them, just as now everything is taken from you. . . ."

Calder listened to this with some derision. "You are saying that we were blood-sucking imperialists, just as Volyen is now?"

"I am saying that you have not always been slaves and the providers of riches for other people."

"And you are suggesting that . . ."

"You are a rich prize for Volyen, and you will be for whoever succeeds Volyen, since empires rise and fall, fall and rise. Volyen will disappear from this planet, just as Maken and Slovin grew weak and disappeared, and just as you grew weak and were overthrown from the planets you had conquered. But whoever succeeds Volyen"—I could not, of course, even hint at Sirius here, for that was a word that could be breathed only to Ormarin, he was as yet the only one strong enough to hear it, and Krolgul himself does not know how soon Volyen will collapse in on itself and become a subject—"whoever will come after Volyen will use you in the same way, if you don't make sure they won't. But you could make yourselves stronger. You could become farmers as well as miners and—"

Krolgul was laughing, sobbing with laughter. "Farmers," he cried, while Calder's followers laughed. "Farmers—on this ice lump of a place." But his contempt for the planet suddenly showed too plainly, and Calder did not like it.

"Farm what?" he asked me, directly.

"If you will listen to me, you and your people, I will show you. Yours is not the only planet with these conditions."

"And what makes you think Volyen will allow us? She wants to keep us as we are; she's interested in our minerals, and nothing more."

"But," I said, "you have a Governor-General who in my view would listen to you."

And at this Krolgul was shouting, "Grice the Greasy-guts, Governor-General Guts, Greenguts . . ."

And suddenly Incent was on his feet, once again alive and alert and Krolgul's creature.

"Down with Grice," he was shouting. "Get rid of Grice and . . ."

I, across the din, looked hard at Calder and said, "Remember, Calder, I can help you. Remember I said this."

Calder did not allow his eyes to meet mine: always a sign that you have ceased to be real for these people. And, indeed, for a few minutes I felt as if I had suddenly become invisible, for all those hard, antagonistic grey eyes from the workers' benches, and of course Incent's passionate black eyes, avoided me, were directed at one another. As for Krolgul, he lowered his head as if gazing thoughtfully at the floor, while in fact keeping a heavy-lidded, hypnotic pressure on Incent, now again his subject.

"It is quite evident," Incent was saying, or chanting, in a low voice that gathered power, "that we are here at the fulcrum of a dynamic! What perspectives stretch before us as we stand with one foot in the shameful and turgid past and the other in a future where the forms of life will become ever more vibrant and luminous and where, grasping opportunities in hands that have lost timidity, we build happiness where nothing is now but sullen misery . . ."

Calder's group began to emit angry noises, and Calder shouted, "Come on, lad, let's hear your concrete proposals."

Incent, brought up short, stood smiling vaguely, his Rhetoric jumping and jolting through him so that his hands twitched, and so did his mouth.

Krolgul said in a low voice: "A concrete proposal! You ask for an action, an act! I'll tell you what act waits for you to—"

"—to fill it with the inevitability of history . . ." said Incent, almost tentatively, for his impetus had been checked and he could not regain it.

"Yes," said Krolgul, more loudly. "An act which will speak for you to the tyrants who—"

"—fatten on your anguish!" shouted Incent.

Krolgul: "Grice the Guts, Volyen's minion, Volyen's symbol, he stands here among you as Volyen; seize him and—"

"Grab Grice!" shouted Incent, jumping up and down. "Drag him before the . . . before the . . ."

"Bar of History," prompted Krolgul. And, with an almost unnoticeable gesture of his hand, he made Incent keep quiet, so that Incent stood with his mouth loose, his eyes half closed: the image of a sleeper, or of someone in a trance.

Suddenly from the band of workers came the shout, "Yes, that's it, drag him to judgment, let's try *him*. . . ."

"Down with him," shouted Incent. "We will drag him from his palace, we will make him stand here among us all—"

"Among the *people*," prompted Krolgul—and Incent was lost. Standing there among us, his arms raised above his head, he seemed to flicker and shine with the life that Krolgul was feeding into him. No check there now; Incent was his, and everyone in that courtroom leaned towards him in a kind of yearning, a hunger. And, Johor, I must tell you that I was affected myself. Oh, how small and meagre and pitiful suddenly seemed to me all our efforts, above all our language, so cool and measured and *chosen*. I saw myself as, I knew, those miners saw me at that moment: a figure apart from them, their lives, their efforts, an alien figure sitting quietly on a bench, indifferent and passionless.

But simply because of my distance, and because anything I said must seem so wrong, even brutal, I knew they would listen, and I remarked, with no raising of the voice, no show of willing self-immolation and sacrifice: "And once you have dragged Grice from the Residency, and even killed him, what difference will that make to Volyen? You will have a new Governor at once, and possibly one much worse."

A growl, a groan from the men, who looked, as if at their own lost potentiality, at the exalted Incent. But Calder did allow his eyes to flicker over me, just once, with a look of dislike that I was weak enough to find painful.

"And," I inquired, "just how do you propose to drag him from his palace?"

Krolgul said: "We shall go out into the streets and the meeting places and we shall say to the people, Come with us. . . . And that's all we shall need."

"I think perhaps not quite all," I remarked, in the same flat voice. Meanwhile I had turned my head just enough to see that Grice was visible to anyone who chose to glance up at the little window. He was leaning forward, gazing with sombre passion down at us. And particularly at Incent, the ennobled youth, who was chanting softly to himself: "Freedom or death, death or freedom."

I laughed. Oh, yes, it was a laugh as calculated as anything Krolgul went in for.

Through the mutters, then the shouts of indignation, I said to Calder, who alone of the miners was still sufficiently his own master to keep a connection with me, "Shall I tell you the last time I heard that cry, freedom or death? Calder, would you like to hear?"

Still those stony grey eyes refused actually to engage with mine, went past me again, and I said, "Calder, do I have the right to speak?"

With the same dislike he at last looked at me and nodded.

"Go ahead, then," he said.

And while Incent chanted, "Liberty or death!" I said, "It was on another planet. The people of a certain country were impoverished and the economic conditions chaotic. They wished to rid themselves of a variety of parasites who lived off them, one of these being a something called a church, which at least you have never heard of here. While they debated and conspired and conferred, always at great risk, certain professional revolutionaries took charge, using words like Liberty or Death, We can be reborn only through blood—"

"Reborn through blood . . ." chanted Incent, and it was as if the words were feeding strength into him. He seemed positively to float there on the power of the words he was using, or which used him.

"The King and the Queen, who were in fact quite well meaning and responsible people, were used as scapegoats, and the revolutionaries directed popular rage and resentment against them. The lies and the calumnies created a picture of monstrous personal self-indulgence that was strong enough to last centuries. The revolutionaries murdered the King and the Queen and the people around them as representatives, and then as the populace became more and more inflamed with words, words, words, the murdering became indiscriminate and soon the revolutionaries were killing one another. An orgy of killing went on, as the degenerates and criminals who always flourish at such times became powerful and could do as they liked. In the frenzies of killing and revenge, and the orgies of words, words, words, that everyone took part in, the reason for the revolution, which had been to change the economic conditions and to make the country strong and wealthy, became forgotten. Because in every one of us lies, only just in control, the brute, the brute that in this planet here was so recently one that ate raw flesh and drank raw blood and who had to murder to live at all. The energies of the poor country had gone into killing for killing's sake, into the enjoyment of words—"

Incent was chanting: "Kill, kill, kill . . ."

"And soon there was chaos. Into this chaos came a tyrant, using inflammatory words, uniting the disunited people by words, and he took control, reinstated the class that had fattened on the poor and even added to it, and then set about conquering all the neighbouring countries. He too, having risen by the power of words—*lies*—fell again, having murdered and plundered and destroyed. And the country where the words Liberty or Death had seemed so noble and so fine was in the hands again of a hereditary ruling caste that controlled wealth. All that suffering, killing, heroism, all those words, words, words, for nothing."

Calder and the miners now had their attention fully on me. They were taking no notice of the unfortunate Incent, who still stood there chanting. They did not look at Krolgul, who was inwardly conceding victory to me and quietly working out plans for another day. A modest figure, with his chin in his hand, he was watching the scene with an ironic smile: the best he could do.

"Calder," I said, "there are those who exist on words. Words are their fuel and their food. They live by words. They make groups of people, armies of people, nations, countries, *planets* their subjects, through words. And when all the shouting and the chanting and the speeches and the drunkenness of words is done, nothing has changed. You may 'rise' if you like, you may drag Grice or some other puppet to the bar of history or geography or 'revolutionary inevitability,' and you can make yourselves and your entire people drunk on shouting, and at the end of it all, nothing will have changed. Grice is about as guilty as a—"

At that moment I noticed everyone was looking, not at me, but past me. I noticed that the pale blur on the high, shining wall had disappeared. I saw Incent's face change from the exaltation of his *Blood . . . Death . . . Liberty . . .* into a perfectly genuine scowl of hatred. Grice was standing there among us, beside Incent. As exalted as he, as pale, as ennobled, in the same pose of willing suffering, arms raised, palms forward, chin lifted, eyes shining, he said, "I'm Grice. I'm Grice the Guilty."

"Rubbish," I said. "You are nothing of the kind. You are a person who has been doing his job, and not too badly. Don't get inflated ideas about yourself."

There was by now an uncomfortable silence. Even Incent had stopped his chant. The actual physical presence of Grice was a shock. No one had seen him except half invisible behind the various kinds of Volyen uniform, all designed to obliterate the individual. Of course, everyone knew that he was not some corpulent monster stuffed with the blood and flesh of his victims, but what they were actually looking at now was hard to assimilate. Grice is a weedy individual, pale, unhealthy, with a face ravaged by undirected introspection, weakened by unresolved conflict.

Grice said, with dignity, "Subjectively I can say I am not guilty. I do not stuff myself; in fact, I have been on a diet recently. I do not care about clothing. I am not interested in luxury, and power bores me. But objectively, and from a historical perspective, I am guilty. Do with me what you will!"

And, spreading his arms wide, he stood there before us, waiting for some apotheosis of fate.

"Just a minute," said Calder, disgusted by him, "where's your bodyguard?"

"They don't know I'm here. I gave them the slip," he said with pride. "I've been attending your meetings in disguise. Not as often as I'd like—I have so much to learn, don't you know! But I'm your greatest fan, Calder. I simply love what you do. I'm on your side."

Incent had collapsed. He was sitting on his bench, staring at this villain, and I could see he was in a state of clinical shock. I had to do something with him. I got up and pulled him to his feet.

"Well, I'll leave you to it," I said to Calder, who was conferring with his colleagues. As I left, dragging Incent with me, I heard Calder saying to Grice, in a disgusted, irritated voice: "Now, you run along back to your palace, Governor. And be quick about it. We don't want it to be said we've been kidnapping you, or something like that."

I took Incent back to our lodgings. He was really in a pitiable condition, fevered with Rhetoric, for he had not been able to let loose all the words that were in him.

I sat him down and said to him, "I am sorry, Incent, but I have to do it."

"I know I deserve it," he said, with satisfaction.

Total Immersion it had to be, then. "I shall cause you actually to live through the horrors of the events I described to Calder in the court," I said.

I made him a metalworker in Paris, not in the depths of poverty, of course, because it is essential for a revolutionary of a certain type to be free from the worst of hunger and cold and the responsibilities of a family. The most energetic revolutionaries are always middle-class, since they can give their full time to the business. He met with others like himself in a hundred poor places, foundries, cafés, dens of every sort, made speeches and listened to them, ran through the streets with mobs shouting out *words:* Death . . . Blood . . . Liberty . . . Freedom . . . Down with . . . To the Guillotine with . . . He greedily assimilated every bit of *news* about the King and the Queen, the court, the priests. He was like a conduit for words, words, words, he was in a permanent high fever of Rhetoric, he fell under the spell of all the wonder-workers, the hypnotizers of the public. Then, as words took power completely, and the madness of words had all Paris in its grip, he ran with tumbrils to the places of ritual murder, he shouted filth and abuse at King, Queen, aristocrats, he screamed hatred at former allies like Madame (We-can-be-reborn-only-through-blood) Roland, and soon he was screaming with the mob as former idols fell. It was he who was the loudest, the most vociferous, as Paris exulted in the details of cruelty. When the Parisians, on the call of the Commune, broke into the nine prisons and for five days killed in cold blood fourteen hundred people, it was he who carried Danton's message when told of this: "To hell with the prisoners, they must look after themselves." And he killed, and killed, always chanting as he did, "To the death with . . . death death death . . ." After the killing had exhausted itself, and people were sickened, he sang sentimental songs about the fate of the murdered, and ran about the city like a rat or a beetle because running and shouting had him in their power and he was unable to stop. And when the new tyrant took power, he ran and shouted and praised, "Up with . . . Glory to . . ." He struggled and lied his way into the armies of the tyrant, for he was now no longer a fervent, handsome, eloquent youth, but a rather fat man bloated with words and indulgence and cruelties, and he marched with armies into country after country, murdering and raping. And, finally, he went with the armies on the tyrant's last war of conquest, which failed, and he died of starvation in the snow with thousands of others, still mouthing *words*, abuse of the people whose country he had invaded.

And returned to himself, sitting in the chair opposite me, blinking and staring as the reality of his present situation became stronger than the life he had just left.

He began to weep. First almost silently, sitting there with blank, frantic eyes, water pouring from them, and then with abandon, lying in his chair, his face in the crook of his arm.

I left him there and went out into the streets. Everything seemed as usual. That is to say, the better places of the city—gardens, restaurants, cafés—were full of Volyens, and the Volyenadnans crowded the back streets, with their cafés and clubs. There seemed no more of the armed patrols than usual. In the Residency, a single light burned high up.

I looked in at Incent: he was asleep in his chair.

I walked across the square to the Residency and asked to see Governor-General Grice. I was informed that he had unexpectedly left for Volyen.

I left messages for Calder in all the places I knew he frequented that I was available if he wanted to talk to me, and waited for several days; nothing happened. I listened to Incent, who needed to tell me about the life he had just lived: the fever had—only temporarily, I am afraid—left him. Nothing burning and inspired about these halting, fumbling, painful words. He was shuddering and trembling, sometimes rigid with horror at what he had seen and at what he had done.

But I need to go to Volyen itself, that is clear. I cannot give Incent any more time to recover. Giving him *choice*—as, of course, I have to do, even when it would be so dangerous for him now to make the wrong one—I told him that he could go with me or stay with Krolgul. But at Krolgul's name he shuddered.

We are leaving at once.

KLORATHY TO JOHOR, FROM VOLYENDESTA.

I dropped in here on my way to Volyen, to see Ormarin.

The Sirian presence is very strong. Roads, bridges, harbours are everywhere being built. Everywhere are the camps of the slave labourers. In the skies are positioned Sirian craft of all kinds. There is nothing to be heard but talk of the coming Sirian invasion. Sirius, Sirius, they say. But who is Sirius? While I was there the spacecraft all vanished, leaving the skies empty, and reappeared the next day. Some shift of power on the Mother Planet. But they know nothing on Volyendesta of the struggle there; for them it is simply "Sirius."

Ormarin, our main hope, is in hospital! A setback! His medication could have been better judged. They subjected him to Benign Immersion, choosing five different historical episodes, all aspects of the conquest of the weaker by Empires at the height of their outward sweep. All short-lived Empires, and all from Shikasta at the time of their numerous and so short-lived Empires based in the Northwest fringes. Since it was Benign Immersion, he was not a participator in events, only an observer, but I am sorry to say that this course of treatment has plunged him into a state of mind that is only slightly better than Incent's condition of Undulant Rhetoric. Ormarin sits at the top of the hospital, gazing out over the desert weeping, and in the grip of a severe attack of What Is the Point-ism, or The Futility of All Effort.

"Come, take hold of yourself, man!" I exhorted. "Pull yourself together! You know quite well the Sirians, or somebody, will attack soon, and here you are in such a feeble condition."

"I don't care," said he. "What is the point? We will fight them—or not; we will struggle against them once they are here—or not; we will die in our thousands—millions—in any case. Those poor wretches, the Sirian slave labourers, will die in their millions, since that is their function. We Volyendestans will die. And then the Sirian Empire will collapse, since all Empires do sooner or later—"

"In this case, very much sooner than later," I interrupted.

"And then? Another example for the history books of a failed enterprise, a uselessness, something accomplished in blood and suffering which would have been better never attempted . . ."

He went on like this for some time, and I listened appreciatively, for seldom have I been able to hear such a classic case of this condition, with all the verbal formulations that are the most easily recognized symptoms, so beautifully and elegantly expressed.

In fact, I was having the interview recorded for the use of the doctors.

But what I had been hoping was that I could take him with me to Volyen to assist me with poor Incent.

The doctors assure me that Ormarin will soon be himself again, and ready to play his part in our celestial charade—a phrase he repeats over and over again. I find it quite an attractive one, appealing to those aspects in me which I know *my* immersion in these events is designed to cure or at least to make more easily controllable.

"This celestial theatre of yours," said Ormarin, his honest face full of the exhaustion that is the result of an overindulgence in irony, "this peep show for the connoisseurs of futility! This play staged by planets and constellations for the benefit of, one presumes, observers whose palate needs ever and ever stronger stimulation by the absurd—"

"Ormarin," I said, "you may be ill, our good doctors may have overdone things a bit with you, but I do have to congratulate you on at the very least an increase of overall understanding, a widening of perspective. I look forward very much to working with you when you are a bit better."

He nodded sombrely, his eyes fixed on visions of ghostly conquering armies destroying all before them, these armies almost at once being swept away and vanishing, to be replaced by . . .

I remember I myself suffered a prolonged and intense attack of this condition, and while it caused those responsible for me—you among them, of course, Johor—a lot of trouble, I can report that it is not without its consolation. There is a proud, locked-in melancholy that accompanies the contemplation of what must appear to the infant-mind as futility, which is really quite pleasurable. Very well, then, remarks this philosophical spectator of cosmic events, immobilized by cosmic perspective, and addressing the Cosmos itself; very well, then, if you are going to be like that, be it on your own head, then! And you fold your arms, lean back in your chair, fix a sardonic smile on your face, and half close your eyes, ready to watch a comet crash into a pleasant enough little planet, or another planet engulfed by—let's say—a Sirian moment of expansion due to a need for some mineral or commodity, a mistaken need, as it turns out, the whole thing a miscalculation on the part of the economists.

"I'll see you soon, Ormarin," I said. "On the whole I'm very pleased with you. You are coming along nicely."

But he has brought himself to ask, "Very well, then! If you are not Volyen, if you are not Sirius, who are you, with your authoritative ways?" When I mention Canopus—rarely—his eyes slide: he doesn't want, finally and definitely, to know.

FROM KLORATHY, IN VATUN
ON VOLYEN, TO JOHOR.

I went at once to see poor Incent. It had not been easy to find the right place for his recovery. What he needed was an absence of stimulation. But on present-day Volyen, where even the most secluded rural retreat will at any moment begin to vibrate to the din of machines or of recorded or transmitted noise? One of our friends runs a hotel in the centre of Vatun. Yes, it was in the capital itself that I was able to arrange what I was looking for. A large room in the heart of the building, well insulated, and above all without apertures into the outside world. As you will remember, Vatun is full of parks and gardens, though they are perhaps not as well kept as they were at the height of Volyen's power, and I wanted above all to protect Incent from the debilitating thoughts inevitably aroused by the processes of nature. The cycles of birth, growth, decay, and death, the transmutation of one element into another, the restlessness of it all—no, these were not for Incent, not in his condition. The slightest stimulation of any unhealthy kind was contraindicated.

I told our friend the proprietor, in the letter I sent by Incent, that of course no force of any kind was to be used, but that Incent would probably be only too ready to accept bland and unstimulating surroundings.

And so I found him. Leaving behind the crash and the grind, the shouting and singing and screaming of Vatun's streets, and the disturbing thoughts inevitably aroused by Vatun's gardens, I entered—perfect silence. I approached a tall white door at the end of a thickly carpeted corridor, opened it, found a tall white room, and Incent, lolling in a deep chair, gazing at the blank ceiling. In this haven of a room there was not one natural object, not so much as a thread of plant fibre in a carpet or the bed coverings, not a reminder of the animal world in the form of skins or parts of them, not so much as a flower or a leaf. What perfect peace. I myself was much in need of a rest after adjusting my inner balances, which had been, I must confess, disturbed by the philosophical torments of Ormarin, and I sank into a recliner near Incent and gazed with him at the whiteness all around, and listened with him to—nothing.

"I shall never leave here!" said Incent. "Never! I shall live out my life within these four walls, tranquil, alone, and doing no harm to anyone."

I did not bother to reply.

"When I think of the horrors I have seen and been part of—when I . . ." And tears flooded from his great dark eyes.

"Now, Incent," I said, and offered a selection of the soothing and useful phrases I had so recently offered Ormarin.

"No. I've learned what I am capable of. I've decided I'm going to apply to go home. But first I have two things I must do. One is, I must apologize to Governor Grice."

"Ah."

"And second, I want to find Krolgul and . . . and . . ."

"And what, Incent?"

"I thought—I would like to have a try at reforming him."

"Ah."

A long silence.

"Well, as you know," I said, "you can do whatever you feel you have to. That is the law. Freedom. Of choice. If you feel it is your destiny to reform Shammat, not to mention Puttiora, then . . ."

"And now you are laughing at me! It isn't kind!"

"Ah, well," I said, "perhaps it is too soon. In my view you should stay here a bit longer and have a nice rest. I wish I could do the same. But if you want to leave, then of course you may."

I left then myself, noting with relief that Incent stayed where he was. If a reclining position, feet on the same level as the head, can be called heroic, then Incent's approached the heroic: arms folded defiantly, chin confronting the ceiling, feet at attention.

After I left the hotel, through a lobby all excitement and noise—a trade delegation from the Sirian HQ on their planet Motz were just leaving, looking pleased with themselves—I walked straight into the park opposite. Some freely wandering gazelles came to greet me. They originate, as it happens, from Shikasta, stolen by Sirius and presented as part of a state gift. They licked my hands and nuzzled them, and I knew my emotional apparatus was nearly at Overload. Plant life in every stage of growth. The songs of birds. In short, the usual assault on one's stabilizing mechanisms. So hard did I find it to keep my emotional balance that I nearly went back into the hotel to join Incent.

Oh, the glamour of the *natural* life! The deceptions of the instinctual! The beguilements of all that pulses and oscillates! How I do yearn for Canopus and for its . . . but enough of that. Forgive my weakness.

I was, of course, on my way to Krolgul, and in fact had nearly gone to him first, before Incent.

Shammat has set up on Volyen a School of Rhetoric. This is along the lines of the very successful School of Rhetoric that flourished for so long under Tafta on Shikasta during its latter days, positioned there to take advantage of the emanations from the Religions and Politics. But when Tafta made his miscalculation and backed the wrong junta on Shammat, the school on Shikasta was neglected and became useless. It was Krolgul who studied the history of that school, and who applied to the new Lords of Shammat to try to make one work on Volyen. It has been in operation since just after your visit here, fattening on the effluvia from the turbulences of Sirius.

I do not remember your mentioning Tafta's school on Shikasta. It had two main branches, one disguised as a theological seminary, one as a school of politics. The first building was ornate, grandiose, providing every kind of gratification for the senses; the second was unadorned and functional. In the first, students used robes and accoutrements of great richness and variety; in the second, clothing was austere. But the kinds and types of speech used in the two apparently so different seminaries were almost identical, so that students could, and indeed were encouraged to, translate the religious into the political and vice versa, a process that usually needed no more than the substitution of a few words in a passage of declamation.

It was not possible to copy this exactly on Volyen, because Volyen's "aspirations for higher things" have always been identical with its political aspirations. But there are two main branches of Rhetoric, and the buildings that express them are quite different, one being severe in style and the other using all the aids of a sensuous kind you can imagine, from the artifices of lighting and colour to indoor plant-growing and culture. Sound is of course fully exploited. Thus a visit to the branch of Rhetoric described by them vulgarly as "with-all-the tricks" has the effect of reminding you of the Religious Seminary on Shikasta; while the one housed in a spare, undecorated building, full of students in plain clothing, induces comparisons with Shikasta of a different kind. If you remember, it was enough for a politician of the most crassly power-seeking sort to wear simple clothes and employ the speech of the common people to impress the muddleheads with "honesty" and "sincerity."

But since politics has accommodated, and still does, all Volyen yearnings for the better, it really is "as rich as life itself," to quote the slogan painted over the entrance to Krolgul's school. Volyen has been a subject planet several times in the past: its thoughts and beliefs are full of the vestiges of the Rhetoric of slaves. It has been an independent planet, using minimum contact with its planetary neighbours: the language of proud and self-sufficient isolation is still in use, even though self-sufficiency is long past. It has been a rapidly growing and ruthless Empire: songs, poems, heightened and emphatic speech of all kinds, still in use, remain as evidence of this phase. It is an Empire falling apart and disconsolate in its present state: but its language has not caught up with its condition. It is soon to be a Sirian colony: well, it will not have to invent new means of expression, for the commonplaces of its epochs of servitude will only have to come forward again and find new life.

But the recital of this cycle, I see, is beginning to induce in me symptoms of Ormarin's complaint, and I shall desist.

It turned out that I arrived at the school at a good time, for examinations were being held. I found Krolgul with some fellow examiners sitting behind a table at the end of a large hall, while students came forward one after another to show what they could do.

The examination hall is a simple rectangle, white, with no means of exciting the emotions by form, colour, scent, or any type of sound. In order accurately to test the effects of speech on the subjects, any other stimulus has been ruled out.

As I entered, I passed through a lobby crowded with the anxious examinees. They were from Volyen, Volyenadna, Volyendesta, and the two outside planets Maken and Slovin. Among them were several of our agents, notably 23 and 73—but you will already have had my reports on them. Since they were so young in the Service when they were captured by Shammat, they never had time to become fully Linked, and therefore are of no use to Shammat. Krolgul does not understand at all why his attentions to these two, who are just as enthusiastic as Incent, have no results. Because, the conflict in them being less, they seem to be so much more stable and consistent, he expects from them more than he does from poor Incent. . . . There is luckily so much Krolgul does not understand!

I greeted our two (temporarily) lost members and received their embarrassed greetings. For in their hearts they know themselves to be of Canopus, and in some devious way believe that their service with Shammat is still service with Us. The other agents did not recognize me.

As I entered, a young examinee had just failed. Krolgul and his associates had signalled to have her disconnected from the apparatus when he saw me; he jumped off the platform and came to greet me.

Beaming. Krolgul is always pleased to see me! Surprised? I was, and had to think it out. For one thing, our presence seems to him a guarantee of the importance of what he, what Shammat, is doing. On planets where they have been at work sometimes for millenniums without our—apparently—knowing it, they get quite downcast and wonder whether their efforts are worth it. No, my arrival in the Volyen "Empire" gave them all a great boost.

And the other thing is that they know quite well how partial their information is, and that our plans for any planet are based on blueprints that are far beyond them. Krolgul, working with considerable skill for a mass uprising "all over the Volyens, all at the same moment —and that's all and that's enough," to quote from a recent speech, knows in his heart of hearts that my expectations are almost certain to be quite different, because of *what we know.*

He hurried towards me with his hand out, grinning a welcome, looking rather apelike, and this pleasure was genuine.

He was wearing another semi-uniform. These are not uniforms *of* or *for* anything in particular, but most young people throughout the Volyen "Empire" wear self-invented uniforms. This is because they have been conditioned by recent wars and colonial uprisings which were all fought in uniform. Every army, even if no more than a guerrilla group, used uniforms, imposing uniformity down to the last fastening and belt and neck opening, and any infringement, even the slightest, earned penalties, sometimes death. In fact, it is no longer possible for them to think of war except in terms of uniforms. This mental set now infects every aspect of their lives. There is a certain type of covering for the lower limbs, in thick, unyielding cloth, always of the same colour, and very tight, emphasizing the buttocks and the genitals. It is not only worn in every corner of the "Empire," but has spread to the near planets of Sirius as well. A young person who for some reason or another does not own this garment will regard himself or herself as an outcast, and will be so regarded by others.

This particular uniform of Krolgul's is original in that the lower part consists of a skirt, similar to that worn by unskilled labourers— usually foreigners—on Volyen. On them it is hitched up between the legs into a waistband, but Shammat legs are too hairy and knotted to be displayed, so it is left to hang free. Also, it is coloured; the real reason is that Shammat loves strong colours, but the excuse is that "to wear black, the colour of the working clothes of the working masses, is a false identification." Over scarlet, blue, green, yellow flimsy cotton skirts are worn crisp brown tailored tunics whose main feature is that they are crammed with buttoned pockets all over the front and at the lower back. This gives the impression of a person who needs two free hands, probably to hold a gun of some sort.

Krolgul wore a bright-blue skirt, and his tunic was bulging with papers and writing instruments and various electronic devices.

"Servus," he said, shaking my hand. "You are welcome. Do you want to listen?"

"Do you think I have much to learn?" I teased him.

"Who knows?" he said, pleased. "We flatter ourselves that . . . but you will see for yourself." He signalled for the entrance of the next candidate, but stood beside me, giving me quick, almost pleading glances, of which he seemed to be unconscious.

"You are wanting to ask me about Incent?"

"Yes, yes," he said, all eagerness, but trying to sound offhand.

"He is by no means recovered," I said. Krolgul brightened. Extraordinary, when his own personality is not being governed by some impersonation or other, how transparent he becomes, how easy to read. "Nor, to my mind, will he recover soon. It is a very great strain on him, as of course you know, when you use him as a conduit as you do." Here there were a variety of flickering glances at me, doubtful, triumphant, apologetic, even embarrassed. For Krolgul seemed to believe that we did not know of Incent's importance to them in the battle between us, between Canopus and Shammat, though all our actions, both Shammat's and mine, since my visit here began, proclaimed it. "You risk making him very ill," I said. "At this moment he is undergoing treatment."

"Well, he is just one of your agents, as far as we are concerned," said Krolgul, in a bluff liar's style which even he knew was hardly convincing. And he took out a pipe and lit it.

"Krolgul," I said, I hope temperately, and with the "humour" without which one cannot survive a day in this place, "you are giving us an awful lot of trouble." At this he brightened, flattered again, jerking and writhing a little with pleased laughter. "But you really are on the wrong track, you know." I said this to observe how discouragement took possession of his whole person, and how suddenly, so that there stood this visibly dismayed person who, without any outward feature's betraying it, reminded me so often of the ape, the animal; a blinking, open-mouthed Krolgul, Shammatian Overlord for the Volyen Empire, stood drooping beside me, and his eyes a single craving plea: Tell me, tell me, tell me.

But the attendants had wired up the examinee, and Krolgul had to return to his place on the platform. I refused to go with him, but stood near the wall by myself.

It was a young male from Volyenadna, a stocky grey-green stolid creature, who showed no sign of nervousness, but began at once, raising his hand carefully so as not to disturb the wiring of the monitors.

"Comrades! *Friends*. I know I may call you friends, because of what we are going to undertake together."

The graphs and print-outs showing his emotional responses to what he was saying were displayed, not where he could see them and perhaps become influenced by them, but behind him, on a large, high screen. I, and the examiners on the platform, could watch him and, at the same time, note the precise condition of his emotional apparatus.

It was already evident that this one could not last for long, despite his apparent heaviness and stolidity: at the word *friends* every part of his organism had responded, and *undertake together* had lifted him almost to the limit.

". . . No, you are not asking yourself, 'And what is that?,' for you already know. *We* already know. . . ."

But the young man had already failed. On this *we* his voice had cracked with feeling; and the *Failed* buzzer went.

He was replaced by a strong, handsome young woman, from Volyendesta, full of assurance and calm smiles for us all.

She survived the first passage, with that dangerous and deliberately planted *friends*, very well; she went past that *we* while the machines registered hardly a flicker of response. But then it began to build up in her: ". . . If we do not agree on the reasons for what has come to pass, then we shall on the cure. We stand together here united in one thing, that the situation cannot go on like this. Why are we surrounded by gross inequalities, by appalling injustice, by dreadful poverty and cynical wealth. . . ." Her voice had acquired a timbre that meant tears were in her throat, and she could not last long. But she persisted, although we could see by the impatience and irritation with herself on her face, that she knew she was defeated. ". . . Why are we afflicted as we are by the bumbling stupidities of a bureaucracy groaning under the weight of its incompetence? Why in one street do we see the faces of young people who have never known what it is to open their own pay packet for their own honest work . . ."

Her voice cracked on *work*; the buzzer went. She strode off, bravely, but in tears of disappointment.

The next was one of the frail, pale citizens of Slovin, who always have so much difficulty in getting the solid, stolid, robust denizens of the other planets to believe in their strength. Tough and enduring and with a nervous system much less susceptible to emotional inflammation than most, they are in fact, once one has experienced them, much prized. The platform expected great things of this apparently fragile revolutionary; and in fact she went easily past all the trigger words that had undone the others. ". . . honest work, and in the next sicken at the sight of the overindulged and the purposeless. Why? Why?" These two *why*s caused all her recordings to rise almost to danger level, but she recovered herself. "Why? We all know why! But what is to be done? We know. Again we know. Do we not? Our situation is bad. It is dreadful. But it is not hopeless. What we need, what we must have, is sacrifice." And she was over the top. But so sudden was the swoop upwards of the recording needles that the platform conferred, and said to her that she could go off, rest, and come back for another try. (In fact, she then succeeded easily.)

The next was a Volyen indigenous worker. They are not the most attractive breed, being a dingy putty colour, and built heavily and on the whole without much grace. But they are known for their lack of emotional volatility. The needles flickered badly at *friend, work, sacrifice*, but recovered. "Yes. Sacrifice. And what is being asked of us is not only a tightened belt, though that *is* being asked; not only that we should work eighteen hours a day, even twenty-four hours a day, but also that we should agree to sink our separate and pitiful little individual wills and thoughts in the great whole, the great Will, the great purpose, the great *Decision* . . . that we must agree once and for all that things cannot be allowed to go on like this. Yes, once and for all, comrades . . . brothers . . . sisters . . . *friends* . . ." Up swept the needles. The examinee himself put up a hand and begged for a later rehearing. It was granted.

The next was another Volyen. "And where shall we begin? Where? Why, with ourselves! How can we build a new world with old hearts and old wills? We need new, clean, young hearts. . . ." *Hearts* is where that unfortunate was lost. But all those who survived that far were granted a second chance.

There followed several who failed very early on, at the first testing words. Then, at last, one survived the whole course. It was another of the silvery, fragile, apparently so vulnerable Slovins. "We are surrounded by the heights of colossal events, in the light of which future generations will view their own fate. There cries out in the merged thunder of the times the present fate of planets. We need clear eyes and an unflinching purpose. We shall begin and complete our work to the sound of workers' hymns and songs. Your work is not slave labour, but high service to the fatherland of all the decent people. Sacrifice! A united will! Only on this road shall we find the way out, to salvation, warmth, contentment. Sacrifice. And clean hearts. Clean hands. *Love* . . ."

This first wholly successful candidate retired, full of the shy modesty that is the convention here for people who have succeeded, and then the platform conferred. I could see that there was going to be a break. And I knew it was because Krolgul had been sitting up there biting his fingers and crouching in his seat, leaving the actual work of attending to the prowess of the examinees to his associates, while he brooded about what I had said. He wanted to come back to me and to press and to wheedle, until I told him what I knew. Until he knew what the plans of Canopus were, what the information of Canopus was . . .

But at this moment something unexpected happened. Into the examination hall walked—quietly enough, dressed unremarkably in a variation of local administrative-class dress—Incent. He saw me sitting there and made a gesture to me: Do not worry.

He did not meet my eyes, though. A bad sign; this meant that nothing I could say would affect him. I settled back so that what must happen, could. . . .

Krolgul had leaped up at the sight of him, all renewed energy and purpose. Then, having cried out, "Incent . . . ," he remembered my presence and glanced towards me, but in the same way as Incent, not allowing his eyes to meet mine.

Incent's manner with Krolgul was—there is only one word for it— lordly. He stood in the examinee's place and signalled to the attendants to wire him up.

"I intend to pass this examination," he said, in the calm, almost indifferent way of his illness; for of course he was ill, though this need not be obvious to the examiners. He was depleted of emotion still; he was empty, after such an excess of it. No one recovers from Total Immersion in a few days, or even many. His emotional reservoirs were low; therefore he seemed calm; therefore did he give this appearance of benign urbanity.

When he was standing upright there, all the wires and leads in place, he smiled confidently at me.

"I am ready," he said.

Well, it was very bad.

"Comrades. *Friends* . . ." I think Krolgul expected him to be lost at that very first trip-word, but what happened was much more alarming. Behind Incent, on the monitors, we could see that the needles, far from registering alarming peaks and jags and heights of emotion, were often out of sight at the bottom of the scale. So low was Incent that his whole system had gone into reverse. The word *friends*, which of course he spoke at the right interval after *comrades*, so that the nerves of the auditors had to vibrate in expectation, only caused what little emotion that was left in him to drain suddenly away. The needles flickered back into sight again at the bottom of the graphs. He was speaking in a flat, almost amiable way, though he got all the tones and intervals perfectly. He went through the gross inequalities and the injustice and so on very well, though there was literally no fuel left in him at all. I could see the examiners stirring and whispering. Krolgul was frightened out of his wits, looking at me the whole time: he had never seen anything like this, and had not known the condition existed. He was afraid I was going to punish him.

But Krolgul, of all the creatures in our galaxy, is not likely to understand free will. Not yet, at least; not for a long time.

Incent was droning on. "Sacrifice. Yes, sacrifice . . ." And suddenly he fell, the wires pulling free.

I went over to him and brought him to himself.

He did not inquire where he was, for he knew at once, and stood up, weak but himself.

He looked at me with such shame, and said: "You had better take me back to the hotel, Klorathy. I've made a real fool of myself."

And to Krolgul: "All right. But I haven't done with you all yet. I was going to show you that I could pass your test and *then* reason with you on the basis of being immune to . . ." And he wept, but the tears of weakness and emptiness, small, weak, painful tears.

Krolgul was running round us as we went to the door, panting and exclaiming: "But . . . but . . . I hope you aren't going to hold us to account; I knew nothing about Incent's coming here, I absolutely absolve myself of any responsibility."

Incent was too weak to leave the building at once. We sat in an antechamber for a while, watching the examinees prepare themselves for the Examination in Rhetoric, which they did by using one another as sounding boards and checks on themselves in a piece which, for emotive words and general tone, was more taxing than the set piece in the actual examination hall.

"What, then, is it that we are aiming at? What? Why, nothing less than the whole, perfect, radiant future of us all and our children! What is there to prevent this paradise? We all know there is nothing! In our soil lies the wealth of harvests and of minerals. In our seas and in the air, food. In our own hearts, love and the need to live happily in a happy world where sorrow is forgotten! What is it in the past that has given birth to sorrow, has bred unkindness? Why, only the lack of the will to abolish these things. And now everything has changed, for we have the will, and we have the means. Forward, and let us lay our hands on our rightful heritage—happiness. Happiness and love."

Incent listened to this not totally without emotion: which I was pleased to see was scorn.

"What horrible drivel," he was muttering.

"I'm glad to hear you say it. I hope you will continue to think so."

"Well, I would have got through the test piece if I hadn't passed out, wouldn't I?"

"Yes, but Shammat has words-of-power they didn't use there at all."

"Have they? What? No, don't tell me, or I suppose I'll succumb. I really do feel so awfully ill, Klorathy. I'm giddy, I must lie down."

He lay face down on a bench, his hands over his ears, and I continued to watch the lively scene. Not—as you can imagine, Johor—without mixed emotions! What an attractive lot they were, these chosen ones from all over the Volyen "Empire." Chosen, first of all, because they were for the most part from the privileged: the poor and deprived seldom have the energy to will for themselves positions of power. Chosen because they had natural ability. Chosen because natural abilities are matched with opportunity; plentiful opportunities now, with the "Empire" falling apart. Young, for the most part; educated as far as such backward corners of the Galaxy understand the word; lively; full of the determination to succeed. Of the candidates I watched, while Incent lay there trying to recover his inner and outer balances, few succeeded in getting to the end of the difficult piece they set themselves. Fewer would pass the examination itself. But all would return to enrol for further sessions of study in Krolgul's school: they believe in themselves, and the future that Krolgul promises them.

Shammat prowls through "the Volyens"—to use the colloquialism —watching every public gathering for signs of talent. Some young person, who has perhaps leaped up to orate because of a genuine anguish over the lot of the unfortunate, because of a real vision of radiant futures, finds at his side this personage who understands him and his innermost thoughts, dreams, aspirations. "How wonderful you are," say the eloquent, compassionate eyes of this new friend. "How your beautiful ideas do you credit! Please go on. . . ."

This chosen one, chosen now by Shammat, finds efforts encouraged, speeches applauded, above all in every word the implication that these two, these new comrades, these *friends*, understand where others do not; finds that he is considered to be of finer, nobler, *braver* substance than most. Oh, how cleverly Shammat uses the instincts for evolution towards the better that are implanted in every creature in the Galaxy! But while a generous and imaginative understanding supports this neophyte, there is also judicious and intelligent criticism. "You might have phrased that a little better," breathes Krolgul, if it is indeed he, and it often is, for his energy is superb. "Perhaps if I might suggest . . ." Only too happy is this aspiring one to find a genuine friendship, which is able to teach as well as to support. And so a career develops that has no future in the existing order, but relates only to an idea; the aspiring one, as he or she looks about at the chaos, the ugliness, the disorder of a time of disintegration, sees beyond it some infinitely noble society ruled by himself. But Shammat has never said, in any of these competent criticisms, "You aspire to power over your fellows." Only "You yearn to serve." With Shammat at their side, these young people learn the business of arousal by Rhetoric to the point where, judged ripe, they are offered a course of training. . . .

"You are very good at this," says Krolgul, with that modest and comradely complicity in which Shammat specializes, and which indicates in every look, smile, touch of the hand, *You and I together against those others out there, the others without understanding.* "Would you like to be even better? We can teach you, you know. We? Let us say, *friends*. But you have a handicap—do you mind my mentioning it? It is a wonderful thing, it is great, it is truly inspirational to watch you carry others away, watch you being carried away to such heights of fervour, to watch you becoming drunk on your own visions. But if you want to ascend to the control of real professionalism, that is a stage you must leave behind!" And here Shammat cushions the shock, cradles in understanding the neophyte's moment of disillusion. For throughout "the Volyens"—Volyen itself and its colonies —thanks to the influence of Volyen, emotion is much prized. It stems from the hypocrisies of Empire, from the predominant emotion of the ruling class of that ruling planet. (Though from our point of view this rule has been so short, it has been long enough to infect a group of planets with the malady.) This emotion: "We are sacrificing ourselves, we Volyens, to bring to you, our children, the infinite advantages of our guidance in your development." Unreal emotions breed others: to weep, to emote, to show that you are weeping and emoting, these monstrous perversions are prized. Even by the lively and rebellious young people who see through the hypocrisies of "guidance" and wish only to free themselves "for ever" from Volyen. To hear that they must learn to separate in themselves their yearning for a perfect world, and their verbal expressions of it, from their cool and observant minds . . . no, it is hard to take, and Shammat knows it. "No, no," murmurs Krolgul, all sympathy, "I do not ask you to feel less for the sufferings of others. Can you believe that of me, now that you have come to know me so well? Perish the thought! Never! But to be effective, to become an instrument of the upward strivings of the Galaxy, to address the infinite and legitimate hungers of the poor, the suffering, the unfree—then you must learn to use words but not be used by them."

Oh, yes, it is with the wriest of thoughts that I have heard—so very often, for I have been present when Shammat is at its work, though Shammat has had no suspicion of it—this caricature of Canopus, this shabby mimicry.

And it is because Shammat can use words that *sound* so similar to Ours that so many of our own were among those aspirants for a degree from Krolgul's School of Rhetoric that day. I noted them, I spoke to the two who knew me, using our own quiet words that might remind them, that *will* remind them, when the time comes, that they are not Shammat's, that their future is not to become one of the power-hungry of the Galaxy.

What Shammat does, in short, is to allow "life itself" to throw up its material, encourage "life itself" to develop it, and then, when these people are already well accustomed to assaults of Rhetoric, both from others and as used by themselves, they are taken into Krolgul's school, where they have to learn to become immune to it, so that they may control crowds by the most passionate, violent, emotional language possible, without ever being affected by it.

And never, during the preparations "in life itself" or in the school, does Shammat say to its disciples: "This is a school for the use of power over others, for the crude manipulation of the lowest instincts."

How easy it is for the unprepared, for the innocent, to lose their way: when Incent at last rolled over from his prone position on the bench beside me, he said, "Klorathy, I have been thinking, why not enrol me in Krolgul's school? He need never know that I am here simply to learn what I need."

"And what do you need?"

"How not to be manipulated by words. What else?"

"And you really cannot see any difference in the methods we use to harden you against Rhetoric, and Shammat's?" He was lying there, our Incent, moodily elongated, arms behind his head, legs straight, black eyes brooding, very pale because of his condition. Meanwhile a young Slovin orated, "What, then, is it that we are aiming at? What? Why, nothing less than . . ."

"They certainly seem to have a much more enjoyable time of it than we do," he grumbled.

"Indeed they do. Enjoyable, that's the word. What is more enjoyable than power or the promise of it? *When do we ever flatter you, Incent?*"

A short, bitter laugh. "No, you can't be accused of that, Klorathy. Well, perhaps I *choose* to learn what I need in Krolgul's school and not with you! At least Krolgul won't make me feel as if I'm a contemptible worm without a redeeming feature."

"No, but you *will* be a contemptible worm without a redeeming feature. If you go through Krolgul's school, Incent, you'll come out a first-class little tyrant, I promise you, able to stand on any plinth or platform anywhere, reducing crowds to tears or arousing them to murder, *having them under your will*, and not feel a flicker of remorse or compunction. Oh, Krolgul's school is very efficient, and I was certainly planning for you to see it in operation so that you could make certain comparisons, but only when you were internally strong enough to be able to make the comparisons."

Incent lay there, looking at me: dark eyes, the blankness behind them showing that his degree of exhaustion, though improved, was still severe.

"Some of our people are there, with Krolgul. One of them is reciting now. Agent 73, I know her."

"Yes, and when they've come to understand, through life itself, what they have become, do you imagine it will be an easy task to build them up inwardly, to restore to them what has been stolen? Incent, you are at risk. More than, perhaps, some of the others. Your temperament, your physical tendencies, your capacity for self-projection—"

"Thanks," said he, histrionically. "What equipment I've got, then!"

"Well, *who chose it*, Incent? No, I don't want to hear any complaints that you think free will is a mistake. What do you suppose the difference is between *them* and *us*? It is that *you* choose."

A long silence, while some youth chanted: "And what is there to prevent this paradise? We all know there is nothing! In our soil lies the wealth of harvests and of minerals. . . ."

"Very well," he said. "But you'd better keep me under your eye for the time being, hadn't you?"

I took him back to the hotel, and I do not need to say with what relief we entered the wonderful, all-artificial, cool, stimulus-free white room.

And there we have been resting. Side by side on the recliners, I on my back, he prone and staring at the dull black of the flooring through the lattices of the chair, we recovered together. It was as silent as in a cave deep under the earth, as silent as if we floated in the black spaces between galaxies. The tall slim room reached up into the building, and at its top was a place of quiet light.

At first you are allowed only glimpses of circles, triangles, squares, all a luminous white on flat white, and the shapes darken, turn grey and then duller grey on a white that begins to shine, though softly. These statements of order remain, so that the eye may travel, but resting, soothed, reassured; soon, however, the mind begins to protest against changelessness, longs for relief, and as you understand that this is your thought—a hunger transmuted from a sharp need into the passionless stuff of the mind—the eye is in movement again because up there, at the very tip of the dim shaft, it is not polygons but polyhedrons you are trying to encompass with your gaze. They stand there, as it were waiting in the air, but their solidity is not yet defined and heavy, and you still believe it is a hexagon or an octagon that is enticing your gaze up into itself. But no, there is mass, and there is weight on the faintly gleaming white. Silence and stillness, no movement at all, for a long time, a long . . . And then again, when the restless eye begins to demand change, movement there is, tetrahedrons are changing into octahedrons, and then—dazzlingly!—into those charmers icosahedrons, which transform themselves into icosidodecahedrons, and it seems as if high above you in the tapering dimnesses of your own mind roll spheres that have within them all the luminaries, solid and plane, so that dodecagons tease star polygons, and a decagon may merge into a dodecahedron which resolves into a pentagon which opts, modestly, for the condition of being a cube. Though not for long . . .

Infinitely refreshed, I suggested to Incent that he might turn over and look. He did so, but at once groaned out, "Snowflakes!" and flipped back again, to lie face down.

I continued to amuse myself with the mathematical game, and altered the controlling mechanisms from Automatic to Manual, so that I could at will move from the plane into the multi-dimensional and back again, for no sooner had I decided that I could never be seduced from the fascination of the dance of the polyhedrons, than I knew that I could contemplate for ever a ceiling that had become flat and decorated luminously with the patternings and intricacies of the interlacing polygons.

While I was returning to myself, Incent was also recovering, or at least showing signs of wanting to. "I have been thinking about Governor Grice," he said.

"Oh, no," I said. "Do you have to? You really do have no sense at all of your boundaries, Incent!"

"Oh. Is that it? Is that what's wrong with me?" At the idea that there was some hope of a diagnosis he brightened: it is quite extraordinary how these children of Rhetoric are comforted by the *word*.

When I did not say anything, he said, "Oh, Klorathy, when I think of how unjust I was. After all, Grice was only doing what he had to do. And yet I was wanting to punish him as an individual."

"Incent," I said, "if you'd only do your homework—Do you do it?

Do you in fact study what has been set for you? Because there are no indications in your speech or behaviour that you do anything of the sort! *If* you did, you'd know that when individuals or groups or associations of groups are made exemplar for the populace, they are always blackened and vilified before the ritual sacrifice. After all, you could even look at it as a sign of decency, or of the embryonic beginnings of justice, that it is so hard to get people to kill—even in hot blood—other people who they think are only doing their duty, though misguidedly. No, they have to be told that Grice is Greasy, and that Klorathy is Cruel, and that Incent is—"

"There is something very stale and boring about that," said he, turning over suddenly and lying with his forearm across his eyes, ready to shield them, but gazing into the intricate patternings above us.

"You mean the words are stale," I said. "You have heard them a thousand times in our schools. But they do not seem to affect behaviour, certainly have had little effect on yours, so the *idea* isn't. When you enthusiasts and revolutionaries can withstand Krolgul and refuse to allow yourselves to be whipped into lathers of self-righteousness at slogans like Grice the Greasy, *then* you can use words like stale—"

"I wish I could go and apologize to him."

"There is nothing stopping you."

"Why do you put this terrible burden on us?"

"Why is this burden placed upon us all?"

"You too, of course. I forgot."

"All of us."

"Why, it is too much. We are not fit. I am not fit. Oh, no . . ." And he shut his eyes, away from a vision in the cool shade above of how a pattern of star octagons shifted from the flat into the three-dimensional, and back, lines and planes of dark grey on light grey, then a slight, fine black on shadow that was white only because a sharper white did not lie close enough to contrast with it and contradict. White upon white, or white that was as if a subtle warmth had been withdrawn, a world of strict and formal shapes lived in the spaces beneath the ceiling, which was itself unbounded, seemed to dissolve into nothing.

"Oh, yes, we are," I said. "Everyone of us has felt exactly like you."

"You too?"

"Of course."

"And Johor too—and everyone?"

His incredulity echoed mine. For of course I find it as hard to believe that you, Johor, were ever so feeble, as Incent does of me.

"And then?"

"You'll learn, Incent. But in the meantime—"

"You do rather despair of me?" And his giggle was quite consoling, being full of vitality.

"Oh, you'll do all right. But in the meantime—"

"You'd rather I didn't go running after Governor Grice?"

"If that's what you have to do, it's what you have to do."

"Hmm . . . I can hear that there is something about him I don't know. What is it?"

"If I were to tell you that in some quarters he is regarded as a Sirian agent, what would you say?"

He exploded into laughter, a good coarse crude bray of scornful laughter. I felt an increase of optimism about him.

"I suppose I can take it that you are planning to bump him off, or get someone else to, and that you have to blacken him first."

"Logical thinking," I said. "Congratulations."

"Oh, don't laugh at me. They used to tell me at school that I always had to worry any proposition through into its own opposite before I could let it go. . . . Well, is he a Sirian agent?"

"That is one of the things I am here to find out. You, Incent— though I can tell by the sudden change in the set of your shoulders you find the news a disappointment—are not my only responsibility down here. Though I can assure you, there are times when you are quite enough for me. . . . Do you think you can get along for a while by yourself in here, if I go out and do some fact-finding? Johor is waiting for a report." He watched me, soberly enough, as I prepared myself to leave. "Do you want the ceiling show left switched on?"

"Yes. It makes me think of Canopus."

"Yes."

"And you trust me to stay here alone, after having made a fool of myself so often?"

"I have no alternative, Incent," I said.

KLORATHY IN VATUN TO JOHOR.

If you were to pay a visit to Volyen now, Johor, I wonder if you would be struck most by the changes, or the lack of change? You were here when Volyen reached its peak as an Empire, having just conquered PE 70 and PE 71, and before it began falling back in on itself. It was very rich, self-satisfied, proud, complacent. Its public note, or tone, was the liturgic chant of self-praise characteristic of Empires at that stage. New wealth poured in from PE 70 and PE 71; Volyenadna and Volyendesta were already well integrated into the economic whole. The cities of Volyen itself grew and fattened with explosions of population due to an increase of general well-being: Volyen had been poor and backward for a long time, after having been sucked dry during its previous colonial period under Volyenadna. But the cities were horrible contrasts of extreme wealth and extreme poverty, for even at its richest Volyen was not able, was not willing, to keep its labouring classes in decency. These millions came into existence because of an improvement in conditions; but they were not allowed to live any longer than was useful to the privileged classes who employed them.

This was perhaps the most striking part of your Report, Johor, and one which was used in the Colonial Service classes I was teaching at that time to illustrate that an Empire can be described as wealthy; can increase its wealth many times in a century through loot and plunder; can present an image of itself, far and wide through a galaxy, of splendour and prosperity and growth; yet the bulk of its citizens may still be living as meanly and hopelessly as the most neglected of slaves. These, the poorest classes of Volyen, were worse off than slaves.

Your Report came out just at the time I was on leave on Canopus, and had undertaken to teach the course on Comparative Empires: Sirius, whose Empire had lasted almost as long as ours; and Volyen's, whose Empire in comparison is an affair of moments, provided my material. Your Report made the strongest impression on my students, and on me. I was able to base not only single lectures but also subsidiary courses on a single sentence. For instance:

It can be considered a rule that the probable duration of an Empire may be prognosticated by the degree to which its rulers believe in their own propaganda.

What riches we found in that, Johor!

Well, the complacent rulers of Volyen certainly believed in the image they projected. They saw themselves as kindly, parentally concerned instructors, bringing civilization to the backward populations they were engaged in enslaving and despoiling. And this made them blind to the real feelings that were boiling up under their so tender rule.

I remember how various stages of the Sirian Empire were used as illustration. In the earliest stage of all, they plundered and stole, murdered and destroyed, and this was done in the name only of the good of the Sirian Mother Planet. No pretence about it! (In the very earliest days of Canopus, we too took what we wanted, and blundered, and wondered why it was everything we touched went wrong and at length failed and collapsed, until we discovered the Necessity and were able to do what we should.) But as Sirius developed, not having found the Necessity, that Empire developed Rhetoric. Each new planet, each attractive new morsel of property, was swallowed to the accompaniment of words, words, words, describing theft as a gift, destruction as development, murder as public hygiene. The patterns of words, ideas, changed as Sirius grew a conscience and agonized through its long ages of change, expanding, then contracting, maintaining a sort of stability; then expanding or contracting again, always, always justifying what they did with new patterns of *words*. These word patterns never were anything like this: We are taking this planet because we need its wealth of minerals, or soil, or labour. No, one way or another the conquest was always described in terms of the benefit to the planet itself.

The lying Rhetoric of invaders can therefore, from one point of view, be looked upon as a tribute to morality. . . .

I remember that I used Puttiora and its pirate subsidiary, Shammat, as an illustration of the opposite, a frankness about motive that was even attractive compared with this:

The people of (let's say) Volyenadna, having voluntarily and enthusiastically agreed to our instructing them in the superior ways of our

*civilization, basely and treacherously rose against us, and had to be
taught a salutary lesson by our heroic soldiers.*

Shammat's style is, always has been, more this:

*Those dirty rats the Volyenadnans saw us loading up our cargo ships
with their new harvest and they tried to set fire to it and murdered
two of our men. So we taught them a jolly good lesson, and they won't
do that again.*

The Volyen cities you described were full of new dignified, imposing
public buildings, new prosperous suburbs, newly built forms of public
transport, bridges, canals, places of amusement—were full of a self-
confidence and vitality, all based on this view of Volyen at that time
as "the greatest in the Galaxy," and this consciousness of possession
and dominance was shared even by the poorest female labourer, then
likely to die a third of the way through her normal life span because
of hard work and overuse as a breeder. A loud, bustling, crude vitality;
and, for the most part, these cities were inhabited by people of Volyen
stock, amalgams of the original stock, which had bred with Volyenadnans, Volyendestans, the peoples of PE 70 and 71 (Maken and
Slovin), to make up "We Volyens."

What I saw when I went out from the tall room where Incent lay
recuperating was, at first sight, not very different from your picture.
The great public buildings of Volyen's proud "Empire" are still there,
though shabbied by time. The parks and gardens are generously
everywhere, but if you look close the trees are mostly old, and neglect
shows in eroding earth and in the dirty waters of lakes and ponds.
The prosperous suburbs are now parts of the inner city, for Vatun has
spread out and abroad into new, smaller suburbs and meaner dwellings; and the dwellings of the inner city no longer hold single families
with complements of servants, but several families each. The factories
and workshops of Volyen's greatness decline, and many stand empty.
The general mood is not of unthinking and loud confidence, but,
rather, of a puzzled and even querulous uncertainty. And everywhere
you see how the Volyens who not so long ago held most positions of
public importance are now replaced, often, by the citizens of their
subject colonies; and this goes from some of the most prominent to

the shopkeepers in the large and the little streets: trade was the motive power of Volyen at its peak, and now it is, increasingly, Volyenadnans and Volyendestans who own shops and organize trade.

As the "Empire" grew uncertain, and resistance by the subject planets made ruling difficult and in some places impossible; as conditions worsened in the subject planets—so large numbers of their population came "home" to Volyen to share in the wealth that had been plundered from them. As you walk through the streets and parks and squares of Vatun, you see as many aliens as you see Volyens. And perhaps that is the most immediately striking difference that you would see, Johor. As for the other differences, the primary ones, they are less easily described.

To say: This is an Empire in collapse—that is easy, and we have seen it all a thousand times before. To say: As an Empire collapses, those people who have been displaced and deprived tend to be sucked into the centre—nothing new about that. But each collapsing Empire has its own "feel," its atmosphere, which cannot be conveyed simply by talking of an uncertainty of will.

And in this case, of course, it is an Empire that will shortly fall apart as it is taken over by Sirius in a phase of its own implosion—and this brings me to the next and perhaps most important part of this, my Report to you.

As a consequence of a long contact with us, our slow education of Ambien II, the Sirian Empire developed a crisis of self-examination and questioning about its role, its motives, its *function*: it trembled on the edge of the real question, the only question: *What are we for?* The Sirian Empire, in one of its stages of contraction, so that its physical size was a fraction of what it had been at its height, was riven into two main factions, one supporting Ambien II in exile and the other Four who had followed her there. (That ex–ruling junta, the Five, have been in exile not far from here, on their Planet 13, for two S-years, fifty V-years.) This faction demanded an approach to us, to Canopus, with a request for an education in fundamentals, an understanding of the Necessity. Meanwhile, a decision to inquire into the possibilities of acquiring Virtue (their name for it) led to a premature conviction that they were already in possession of the real qualities. This faction, during the (brief) period it was on top, enthusiastically expanded, overrunning not only planets Sirius had previously colonized and abandoned, but planets previously not colonized because they were not thought to be of enough value. But in this new mood of "Virtue," in which they saw themselves as the bringers of benefits, even second-class and third-class planets have been forced to become reluctant members of the Sirian Empire.

While Sirius has been seeing itself as the bringer of *new* benefits, because of its *new* description of itself, its victims have been unable to distinguish between this fresh expansion of Empire and previous expansions, for all have been accompanied by torrents of self-lauding words, and in fact there has been no difference at all in practice. You will already have noted, of course, that this faction on Sirius illustrates the law to which you drew our attention: A governing class that are victims of their own Rhetoric are not likely to survive for long. The faction opposed to the exiled and imprisoned Five, whose ideas exerted powerful influence even though they, the Five, were unable to use any channels of communication whatever, were not able to combat these ideas, and from one end of the Empire to the other, everyone was chanting slogans about Necessity, and Virtue. But it soon became evident to nearly everyone that nothing had changed: the Empire was in a phase of expansion, and planets were falling victim to savage exploitation, as usual to the accompaniment of Rhetoric. The opponents of the Five, who had been conferring without cease as to the choice of the *right words* with which to discredit the Five, found that the Five were discredited by life itself, for talking about Virtue had not changed anything. The Five, together again in exile on their Planet 13, understood that they, again and for the thousandth time, had been deceived by their own verbal formulations. This time, however, there was a new influence, namely ours on Ambien II, and this did not cease because we were not in actual physical communication. The Five, in their enforced isolation and contemplation of events, came to understand that by being responsible for the use of *words* that distorted and perverted what Canopus stands for, they had been responsible, because of their misguided and premature advocacy of Canopus, for the discrediting of Canopus; but that this fact did not, could not, change the nature of Canopus and what Canopus could offer. The Five learned to hold fast to the truth that *when* Sirius was up to it, Canopus was there, would remain ready to instruct. And the

Five left it at that, refusing to issue new manifestoes, proclamations, theses, analyses of the situation, which they were always being pressured to do because every kind of clandestine messenger and envoy kept arriving on their planet from dissident groups everywhere in their Empire, and of course there were—and are—plentiful spies as well from the Opposition, mostly wanting to get formulations that can be used for their own purposes, and of course wanting too the benefit of the Five's many thousands of years of experience. There are also historians, archivists, recorders, and Memories of every sort. So the isolation of the Five is relative.

But not a word can be got from them of an excitatory, inspirational, provocative, *rhetorical* kind.

It might be said—is said, and often enough by the Five—that this is slamming the reactor door after the electrons have escaped.

For meanwhile, the whole Sirian Empire is in a fervour of words and phrases and slogans, all originating from the Five in their idealistic and Virtuous phase, now disowned by them; all of Sirius is word-fevered, and it expands desperately, frantically, partly because the sober and tempered guidance of the Five is now absent, and their successors are supported only by an idea of themselves as Rulers, an idea with nothing solid underpinning it, partly because expansions of Empires have their own momentum, partly because the present rulers of Sirius—a hotchpotch and a rag-bag and a miscegeny and a rag-galaxy if there ever was one—are the prisoners of their own Rhetoric and can no longer distinguish between fact and their own fictions.

And the word formulations they use are all, because of the period when the influence of the Five conduced to convictions of Virtue, of the most high-flown, simpering, sentimental, nauseating kind you can bring to mind, all based on the rewards of Virtue. I must say that I thought, before this visit to Volyen, I had suffered the worst that was possible in the line of verbal effluvia.

At the time of your visit—so recently, even in Volyen terms—the young of the expanding upper and middle classes all were educated for, dreamed of, and found a place in the administrative machinery of the Empire. Education matched expectation, expectation matched achievement.

But for the last thirty years, since the last war, when Volyen fought a dissident group from Sirius which planned to use this weakening Empire as a possession from which to begin its own adventure in Empire—fought and won, but at heavy cost, because that "victory" in fact weakened it and left it unable to recover—since then, the educated youth have had to face a very difficult future. Yet the education is still largely based on the past: that is, on a conviction of Volyen moral superiority over lesser breeds. Year after Volyen year, the youngsters emerge from the training establishments with all the equipment, practical but mostly moral, for running, administering, advising, *ruling* others, and find their occuption gone. Also, because of the savagery of the war with the Sirian dissident group, because of the lying propaganda on both sides, so soon to be exposed by "life itself," these successive generations of the youth have had a valuable but painful education in de-conditioning, in the use of their minds in analyzing propaganda, that of their own side as well as that of any enemy.

It was as a result of that war that a new mode or pitch or style came to characterize the training establishments of the young on Volyen, one that would previously have been impossible. It was a savage and angry criticism of their own elders, but a cynical criticism as if nothing else could be expected. It was a sneer expressed not only in the tones of a voice, but in characteristic shrugs of the shoulders, a superior tightening of the lips accompanied by a nod and the lowering of eyelids, as if to shield the associate or accomplice from the tedium of thoughts whose banality *of course* was not one degree better than has to be expected. The flavour *of course* pervaded these interchanges. *Of course* this incompetence, this indifference to public good, this venality, this corruption; *of course* the lies of skilled and cynical propagandists had to be expected. But not endured . . . For over the horizon, no farther than the next star and its friendly planets, was Sirius. Sirius the new civilization. Sirius the great and the good, the hope of the Galaxy. For the absolute readiness to see nothing but evil in Volyen was matched by a need to see everything good in Sirius.

And the Sirian agents, everywhere even then, noted this new mood among the youth, the future class of public administrators (though few of them would in fact find such work in the dwindling Empire of Volyen), and reported to the representatives of Sirius on the near planets, who then reported to Sirius (in the hands of the junta who had supplanted the Five) that the entire youth of Volyen, sickened by the flagrant corruption of the ruling class, revolted by the depredations of their Empire (you will recall that Sirius was again in the grip of fantasies about its own nature as a ruling power, and saw itself only as a source of virtues), were only too ready to betray their planet and become agents of Sirius. This without money, for the most part; without reward, other than that of a conviction of Duty well done; and purely out of idealism and love of Progress and Future Harmonious Development, not only of local galactic populations, but of peoples through the Universe . . . You will forgive me if from time to time I seem infected by the style.

That war of thirty V-years ago was truly horrible. A developing technology introduced new and awful weapons. The Sirian Rhetorics, and the Rhetorics used as counterforces by Volyen, were sickening. On Volyen there is a time when the young are able to see through local Rhetorics, though this is usually for only a short period before they have to earn a living and thus to conform; before they can be accepted as members of a governing class—and thus must conform; and now, when there is so small a governing class to belong to, before they join one or another of the innumerable political groups, each with its own Rhetoric, which they cannot afford to criticize, for if they do they will forfeit membership in the group, which is their social base, the only base they have for friendship. For Volyens, evolved so recently from animal groupings, for the most part cannot function outside groups, packs, herds, and each of these has its own verbal formulations which are sacred; they can be changed, but only with difficulty, and while they are being accepted cannot be questioned.

Rhetoric rules these youngsters again, when they have sought to escape from it. Shedding the Rhetoric of Empire, which they are prepared to analyze with acumen and to reject with scorn and contempt, they become prisoners of the Rhetoric of oppositional groups whose only aim is to become, in their turn, rulers who will govern through Rhetoric. Through the formulations and manipulations of *words*.

Sirius, skilled in group psychology, in manipulation, in the uses of ideology, knew how to subvert the young people at just that moment in their lives when they had turned their powerful youthful scorn on the Rhetorics they were refusing.

On Volyen these youngsters became Sirian agents in considerable numbers. This, long before it became part of the public consciousness that Sirius was a real physical threat, might actually physically invade and conquer; though why it was so difficult for Volyens to accept that it is hard to say, since they had themselves overrun and stolen other planets so recently. No, how these young people saw themselves was not "I am paving the way for an invasion by Sirius," which struck them as a laughable idea; but "I stand for the noble, true, and beautiful ideas of Sirius, which will transform this shoddy and pitiful and corrupt and lying Volyen into something not far from a paradise. These ideas will abolish the already disintegrating Empire of Volyen, and the sooner the better, for empires are wicked and disgusting. Sirius stands for the ever-upward march of evolving galaxies. Sirius means Justice! Truth! Freedom!" (And so on *ad nauseam*.)

While hundreds of thousands of "the flower of Volyen youth" have been dreaming of the virtues of Sirius, the fact is that this Empire is at this stage as brutish a tyranny as we have ever seen. At various times of expansion in the past, Sirius has simply decided that a certain planet would suit its purposes, sent in its armies, established a ruling base, exterminated those who resisted, and adjusted the economic conditions to its advantage. But under the influence of all this "Virtue," the pattern has become more like this. A planet lying somewhere in the path of expansion becomes next in the line of conquest. Agents and spies enter it in all kinds of guises and spread information about the advantage of Sirian rule. This operation is a mixture of purest cynicism and purest muddleheadedness and creates maniacs by the planet-load, for it is necessary both to know that the conditions you are describing conform to the classic descriptions of tyranny anywhere at any time, and yet to believe that these constitute "Virtue." Local populations "believe" at first in these fairy tales about Sirius to a greater or lesser extent. When Sirius invades, there is a core of believers ready to commit any crimes against their own people for the sake of "Virtue." They form part of the new ruling machinery. Some, if not most, soon become disillusioned as they see what horrors are being perpetrated around them, and these are at once murdered.

Others, blinding themselves, become willing tools of Sirius. The wealth of the colonized planet becomes available to Sirius. This process, of course, is nothing like the well-planned, thought-out processes during the times of the Five, who at least understand long-term planning of an economic kind, if nothing higher. No, all is muddle, confusion, inefficiency. Miserable exploited populations, refused any means of protesting, have to listen to the chants of self-praise of the Sirians and their local captive minds. Anyone who tries to use language accurately to describe what is in fact happening vanishes into torture rooms and prisons or, diagnosed as mad, into mental hospitals. There is soon a sharp division between the masses and the small, obedient governing class, one living in direst poverty, the other given every advantage. A major occupation is the fabrication of verbal formulations to disguise this very ancient organization of a country and to describe it as some sort of Utopia; a large part of the time and energy of the administration is concerned with nothing else.

That is the truth of all the Sirian colonies near Volyen. They can be described as prison planets. If this Report were to be stretched to twenty times its length, I could not begin to give an idea of the suffocating, lying, claustrophobic atmospheres of such planets: the poverty, the misery, the exploitation of every possible resource for the benefit of Sirius.

Meanwhile, on Volyen, a thousand groups of energetic, educated youngsters base their hopes for the future on the Sirian rule; and, as every year the training establishments spill out their occupants, they form new groups, new societies, new parties, all with one idea, to make Volyen "like Sirius," though each group chooses a different example from the near planets to use as inspiration. For, of course, information comes out from the Sirian slave planets about their real condition; unable to jettison the dream, these groups will at once change the formulations and announce that such-and-such a planet has unfortunately "left the correct path" but that another planet, probably just conquered (so that news of its real condition has not yet come out), is now the inspiration for all.

And the generation of Volyens who became agents for Sirius have become middle-aged or old. Everywhere through the administration of Volyen are people who became agents to one degree or another, and who then, through the processes of "life itself," saw what a nightmare they had been so anxious to introduce into Volyen. Some fled to one of the Sirian colonies, knowing they would get favoured treatment, even if it was only the comfort and contentment allotted to an imprisoned animal whose function it is to provide some kind of nourishment for its owners. Some were caught and imprisoned. Some were found out—and were not punished; for it was soon discovered how widespread was this weakness of the Volyen governing fabric and how many would have to be exposed, thus advertising everywhere the extent of the weakness. Some were never found out, but lived out their lives—still live out their lives—in dread of being discovered. But the citizens of Volyen are only beginning to suspect how many of their trusted rulers were ready to betray them, to the extent that even their secret services, whose first task, of course, is to keep a watch on the ever-expanding Empire of Sirius, were full of Sirian agents; to the extent that at a certain point the head of these secret services was a Sirian agent. . . .

And so—there it is, this fact that I think is perhaps of the most interest. It is here that we have this phenomenon—I believe unique, for I cannot remember another case of it, either in our Archives or in anything that has come to our notice from Sirius in the past—of an Empire (Volyen) being sapped and weakened by the thousands of its citizens who admire one of the worse tyrannies the Galaxy has ever seen; admire it not for its tyranny, but for its idealism, its "Virtue." The irony is that Volyen itself—not its colonies, which it has always reduced and enslaved—is rather a pleasant place. The extremes of poverty have been abolished, and you would not see now, Johor, if you were to pay a visit, streets full of people with all the obvious marks on them of hunger and illness. You would not see children ill-fed and cold. Nowhere is to be seen what you wrote of so sorrowfully, the use of children as labour in conditions that meant they must die, the use of females in cruel occupations. No, for just this small space of time, no more than a few of their decades, Volyen has been, still is, a place where there is adequate if not perfect health care, adequate education, enough food for everyone, shelter of some kind for most. And above all, an absence of that immediate oppression that keeps the Sirian colonies in sullen quiet, afraid to use words to describe anything at all as they actually see it.

This rather pleasant, if recently achieved and of course temporary condition, is what their idealistic youth long to overthrow.

And their idealistic ex-youth. Like Governor Grice, who came to adulthood at the height of the recent war and was appalled at the propaganda, first of the Sirian would-be invaders, and then of his own side, for he found it cynical and opportunistic. Who then, looking around him at Volyen's treatment of her colonies, felt he had been tricked and betrayed—by words cunningly deployed against him. Who then, meeting a member of his peer group who had become a Sirian agent, agreed to "give information, but only what I choose to give, mind, and when I choose!" (This formulation is only possible to a young male member of a ruling caste accustomed to choosing his times and his places.) Who, at last, finding himself deeper and deeper in the toils of Sirius, and learning of the real conditions in one after another of the Sirian near-colonies, gave himself up to his superiors for punishment. "Do with me what you will. I deserve it." They, recognizing a state of mind that afflicted at least some of their number, reflected, decided it was a pity to waste his real qualities, and made him first a minor functionary in their colonial administration, and then Governor. Thus Governor Grice, Greasy Grice, came into being.

But he has had to be sustained by salutary incidents. Such as visits from a certain Trade Representative, at whom Grice has learned to gaze as if into a horrible mirror, for an attractive and affable companion alternates with another, a writhing misery of a man, who begs Grice for sympathetic understanding. "That's all I want," he cries in the moments when he is not being the social adept; it is amazing how fast the two souls can switch places inside the carefully maintained flesh and well-tailored clothes of the spy. "All I need is to talk to someone who understands me, and what a hell I live in! But you know what I mean."

This is a Sirian agent who was trained to undo Volyen in any way he could. Picked as suitable material from an elite school on his own planet and sent to the Sirian Mother Planet for training, he was then instructed to make himself at home on Volyen, to insinuate himself into high places—and so on and so forth, as usual. Energetic, clever, ambitious, and above all dedicated, he pleased his superiors and delighted himself with his accomplishments. Meanwhile, he enjoyed life on Volyen, so agreeable a contrast to the gloomy fanaticisms of Sirian rule. It was some V-years before, as he described it to Grice, "all at once and in a single moment" the scales fell from his eyes. What was he doing, trying to destroy these amiable if feckless people, this pleasant if declining and badly organized society, in order to introduce the hideousness—as he now recognized it—of the Sirian Empire? He broke down. He suffered. Unable to confess to his own side, who would of course have had him murdered at once in the name of the Virtue, he confessed to the secret services of his host country, who were sympathetic with his moral predicament and who, when offered his talents, not to mention his "total dedication," as a double agent, temporized. Like so many of his opposite numbers in the Volyen services, he was left in a condition of wondering whether he was, or was not, "really" a double agent. Meanwhile, he was indeed being found useful by his confidants, in keeping people like Grice up to the mark.

Grice suffers bad times when he wonders whether he is a big enough person to sustain the ambiguities of his position. A Governor who hates governing; a Volyen who loves Volyen at home but not abroad; an admirer of the Virtue, but only in an abstract, pure, and ideal way, for never yet has the Virtue been applied on any planet in a way that deserves the name; a hater of Sirian Virtue, not to mention the Virtue of the Sirian colonies . . .

At such moments, when he tells himself that it is all too much for him, a visit from X never fails to convince him his own position is a paradise in comparison. "This is your pal, Mr. X," is how he announces himself to Grice, who has to shudder, not least because he wonders how "they" seem so infallibly to sense when he is low in spirits.

Grice is now on Volyen, demanding to be heard "at the highest possible level." This high level, recognizing that, indeed, it would probably be to their advantage to see Grice, is engaged in checking him out from the point of view of possible renewed defection: once an agent, always an agent, is how they see it. Besides, it is known to them that he has been observed in disguise at meetings of Calder and his men.

He is sending in one message after another, as he hovers in outside offices. "It is Urgent! You should hear me At Once! There is a Critical Situation!"

Krolgul has found all this out and is brooding about how to use the situation for his ends.

KLORATHY ON VOLYEN, TO JOHOR.

Yes, my information confirms yours. We may expect a Sirian invasion of Volyen earlier than we thought, *but by which planet?*

I have been following Grice, as I did Incent on Volyenadna: Grice has been no less fevered in his efforts. But Grice has been leaving a very different trace. Trying to ascertain from person after person what Grice is planning, I have had to conclude not only that he is disordered mentally, but that everyone can see that he is.

This has meant that his old colleagues, responsible for his being Governor, and who are mostly in the same delicate position *vis-à-vis* Sirius, have dealt with him by making excuses. Yes, yes, their attitude has been, what brilliant ideas he has brought with him for the well-being of Volyenadna; meanwhile, why doesn't he enjoy a pleasant holiday away from the provincial tediums of that planet?

Unable to make anyone in his own generation listen to him, Grice is now approaching one after another of the revolutionary groups that are his generation's successors.

I at last met up with him in a small town in the north of Volyen. He sent invitations to the Virtuous Party, the Party of Real Virtue, the Party for the Support of Sirian Virtue, the Party of Opposition to Sirian Virtue, the Friends of Alput (the Sirian CP 93), the Enemies of Alput, the Friends of Motz (the Sirian CP 104). These groups, every one of which is devoted to the future well-being and good government of Volyen, spend all their time quarrelling viciously among themselves.

When I arrived at Grice's hotel room, he thought I was the last of a long stream of young revolutionaries, and simply went on with a speech that he had been delivering for hours.

Striding up and down the room, his lank, pale hair flopping over a face inflamed with emotion, his pale eyes gleaming, gesticulating wildly, he was painting a picture (accurate) of the sufferings of the Volyenadnans, and (inaccurate) of the successes of "dedicated experts on colonial revolutions from Sirius." Meaning Incent.

"Grice," I kept having to say, "Grice, come down to earth. I am Klorathy. We saw each other there, don't you remember?"

He did and he didn't. He came stooping towards me, blinking and peering, literally vibrating all over from the effects of having to stop in the middle of his verbal self-stimulation. Then he sank into a supine position.

I talked and talked, more or less at random, until he was able to listen, and then I put to him that:

We, Canopus, could cause to arrive in Volyenadna everything necessary to start a new agriculture. In a very short time that poor planet would be enabled to feed itself adequately and be able to export as well. This would have all kinds of important consequences. He, Governor Grice, could cause the Volyen rule to be associated with this beneficial development, but he would have to be quick about getting the approval of his superiors.

He came, minimally, to life—"Them? You're joking!"—and slumped back into enjoyable gloom. "Rotten, hopeless, decadent . . ."

I let him run on for a while, and said, "Very well, but do you want these improvements—which would amount to a revolution of a kind—to be associated with a Sirian influence?"

This caused him to stiffen all over, in fright and shock; then to lift his head cautiously and give me a swift glance, and then lie rigid again.

He said nothing. But he was searching for a suitable formulation.

I had been hoping the shock would bring out of him some news of his exact involvement with Sirius, but it did not.

At last he said: "Well, there'd be plenty of people glad enough if that happened. . . ." And he burst into shrill laughter, then tears. For his conflict over Sirius was profound, even worse than I had feared. ". . . You have no idea how many people—I've been meeting them all day and every day since I came. It's strange, isn't it, we know exactly what Sirius is capable of now, but all the same it's as if they don't want to know." And again the reaction of mixed laughter and tears. "Oh, I know what you are thinking, I was taken in by it all long enough, but at least I . . ."

What I want to know, of course, is exactly the hold Sirius has over him. Is he held by blackmail? I think not. It seems to me the ruling class of Volyen, when it discovered the extent of its servants' subordination by Sirius, and how many were being blackmailed, simply took the power out of that threat by telling the same servants: Very well, you come clean about what you've promised Sirius, what hold they have over you, and we will stand by you—that will dish them, in ways they've never even imagined! For *they* are not the sort to stand by their own in similar circumstances, not at all; more likely that any hapless employee of theirs would get a knife in the back some dark night, or a dose of poison. An *"accident"* . . . No, I can see that Sirius, after so long and so skilled a process of involving hundreds of key Volyens in their plots, and then finding that Volyen had foiled them in this way, must have been at least temporarily nonplussed. Probably admiring too. Yes, I think I can imagine Sirius admiring their opponents' cheek in this game. For what tricks and traps and toils and snares were revealed then! And what nets and snares were left unrevealed! For some agents would have confessed all to Volyen; some part; some not at all; some falsely. Probably some highly placed ones would also have believed that, once they had confessed to youthful folly—"Please, I didn't know what I was doing" —and been forgiven, there was an end to it, only to discover later on that it was not an end at all! Sirius might say, "Yes, but you didn't confess *that* to them, did you? What will they think now if you say you simply forgot? You plan to say you didn't know anything about it? How naïve you are! Or how culpably careless!" Sirius might say, "Yes, but now that we are poised to invade, now that we are all around you, what do you feel about having betrayed *us*, who represent your real allegiances, to them, who are due only a sentimental loyalty? Shortsighted, wouldn't you say? No, no, we go in for the long perspective, the historical view. We'll give you another chance, if you will agree to . . ." Sirius might say, "You thought we'd forgotten all about you! But Sirius never forgets! Very well, but you know all we can do in the ways of punishments, don't you? And you'll feel the full weight of them unless you . . ."

And where was Grice in this spectrum of loyalties, or disloyalties, according to how you look at it?

"Grice," I said, "if I told you that Sirius would be invading Volyen very soon, what would you do?"

"Do? I'd throw myself off the nearest high building." But this was said with such painful relish that I waited awhile. "What difference would it make to a Volyenadnan—or a Volyendestan, for that matter, from what I hear of the place? Would the Sirian rule be worse than ours?"

"You could of course improve yours. Is there any chance of your colleagues' listening to you?"

"Them? They don't give a damn for their colonized planets!"

And suddenly he sat straight up and looked at me tragically, lips quivering.

"And they don't give a damn for me. Not one of them. And neither do the others."

By this he meant the young groups. They had rebuffed him.

You will note that their not giving a damn for *him* was what really reached him.

"Yes, but do any of them care about Volyenadna?"

"If you told some of them to go out there and join the revolution, they might listen to that."

"You are referring to Incent, I suppose? To Krolgul?"

"If they would have me, I'd go like a shot and throw in my lot with them, with Calder! But they don't want me! No one does. It's always been like that, Klorathy! Ever since I was small. I've never really fitted in. I've never been wanted. I've never been . . ."

And he flung himself down and wept, loudly and painfully.

I could see we can expect nothing from him, so I told the hotel to send medical assistance, and came back here to Vatun.

It is my belief that I myself should, as Canopus, try what I can do with Calder. I put this forward as an official request.

KLORATHY ON VOLYENADNA,
TO JOHOR.

I had hoped to meet Calder with his colleagues. He sent a message that he would come alone, to a place that turned out to be a settlement of a few clans in a cold valley far from the capital. Grey stone houses, or huts, and a grey tundra rising all around us to a grey sky.

It was a miners' club, but at an hour when they were at work. A woman served us the thin, sour beverage of Volyenadna and went out, saying she had to prepare a meal for her children.

This is the conversation that took place.

He was in that condition of irritable gloominess that indicates, in this species, an extreme of suspicion.

"Calder, would you describe this tyranny you live under as an efficient one?"

He slammed his great fist onto the table and exploded: "Tyranny, you say! You can say that again! Filthy exploiting callous swine who . . ." He went on for some minutes, until he ran into silence. "But you know what they are like," he added.

"What I asked was, is it efficient?"

He sat blinking at me, confused; then, feeling himself attacked, growled, "You forget, I've never been out of this planet. How can I make comparisons? But I take it you can. *You* tell me, then, is it efficient or not? From where we sit, it is efficient enough: it drains all that we make with the sweat of our brow and leaves us . . . as you can see for yourself." And he sat there triumphant, as if he had made a good point in a debate, even shooting glances to either side as if to check up on the reactions of an audience.

But I could see that his need to speechify was fed, temporarily at least; and that now we could profit from his attention to me. For he was sitting there, leaning a little forward, his grey, flat eyes searching my face. A solid, heavy, slow man, his thoughts slowly at work in a mind that had learned only distrust.

I said, "Calder, it is an inefficient tyranny. And has been for a long time now—for all your life, certainly. It is inefficient, as tyrannies are in their last stages." I stopped to let this sink in.

"I haven't noticed signs of their deciding to leave us in peace!"

"When the Volyens first came, they knew of everything you thought, planned, let alone did. They were everywhere. And where are the nearest Volyen police to us today?"

He nodded. "Still, they do well enough."

"But not for long . . ."

"So you say!"

"Tell me—a specific question. If the rocks, let us say these flat rocks lying all around us on the hillside, were to change colour from grey to a dull red, do you think the Volyen administration would notice it?"

Here he heaved with laughter, again sharing the joke with the invisible audience at the expense of my stupidity.

"No, I don't think they would, no. I can say that much." And he pulled out a pipe and lit it, slowly and with emphasis.

"I can offer you a form of food that would make you independent. It is a kind of plant, like one of your lichens. It grows on rock. A few spores scattered on the rocks of this valley, and they would all be covered with it very quickly. You can eat it raw. You can cook it as a vegetable. It can be fermented in various ways, which will change its nature. With this plant you could be self-sufficient on Volyenadna."

He had slowly leaned back in his chair, and it was as if his eyes had become half their size. A sceptical grin stretched his lips, between which hung the pipe emitting narcotic smoke. He had such command of his invisible audience that he had even sent them conniving glances. He was a solid block of cold, rejecting suspicion. Then he gave a snort of contemptuous laughter, and then a summoning shout, and the woman came from next door and, as he snapped his fingers, said, "Yes, at once," and refilled our glasses.

"Food," he said, heavily. "Well, if it was as simple as that."

At the word *food*, the woman gave us a rapid, clever glance that took in everything about us; until that moment she had not given us much of her attention, being obviously harried with family problems. And now I saw her shadow hovering on the wall beyond the half-open door. Very well, I thought, I had not planned on this, but let us see. . . .

"It is as simple as that."

"We have a saying on this planet—"

"Yes, I know. It is this: 'Never trust strangers when they come bearing gifts.' "

"How did you know?"

"Because every planet has a version of this saying. But is it really so useful a guide, useful under every set of circumstances?"

"Oh, well," he said, wagging his head knowingly, "it's good enough for us!"

"Calder, you are a very sensible individual. I was looking forward to this talk, an exchange with a straightforward, sensible, no-nonsense person. I can call you that because of these hard lives of yours—and you have no idea how terribly hard and deprived and bare they are, Calder, since you have nothing to compare your conditions with—it is because of your hard lives that you are sensible and down-to-earth. No room for the nonsense I find when, for instance, I am on Volyen."

"Yes, well, I see your point. Some of my mates went there on a delegation. A rotten lot there, I'd say."

"Well. But I had hoped I would be able to say a few simple, straightforward things to you, and that you would listen."

He sat silent, slumped forward, looking down at his glass, which was already empty. He seemed to go loose all over. Receptive. For a few moments at least.

"Your situation on Volyenadna is this. You produce only minerals. All your food has to be imported—at this time, by your masters, the Volyens. You are completely at their mercy. You cannot rebel, or even bargain, for the meagreness of your food resources cripples you. Except for the period when you yourselves were a piratical Empire and grabbed food from—"

"You say that we were an Empire and as bad as the Volyens, but why should we believe you?" he shouted.

"Oh, Calder, given the chance, every planet will become an Empire. It is a stage of growth this galaxy has reached. It is a question of what kind of Empire—if you are interested, we can discuss that. . . ."

"Let's get back to this food of yours."

"It grows very fast. Spreads. Yet there are means of controlling it. It will make you independent, Calder."

"You sit there, and just let drop—as it might be, between one glass and another—that there's a plant that will change our entire situation . . . just like that. Well, why did we never hear of it before?"

"Who was to tell you?"

He maintained a kind of stylized sneer on his face, but he was thinking hard.

"Krolgul never mentioned it."

"He has never heard of it. Shammat has as yet to get its hands on this plant. It is called Rocknosh, by the way."

"Shammat! Canopus! You might be a Sirian spy, for all I know."

"And if I were? You would soon find out, by experimenting, whether the plant was of any use to you."

"The place is suddenly crawling with Sirian spies. Every second person, they say, is a Sirian spy."

"With good reason, Calder. The Volyen Empire is at its end. Sirius is about to overrun it."

"We shall fight them," he shouted, as I had expected, for he is programmed for it. "We shall fight them on the sands, we shall fight them on the cliffs, we shall fight them street by street of our cities, we shall fight them on the tundras—"

"Yes, yes, yes," I said. "Though why you should care whether it's Volyen or Sirius . . . Whether it's one or the other, without this plant I am offering you, you are helpless. Whether it is Volyen or Sirius, with the plant you can feed yourselves. You can bargain."

"Why have you—someone—not given us this plant before?"

"Because it is only recently that conditions on this planet have made it possible for it to grow here."

"I don't like it," he said heavily, full of grief, of suffering. The long, dark, heavy history of his planet was weighing on him. He sat there, looking back through his life, the long struggle of it, and thinking too, as I could see, of past generations of deprivation, hunger, the harshness of Volyen rule.

"What have you got to lose, Calder?"

"How do I know what we might lose by it?"

At this point the woman came in from next door with her jug of the beverage, filled up our glasses, and stood there quietly, looking out the door at the sodden dark hillside, where rain was falling.

"I am at my wit's end to find food for the children," she remarked. "There's hardly anything in the shops. The rations have been cut again. And the last Volyen consignment was half the usual."

He was hardly listening. "Yes, yes," he said to her, in the kindly, fatherly way they use with their females when the females are playing their allotted role, which is to work even harder than their men.

"I suppose you haven't had any news, Comrade Calder, of the next Volyen food consignment?"

"No, but it's late. My wife was grumbling about it."

"Strange, I wonder why she'd do that?" She went out slowly. To stand just outside the door, while I watched Calder inwardly writhing in the toils of his suspicion of me.

I said, "In a very short time you will be overrun by Sirius. Yes, whether you fight or not. And then, almost at once, there will be no Sirians, because their Empire is at its peak and is about to collapse."

"How do you know all this? Oh, yes, you say Canopus, Canopus, as if that's an answer to it all."

"From your point of view it is. . . . Shall I go on? The Sirian conquest of Volyen will be brutal and *inefficient*, as I have been using the word, for Sirius itself is riven with debate, conflict, indecision. There have been times in Sirian history when a conquest of a planet was *efficient*: I mean, Calder, organized with certain aims in view, and carried out in accordance with a plan. This will not happen as Volyen is overrun. Because first one, then another group comes to the top on the Sirian senior planet itself, and on all the planets of the Sirian Empire. There is no consistent plan now. The conquest of Volyen will take place almost by accident, because of a temporary ascendancy of a certain viewpoint within the current—temporary— alignment of some planets. And you will be overrun, not by Sirian Mother Planet soldiers, but by a mix of armies who will quarrel among themselves, who will never agree about anything, and who will not carry out orders."

"Oh, this poor Volyenadna," Calder brought out heavily. Tears stood in his eyes, in accordance with this convention in "the Volyens" that tears are a sign of superior sensibility, and even of superior thought. They will make sure you have noticed that they are evidencing these signs of sensibility to a situation, and therefore Calder turned his head slightly so that I could see water glistening in his eyes. "How long will it all last?"

"Not long at all," I said, "because the armies that overrun you will bring hardly enough food for themselves. And will not bring food for you. When they notice that you are starving, they will appeal to the Sirian HQ on Volyen for supplies, but inadequate supplies will arrive, and then none. . . ."

"How do you know all this, sitting there so calmly, announcing this, that, and the other thing as if you can see it?"

"Why should we have to see it? It is enough to know the nature of the species, the races, the individuals involved. The armies that will overrun this little planet—this very little, unimportant planet, Calder —will be in a blind panic, because they will have understood that the Sirian Empire is collapsing around them and that they may find themselves marooned here, forgotten, on a planet that—forgive me—is not the most inviting in the Galaxy."

"O unfortunate planet, planet doomed to misery, to hardship, to . . ."

"Rubbish, Calder. It is not doomed at all. You could have your own food supplies long before then. You could bribe the rabble of soldiery to leave, with food, for there won't be much of it anywhere, I promise you, not even on Volyen, given the mess the Sirians will be making of everything. In fact, if you plan intelligently, you will be able to use your supplies of Rocknosh to buy yourselves not only independence from the Sirians, but real independence for yourselves. You will be able to govern yourselves, use your minerals yourselves, export what you choose to whom you choose."

"There is just one little thing you have overlooked," brought up Calder triumphantly. "It is this. What makes you think that Volyen will let us get away with it? What? You tell me that, now!" And he subsided, chuckling, shaking his head from side to side over my foolishness, and sending glances at that audience of his for whom he had been performing all his life.

"Did I not begin by saying they wouldn't even notice it? You could cover the rocks of half of the planet with a dull-reddish furry plant, and they wouldn't know it."

"Oh, that's what you say!"

"Anticipating that you have become such slaves by habit, I had planned to get hold of Governor Grice so that he could obtain official permission for the introduction of this food. There are plenty of people in the Colonial Administration of Volyen who sympathize with you about your treatment. And Governor Grice is exactly the right man to do it, but . . ."

"And now you've gone completely off the rails, as far as I am concerned."

"It would have been *almost* the simplest way—for the simplest and easiest would have been for you to agree and to do it yourselves. But Grice is not himself at the moment, I am afraid."

"And another thing: I'm not sitting here to listen to you call me a slave."

And he got up, conscious of a hundred pairs of eyes for whom his demeanour, enduring modestly heroic, was intended. Without looking at me, he shouted out: "The Sirian gentleman will pay." As the woman came in, he grinned at her, like a child who has won a point over another, made a grimace towards me that categorized me as a hopeless lunatic, slapped her across her large buttocks as a way of re-establishing his balance, and went out.

The woman stood looking at me. Like all their females, she is a rock and a stone, all strength and ability to withstand. She came slowly across and stood by Calder's empty chair.

The following is a full record of the conversation I had with this female of Volyenadna.

"You say there is this food?"

"Yes. I have spores of it here."

"When I plant it, how do I look after it?"

"You don't. It will grow on any rock. Here is a list of the methods you can use for preparing it."

"Thank you."

KLORATHY TO JOHOR. FROM VOLYEN.

The first thing I heard on my return was that Grice had been kidnapped by Motz. No ransom has been demanded. Questions include: Why Grice? Is Motz aware that Grice in his youth became a Sirian agent? If so, is it important? Is this kidnapping designed to frighten all the other ex- or "sleeping" Sirian agents on Volyen? In other words, was this kidnapping inspired by some Sirian faction? Does the other nearby Sirian planet, Alput, know of this situation?

I hear that Alput and Motz are in serious disagreement over the invasion of Volyen.

Motz represents an almost pre-Ambien attitude, to the effect that a Sirian takeover is by definition an advantage to the taken-over. Might is right. Sirius is good, other planets are all in need of her superior wisdom.

The faction on Alput currently in ascendance debates endlessly about the Virtue.

Waiting for further information about Grice, I paid a visit to Incent. On my way in, our friend the hotelkeeper stopped me to say that he believed, on the basis of sounds coming from the inner room of Incent's convalescence, that Incent was "off again." And so it proved. He was lying on his back in the recliner, and contemplating with giggles, shouts of delight, groans, ecstasies of all kinds, the patterns of the upper part of the room, which he had set into violent motion. Revolving rhombohedrons, tripping tetrahedrons whirled in a dance with oscillating octoids, while Luminosity was set at Full and the Sound Gauge was on Singing of the Spheres, also at Full.

I switched off the apparatus and waited for him to stop writhing and gasping out cries and groans of "Wow! Cool! Neat! Right on! Sensational! I am so *moved!*"

He lay on his back staring at the now empty space at the top of the room.

"All right," he said at last, "there's no need to say it."

"What are we going to do with you, Incent, what!"

"The thing is, I really do feel I have it in me to get well again; I really do believe that, Klorathy."

"Very well, then. Do you want to stay here—only I might be gone quite a while, because poor Grice is giving us a lot of trouble—or do you want to come with me?"

"Oh, *no*, I don't think I could trust myself outside yet. It is wonderful in here. I really was feeling that I was coming to myself again. No, I'll be careful with the mathematicals."

And so I left him.

Our agent on Motz (AM 5) is trusted by Grice's captors; ironically he was a foundation member of the revolutionary group that now runs Motz, being at that time in a sentimental condition. He rapidly recovered, and found himself advantageously placed, from our point of view. I am waiting for a report from him.

REPORT FROM AM 5.

Salud! Servus, as Krolgul would say—and does say, since here he is, stirring it up. Mind you, he is not having it as easy as he likes, because the situation here is pretty clear-cut, and what the Father of Lies likes is already muddied waters he can muddy even worse. The situation? Onto a barren planet unpopulated by higher animals came a population fleeing from another planet, their own, but taken over forcibly by a species evicted from *their* planet by . . . but the account of this invasion was sent to the Archivists. Meanwhile, the deserts and marshes of Motz have been made fruitful. They are a clever, industrious people, full of the energy that results from single-mindedness. What are their minds and efforts directed towards? One thing only, to return to their home planet. For Motz, which they have created, have *made*, is not their home: so their minds have been set. While levelling a mountain or draining a swamp, they are singing: One day we shall go home. Yet the usurpers on their own planet have of course no intention of leaving, unless forcibly ejected. For a long time Motz was not strong enough; recently it has become strong enough. Yet while they talk—dramatically enough—of war, they do nothing about it. The truth is, they have become Motzan, of Motz; they do not really want to "go home." But they can't admit it, at least not publicly. Speeches and ceremonies of all kinds allow them to dream—briefly—of "our home." They decided that their grievance, their just cause, had been forgotten by the Galaxy, and kidnapped Grice to publicize their cause, counting on Volyen making efforts to recover one who is, after all, a senior colonial official. But Volyen, as you know, has made no more than routine protests; and this is because Grice's past as a Sirian agent (admittedly an ambiguous one) makes it hard for them to know what to do. As for Motzans, that he was, is, an agent serves only for them as a guarantee of worthiness, of Virtue.

Krolgul has told them that Grice was a "blood-sucking tyrant" on Volyenadna, and, unable to reconcile these two states of mind, after long and tortuous thought they have concluded that his tyrannical behaviour as Governor was the result of a necessary concealment of his (intrinsically) virtuous nature, so as to make his association with Sirius seem improbable. Because these revolutionaries, who call themselves the Embodiments of Sirian Virtue, believe that, "overall and in the long term and looking at the essential situation," Good equals Sirius, and if anything that opposes Sirius shows any signs of decency, then this can only mean (a) the phenomenon in question is showing, but of course only briefly, Sirian qualities, or (b) it isn't really good and decent at all, "looked at from an objective point of view." This, despite the fact that it was under the aegis of Sirius that their planet was filched from them by conquerors whose own home had been stolen; and that everywhere you look in these Sirian outlying colonies is nothing but confusion, incompetence, lying, and those particularly brutal types of tyranny that result from indecision and conflict at the source: the Mother Planet of Sirius.

These are people who cannot accommodate more than one point of view at a time because of their history, which as I've said is a single-minded concentration on one thing, to return "home." Faced with a fact that does not fit their current view, they attempt to turn it on its head, and, if they fail, simply push it out of sight. Krolgul inadvertently let slip that he has enjoyed perfect freedom on Volyen to run his School of Rhetoric, and since he is currently informing them that Volyen is a total tyranny, they have decided that if there *is* such a school, then he, Krolgul, must be in the pay of the Volyens.

"No, no," cried Grice, "not so. Volyen at this present moment of historical time enjoys a situation of comparative democracy and tolerance for varied viewpoints, though this is, of course, due entirely to the contradictions of historical anomalies and uneven historical evolvement. . . ." (I *hasten* to remind you that I am quoting.) "In short, Volyen itself is the pleasantest place imaginable to live in for the vast majority of its citizens," insisted Grice, quite courageously really, seeing that the Embodiments were getting more and more restless and uneasy as their mentations jammed under the strain of it all.

But it was no use. For Motz, like all of the surrounding planets, is in a war-fever, ready to invade "the Volyens." This war-fever is, of course, equated with the Virtue, and it is too much to ask of these poor bigots that they must invade the "pleasantest planet imaginable" in order to impose Sirian Virtue, even at the behest of "irresistible historical imperatives" (a phrase much used at this "present moment of historical time" here).

No, it is all too much for the unfortunate Embodiments; and so they have simply shelved the problem of Grice. They have locked him up in the sociological wing of their main library, because it happens to have only one, easily guarded, entrance. There Grice is left alone, with nothing to do but read.

I have described *their* state of mind.

I shall now describe Grice's. *He* has been conditioned to believe (by the unavoidable historical accident aforementioned) that to keep an open mind, and to see several points of view simultaneously, and to accommodate "contradictions," is a sign of maturity. This exercise has cost him nothing but discomfort because he has never been informed that he is an animal, recently (historically speaking) evolved from a condition of being in groups, small or large, inside which everything that will conduce to the survival of the group is an imperative, and where individuals can expect to receive what they need; while outside are enemies, who are *bad*, to be ignored if possible, threatened if they intrude themselves, destroyed if necessary. The minds of Volyens, in this brief period of theirs when a calm and dispassionate and disinterested inspection of possibilities is the highest they aim for, are being asked for something that challenges millions of their years of development. No, it is the passionate bigotry of the Embodiments which is what comes easily; "seeing one another's point of view" is a stage upwards in evolution to be made, and then kept, only with difficulty. . . . And there sits Grice, in daily contact with people whom he must by upbringing regard as comparatively simple-minded, and even pitiable; but longing with every fibre of his emotional self to *join*. The Embodiments love one another, cherish one another, look after the weak, reward the strong, watch one another's every thought and impulse. For the only ideas they ever permit themselves are related to how they have been dispossessed of their rights, and of how they will regain these rights on "their own place," how they will turn this Motz into a paradise, "just to show the Galaxy." The Embodiments are people who have barred from their minds all the richness, the variety, the evolutionary possibilities in the Galaxy. Grice watches them, and yearns to be of them, while through his tormented mind pass feebly protesting thoughts. "No, it isn't like that," he keeps planning to say to them "when the opportunity is ripe." "No, but that isn't true. How can you say that? I've been to that planet; it's not at all as you describe it . . . but look, it's a question of *facts*. . . ."

KLORATHY, ON SLOVIN, TO JOHOR.

Bad news about Incent, I am afraid. I left him with revision material, but as a result of remorse over his misuse of the "mathematicals," he overdid things. The information was not properly absorbed into his emotional and mental machineries, but overflowed into a compulsion to instruct. He left me a message and departed for Slovin, commandeering my Space Traveller.

He had reasoned thus: Slovin, having been subjugated so long by Volyen, and having just thrown off its chains (sorry!), must be in a certain easily foreseeable and easily diagnosed condition. Part of the material left with him to study had to do with the Shikastan Northwest fringes. If you remember, that area of Shikasta was subjected for nearly two thousand Shikasta-years to one of the most savage and long-lasting tyrannies ever known even on that unfortunate planet, that of the Christian religion, which allowed no opposition of any kind, and kept power by killing, burning, torturing its opponents, when not able to do so by the simpler and even more effective methods of indoctrination and brainwashing. In the early twentieth S-century this religion lost its hold, largely as a result—because of new technologies—of the opening up of Shikasta to travel by the masses. It was no longer possible for the tyrants of the Northwest fringes to maintain in their subjects the belief that Christianity was the only religion, that their God was the only God. And the truth slowly came home to these recently enslaved ones that the Northwest fringes were in fact provincial and backward, compared with other parts of Shikasta that had older and more sophisticated civilizations.

There followed a period when the peoples of that area (a small area geographically) had the opportunity to enjoy freedom of thought, of speculation; freedom to explore possibilities that had been denied them for many hundreds of S-years. But because they had been conditioned by the various sects of that religion to need domination, "priests," creeds, dogmas, ukases, they sought these things again, in the same forms but under other names, notably in "politics." New "religions" arose, but without "God," which were identical in every way with the sects of the "God"-orientated religions of the past. Each was equipped with priests with whom it was not possible to disagree, whose orders had to be obeyed, and with "creeds" that had to be recited and quoted; and the slightest infringement of the "line" earned savage punishments, from ostracism and loss of employment to death, just as had happened with "Holy Writ" in the recent past. Each new secular religion maintained itself by the use of the techniques of brainwashing and indoctrination, learned from their great exemplars, the priests, who had perfected them through two thousand S-years; techniques continually refined and augmented with the increasing sophistication of psychology.

In short, freedom is not possible to people who have been conditioned to need tyrannies.

This was the message that our poor Incent was impelled to take to Slovin.

The planet has been for several V-centuries a sullenly uniform place, poor, deprived of its own wealth, administered by a Volyen Colonial Service, kept in order by Volyen police, prisons, torturers. Suddenly it has "thrown off the yoke." The small class that was used by Volyen fled or were killed or became patriots. All Slovin seethes with new parties based on military groups that freed Slovin. Each of these has —of course—leaders, an army, and a creed, which it defends against all the other groups, often with bloodshed. One party stands for a united Slovin, another for a regionalized federated Slovin, and so on. The air is thick with the Rhetorics of liberty, for they know they are free.

Groups, armies, sects, parties, factions: Slovin, just like every other "liberated" planet, is full of them.

Incent went straight to the capital, asked for the largest and most influential party, found that every Slovin gave him a different answer; so he caused an announcement to be made that he, "a dispassionate, disinterested well-wisher from a distant star system," would be addressing the liberated peoples of Slovin on such-and-such a day in the public square, this address to be heard by all of Slovin.

Now, the very language he was using had to attract attention, because words like *disinterested* and *dispassionate* had fallen out of use: the qualities they described had been eroded by the corruption and ugliness of Volyen rule, finally destroyed by the violent partisan passions of the period of "liberation." "*Disinterested:* what can that possibly mean?" Slovins were heard asking. And, having looked up the meanings of that and similar words, they scoffed: "What nonsense, what idealistic rubbish!" But wistfully. They felt that they might have lost something.

These tall, fragile, silvery creatures always arouse in foreigners the strongest feelings of protectiveness and compassion, because of their apparent vulnerability; and our Incent was moving around the planet, almost beside himself with emotion as he watched them approach one another with a new tentativeness and uncertainty, probing and asking. Like those exquisite shining insects that live for a night and then, losing their wings, die, so did the Slovins seem to Incent, who *knew* he could save them from themselves, if only he could make them listen. Oh, poor, poor Slovins, mourned Incent, as he mentally worked on the phrases of the address, on the perfect, above all *appropriate*, words that would magically do away with the results of centuries of Volyen oppression and uniformity.

Meanwhile, the Slovins did not know how much they had been attracted by the "otherness" and "difference" of the amazing message. What did *impartiality* mean? What: *magnanimity?* What: *unenvious, detached, honourable, chivalrous?* Somewhere or other, somewhere else, perhaps even once on Slovin, had there been a people for whom these words were everyday words, and had they been able to use them by right?

On the great day, Incent, beside himself with exaltation and the need to persuade, stood on a plinth in the central square of the capital, surrounded by many thousands of whispering, silvery, tenuous, delicate Slovins, who were gathered not in a single mass, but in companies and bands, all armed, all owing allegiance to different leaders, all staring upwards with their great many-faceted glittering eyes, waiting to hear some truth that would once and for ever enlighten them. This was because they unconsciously yearned for unity, because they had known Volyen unity for so long. Also, something had happened in the last few days that was very fortunate for Incent: fighting had broken out all over Slovin between guerrilla groups and armies, and the planet was afraid of civil war.

Imagine the scene, Johor! That vast but infinitely divided crowd, all yearning for inspiring, dedicated, and uplifting words, for they felt that what had already been reported to them of Incent's message was a promise from a star whose existence they had known nothing of, but whose sovereignty they might very well have to acknowledge. Though of course they would have killed any one of their number who suggested such a thing.

Incent began by asking their permission to tell them a sad and sorry story. They would have permitted him anything, and anything he said would have seemed to them exactly what they had been longing for, their expectations from him were so vast. He told them the story of Shikasta, of its Northwest fringes, when its worst and oldest and longest-lasting tyranny dissolved, and all its people fought to re-enslave themselves. And succeeded. He told the tale well enough, making these unfortunates shudder and shiver at how easy it is to fall under the spell of the need to submit, when submission is what you have been taught.

"You people," said Incent, after a long silence, which he held by the sheer force of his difference, and of his astonishing words, which seemed to come from some distant and wonderful sun.

"You people," said or sang Incent, arms outstretched as if to embrace their future, their still-unfulfilled potentialities, "you people are in the greatest danger imaginable, and you seem not to know it. You are in danger of submitting yourselves to a new tyrant, because the patterns of tyranny are in your minds. But this danger has another face: a road to a beautiful future, of a kind you have never even envisioned. It is that you will all remain truly free people, refusing allegiance to leaders and to tyrants, to priests, to dogmas. You will keep your minds open and at liberty, examining possibilities, analyzing your own past conditioning, learning to observe yourselves as you might observe another species on a near planet—as you all observe and criticize, for instance, Maken." (Here there was a groan of dislike, for this area of the Galaxy conforms to the general law that planets loathe and distrust one another according to how close they are.) "Yes, that could be your future! You could say to yourselves, 'We will never again submit to a leader, because we don't need leaders; we understand that we have been taught we must have them.' Long ago, in your animal and semi-animal past, you were groups and bands and packs, and on these genetic inclinations tyrants have built, to keep you in groups and bands and packs; but now you can free yourselves, because you understand yourselves. . . ."

And the conglomeration of separate groups dissolved in an ocean of emotion, into one soul, everyone embracing and entwining in a susurration of dry, papery flesh, so that Incent seemed enclosed in a storm of rustling kisses. And then, in one motion, they swept together around him and bore him into the air, crying, "Our leader, you have come to save us!" And "Incent for ever!" And "Stay with us, O Great One, tell us your Noble Thoughts, so that we may write them down and study and recite them for ever." "O Incent the Great . . ."

Incent struggled and cried, protested, "No, no; no, don't you see, that isn't the point. O Slovins, don't, please, oh dear . . . what can I say that will make you . . ."

These pleas and plaints were of course not heard in the typhoon of enthusiasm. At last he managed to creep away from under heaps of Slovins struggling with one another, even killing one another to pay him honour. He ran weeping to the Space Traveller and returned to Volyen, where he skulked into the safety of the tall white room.

Luckily, Shammat has been otherwise engaged, and was not on Slovin.

I have withdrawn all study material from Incent. He did not need me to explain that it was too inflammatory for him in his present enfeebled condition.

AM 5 ON MOTZ, TO KLORATHY.

Well, I am sorry to have to say so, but Grice has suffered a conversion. He demands "once and for all" to be one of them. "It is not possible," insist these earnest ones in the severe manner that they strive to perfect; "you are a Volyen." "How can you say such a thing?" he cries. "You are contradicting your own best selves. The Sirian Virtue is something that must overtake everything and everyone everywhere! You say that yourselves. How, then, can you exclude me by saying *You are a Volyen*—and at the moment when you plan to take the Sirian Virtue to all of Volyen? You are illogical!"

This jams the Embodiments' mental machinery: it seems to them *logically* to be true. But, on the other hand, he is demonstrably not remotely like them, not physically, not mentally. He may wear their uniform—he has asked for one. He may try to use their conventions of speech. But, as one of them remarked to me (you will remember that I myself am considered to be an Embodiment): "Just take a look at him, will you! *He* one of *us?*"

KLORATHY ON VOLYEN TO JOHOR.

I shall now make an abstract of a very long Report from Agent AM 5.

It is a V-year since Grice was kidnapped by the Motzans, who have now come to regret the act. Every attempt to provoke Volyen into publicity for their cause fails. They hint at torture, and worse—no reaction. Above all, Motzans understand loyalty to their own, for everyone on Motz is "of us." That the rulers of Volyen seem to have forgotten one of their officials: Motzans have given up trying to think about such an incomprehensibility. Grice is still a "prisoner"; the library is his prison, but he is there because he wants to be. This collection of books was pirated from a provincial town on Volyen by the Motzans some time ago—again, to earn publicity. They succeeded. Outrage! Everyone on Volyen talked of nothing but the stolen library, and then forgot about it. How is it possible, wonder the Motzans, that the Volyens can care about books more than about an official? It happens that this library contains the results of research done on Volyens as a species by Volyens. In the high imperial days of Volyen, the subject planets were much studied, and the researchers got into the useful habit of seeing species and races of people as they would types of animal, studying them with the same—or almost—dispassion we use on similar studies of genera and species. It occurred to them at some point that although they observed others dispassionately, they had not made the attempt to do the same for their own patterns of living, but saw themselves always from within their own subjectivity. They turned their tools of research in on themselves, trying—though this is always hard enough—to see themselves as others see them. This provincial library was full of the results.

Grice has spent his time reading. His prior education was largely designed to equip him for ruling, particularly to inculcate the conviction of superiority that in one way or another the administrators of Empire must have. He has had no idea at all of the richness of information available about his own species. You may ask how it is that, once equipped with so much information, the Volyens have not hastened to put it into useful practice, have not taught it to their young—just as Grice is asking. Probably when the historians get to work on this particular epoch, the time before the Volyen "Empire" falls to Sirius, this will be the fact they will single out as the most remarkable: with so much knowledge about the mechanisms that govern them as individuals, groups, conglomerates, why did they never use it? Well, they are a lethargic lot. With much-compartmented minds.

Grice is riven, split, fragmented. No sooner had he decided to give his wholehearted allegiance to the simplicities of the Motzans than he found himself every day acquiring facts that made single-mindedness difficult. His mind is exploding with new ideas, suppositions, possibilities; he lives in a fever which he cools by having loving thoughts of his new comrades, so stern, so austere, so dedicated, so restfully and admirably single-minded.

EXTRACTS FROM A
REPORT FROM AM 5.

Oh, these poor Embodiments! They cannot get to grips with Grice! Sometimes they think they'll drop him back into Volyen and be rid of him. They long to be able to bump him off, but it seems that, when expressing his admiration for them, he accidentally used some verbal formula that is sacred and makes him immune—he is a guest now.

But he is not finally classed as a guest, because they might find him useful after all as a hostage. I encourage them in these rare moments of flexibility, ambiguity, in my (I sometimes feel vain) attempts to evolve these mono-minded heroes.

But Grice admonishes them. "You are being illogical," he says sternly—their manner is now his, for at least most of the time. "Either I am a guest, or I am a hostage. I can't be both."

"That is true," they reply, but continue to treat him as both.

As a guest, he asked to see more of Motz, and I was deputed to take him.

We went by air, back and forth and around this little planet, and Governor Grice—for it was the Governor, the administrator, who was with me, not Grice the Groaner—was ecstatic, and sobered, incredulous, and admiring, at what we saw.

Flying over a steep and rocky mountain, looking down, you see that on every possible slope, in every minuscule valley, has been built a field. The mountain is black and barren; but it holds a hundred pockets of earth, each grain of which has been carried in a basket to be made fruitful by these exiles from a fertile planet. You descend, to be met by a group of strong, muscled, spare people who take you to see fields, gardens, orchards, tramping up and down impossible slopes and escarpments; and as they stand proudly beside some minute patch of glistening green, they will smile with such a passion of protective pride that there is no need for them to say: "There was nothing here before we came."

You fly over a plain patched with healthy crops, and they tell you: "This was a marsh; we drained it."

You see beneath you a desert, but around its edges are belts of dark green. "This is a desert now, but in a short time it will be a forest."

I do not remember seeing anywhere a bleaker planet than this one, as nature made it; I have never seen anywhere such accomplishments, achievement.

They have done it all with their own strength, their own dedication, their austerity, their self-discipline. They possess total confidence: they know they can do anything they decide to do. They fear no deprivation, for they can live on a handful of grain a day, despising those who want more. They wear clothes whose simplicity makes them a uniform.

What magnificent creatures they are! And how pitiful, for they despise, utterly, everyone else.

"Oh," cried Grice, as we descended to yet another settlement surrounded by desert or scree, "oh, look what we could have done on Volyenadna, if we had tried."

"Nonsense," I kept saying. "You could have done nothing of the kind. You can't impose this on a people. It has to be voluntary." You will remember that as far as Grice is concerned, I am an Embodiment, so I must speak in character. But, after all, it is true enough.

"When I think of poor Volyenadna. Oh, poor, poor Volyenadna! We could have done something like this."

"So what is that planet like?"

"It is all tundra and rubble and permafrost."

"You've never, perhaps, heard of a plant called Rocknosh? I believe it thrives in such conditions."

He was in a state of violent agitation and conflict. "Oh, I believe I did. Some type mentioned it, but he was just a—" He had been going to say "just a Sirian spy," but stopped himself. His face, at such moments, as it were disintegrates, crumbles, then convulses in a spasm, as his organism strives to achieve some sort of balance or wholeness.

"A Sirian spy," I've heard him muttering, "but I was so young, I didn't know better . . ." And, at other times, "A Sirian spy? The words sound bad, but after all, if this Motz is Sirius, then . . ."

I sometimes attempt to talk to him of the Sirian Empire, as it really has been. It is no use talking of the long perspectives, the long millenniums of such Empires, to a mind that has called "Empire" the few V-years of the Volyen ascendancy. But I try to describe something of its changing histories, its fragmentation now. I remind him of the forthcoming overrunning of Volyen. He frowns, he sighs, he grimaces. . . .

But he has found a solution to his emotional predicaments. Bizarre! But—you'll agree, I am sure, Klorathy—of a psychological ingenuity that . . .

Grice has decided to sue Volyen for having defaulted on promises and guarantees made to every Volyen citizen in its Constitution.

The problems facing Grice have included: that he had only an approximate memory of the relevant clause in the Constitution; that there was no copy of the Volyen Constitution on Motz; that he has to get back to Volyen to instigate this case; that he could not think of any sort of precedent.

Krolgul heard about Grice's scheme from a baffled Motzan, and at once visited Grice. He entered the library with a sharp triple knock, stood in the entrance silently, stern-faced, till he knew Grice had seen him, and then advanced the length of the room, unsmiling. The grey uniform (a version of the Motzan one), the sombre responsible mien, the tread like a soldier's . . . Grice involuntarily got to his feet, like one guilty, but before he could speak Krolgul shot out his hand with a bark of "Servus!" And then, "I have heard of your plans. I have come to congratulate you! Magnificent! In scope, in courage, in daring. This is true revolutionary creativeness."

After a few hours of Krolgul, Grice was ready for anything, including the task of making the Motzans understand.

Imagine it, Klorathy! Twenty Embodiments, and I, all fresh from our hard labours, with difficulty giving up an evening to this embarrassing request of Grice's, sitting in a half-circle in a hut in the middle of a desert they have decided to reclaim. On a shelf, a jug of water, some chunks of vegetable, a lamp. Grice seated in front of us, but whether as guest or as prisoner, no one has said.

"You say you are going to publicly criticize your own people?"

"Not my people, Volyen."

"What's the difference? How can Volyen be distinguished from Volyens?"

"If it cannot, how is it possible for it to promise and guarantee its people certain rights?"

"But you speak as if you are wanting to publicly criticize an abstraction?"

"How can it be an abstraction if it can guarantee and promise, if it speaks like a parent? And besides, I am not criticizing it, I am bringing it to court."

"What, the Constitution?"

"No, those who represent Volyen at this time."

Gloomy silence; hostile looks; impatience.

"And what will you achieve by this?"

"Achieve? I shall expose Volyen for the fraud it is."

"Volyen?"

"I mean, our ridiculous Constitution. Lies. Lies!"

"But when we impose our Virtue on Volyen, then genuine justice and genuine liberty and real freedom will be theirs."

"Yes, but that won't be yet awhile, will it? And anyway . . ." Governor Grice is quite unable to believe in what he has spent so much of his life dreaming about: the actual advent of revolution, the actual arrival of Sirius in his land. "And besides," he said triumphantly, "if I expose them in the courts, as they richly deserve, then your task will be so much easier, won't it? The hypocritical mask of false justice will be ripped off the face of tyranny and—"

"We don't understand how you, as an official of this tyranny, or even as a citizen, are in a position to take it to court. Which certainly sounds to us like a criticism. And how can you *criticize* a tyranny?"

"Ah, but you see, we have a democracy, haven't we? Of course, only because of historical anomalies and so forth," muttered Grice.

And so it went on, nearly all night. From time to time I chipped in with something designed to remind the warriors of reality; or, as you and our other tutors in the Colonial Service Schools kept describing it, "life itself." For instance:

Myself: "But if I may remind you, you don't actually have a copy of the Constitution. . . ."

In the end, it was decided to send down a team of two to Volyen, disguised as Volyens, to get hold of a copy of the Constitution for Grice.

"And while you are about it," he shouted as they left, "you might as well get me the second volume of Peace's *Laws Governing the Behaviour of Groups*. It was out on loan when you liberated the library, and I need it for my case."

He wrote it all down for them. The Motzans don't read. Or, rather, they read only histories of their home planet, of their eviction from it, of their struggle to develop Motz, of their fight to keep Motz out of the hands of fellow Sirian colonies. They read books of practical instruction, technical books, and—recently—books descriptive of Volyen and its "Empire," but entirely from the Sirian point of view. Never do they read anything that might suggest they and their history, their passion, their dedication, could be seen from any viewpoint but their own. They are not even tempted to do so: they have been so thoroughly conditioned to see other people's ideas as heresy. "That's all, and that's enough," to quote their invariable response if actually faced with some book that might even indirectly criticize them. And "What we have is what we need."

Making the case against Volyen has required the efforts of Grice, myself, Krolgul, and a Motzan introduced to Grice by Krolgul, who felt that this new associate could only do Grice good—from Krolgul's point of view. This Motzan is a young male named Stil. His characteristic is the number of handicaps he has had to overcome. He was born on one of the new settlements, where a marshy estuary was being drained. It was cold, dank, dismal. His mother died giving birth to a third child. The father was working as hard as Motzans do. The children were reared haphazardly. Stil was helping rear the two younger ones, going to school, and working to earn money when he was a child. Then his father died in an accident. Stil's history continues like this; and he matured early into a physically and mentally strong individual, able to do any work or cope with any event. This paragon spends his time with Grice, who is crushed even further into self-deprecation and a sense of inadequacy. As for Stil, he is naturally fascinated by Grice, whose life seems to him pathologically indulged and selfish. At every criticism, Grice agrees and cries out: "I'll get them for it, see if I don't"—meaning, of course, "all of Volyen."

The "Indictment" already runs into several volumes, and there seems no reason why it should ever be concluded; but Krolgul is urging haste. Rumours! Rumours! Mostly about an imminent Sirian invasion. Motz's army is, in theory, mobilized. Since these soldiers are also farmers and miners, essential workers, Motz cannot afford this situation. Protests have gone into "Sirius itself." Where, of course, there are nothing but squabbles. Debates. Disagreements. Changes of policy. No reply from "Sirius itself," so Motz has its army on standby, but tells itself, truthfully, that the self-discipline of its soldiers is such that they can be assembled again in a day. Krolgul says to Grice, "If you don't act now, you never will. There won't be any Volyen to sue."

"Oh, Krolgul," says Grice, "aren't you exaggerating?"

"Do you or do you not want the Virtue of Sirius?"

"I didn't hear anything from you of the Virtue of Sirius on Volyen-adna. Why was that?"

"You weren't mature enough then to hear the truth."

"It wasn't me who had to hear it. How about Calder and his mates?"

"How do you know what I used to talk to them about? You weren't always listening at the keyhole, Governor Grice!"

To such a level of vulgarity has Krolgul sunk with Grice, who is uneasy, but can always cure moments of doubt about Krolgul simply by looking at him: That upright soldierly form! That heroic profile! That air of solitary self-sufficiency! Everything Grice longs to have been, to be, seems embodied in Krolgul when he looks at him. And if his doubts about Krolgul get acute, there nearby is Stil, who either has just come from or is about to leave for a long day's physical labour on a diet of powdered fishheads and some marsh water.

There is also, of course, myself, but Grice simply cannot come to terms with me. Sometimes he feels relieved that a Motzan can be capable of ordinary irreverence, even flippancy; that a Motzan can criticize Motz. At other times he feels that there's something a bit off about me. "Are you sure you aren't a spy?" he snapped once. "Of course I am," said I. "How clever of you to spot me. But it takes one to know one, doesn't it, Governor Grice?"

KLORATHY TO JOHOR FROM VOLYEN.

Since I last reported, I have (a) visited Ormarin on Volyendesta, now out of hospital; he is recovered and ready for the future, which he is preparing himself for by a judicious and sober study of the histories of certain of our planets; (b) flown over Volyenadna, large areas of which show a reddish tinge; and (c) been travelling Volyen from end to end.

Incent sent me a message saying that he was feeling well enough to leave his retreat: he wanted to test himself. He too has been wandering over Volyen. I have encountered him twice.

First, in a small town where there was unrest, rioting: immigrants, settled there from PE 70 and PE 71, were clashing with the locals. As you will have heard, these two planets have thrown off Volyen rule, and by the processes of logic usual in primitive minds, the unfortunate immigrants, who have been happy and loyal Volyen citizens for a long time, were suddenly designated Sirians and possible traitors by the mobs.

I was there with 33, 34, 37, and 38, summoned from their work on Volyendesta, to do what we could to mitigate the worst excesses of the mobs. We were of course in disguise, and I was not recognized by Incent, who was seated on an embankment above the rioters, watching. His very presence could have been taken as an incitement. Sombre, white-faced, tragic in mien, but above all merely an onlooker—it would have taken only an unlucky chance to make him a target. I assigned 33 to watch him, unobserved. Then I sent him a message suggesting that he might care to join me and others in real, responsible work. To this I received no reply. The next time I saw him was yesterday, here in Vatun. Again it was a mob scene. Streets of houses were burning, and a small army of mostly young Volyens were destroying everything in their way, with screams of "Down with . . . ," "To the fire with . . ." The names were those of local shopkeepers, mostly immigrant Volyenadnans. Incent leaped from among them onto a low bridge that crossed the street where houses were burning on either side. Smoke, the tossing flames, the seething crowds beside themselves with rage— and there was our hero, shouting—or, rather, screaming—to make himself heard. "You have to realize . . . no, listen to me . . . you are betraying everything that makes you real, responsible individuals, no, you must listen. . . . You are at this moment at the mercy of your animal brains. . . . Did you know that . . ." Below him the front ranks of the mass stopped momentarily to stare up, their mouths agape, arrested by astonishment, bewilderment—but above all by this check on the flood of their emotions. The shadows of the flames and smoke darkened the mass of faces. For a moment there was a near-silence, in which flames roared and some people at the back chanted, "Down with . . . we'll bring him down. . . ." "Every man of you has in your head two brains, well, more actually, but one is an animal brain, and when that gets control then you become like animals, and that is what you are now, you are a herd of . . ." The mass screamed with derisive laughter. "If we wanted a lesson in biology, we'd ask you," screamed back our 37, from among them, to deflect their rage. As the mass turned to see who it was speaking for them, in terminology certainly not possible to them at this time, 38 ran out to grasp Incent, who was in danger of toppling forward into the crowds, who would have torn him apart. "Listen," Incent was shouting, "listen to me . . . you are all under the control of your primitive brains, can't you see that? You have regressed a million years and . . ." At this he was hauled back onto the bridge by the resourceful 38 and hustled along to where I was. We grasped him by the arms and ran him out of sight along a street the mob had not reached.

"But it's *true*," Incent was reiterating as we ran.

We left him in a small bar that was empty, telling him to stay there till we got back, and at once went out to see what we could usefully do. It was all very bad. The rioting, looting, fighting went on, and when I got back to the bar it was closed, with no sign of Incent.

Do not be too discouraged about Incent! I can feel that he is actually mending, and is no longer an open channel for the depredations of Krolgul.

AM 5 TO KLORATHY.

All of Motz is on full war-alert. Grice is on his way to Volyen: the Embodiments finally lost interest in him. They said, "Governor Grice, just go. Yes, yes, yes, anything you like, but just go." They have sent Stil with Grice, at Grice's request.

KLORATHY TO JOHOR, FROM VATUN.

It has occurred to Grice that the Volyen he has arrived on is not the Volyen he left. Riots and disorders, arson and looting! "But Volyens aren't like that," he keeps protesting. "We aren't like that at all. We are good-natured and kind, we are *reasonable* people."

Yet another impossibility has had to be fitted into his already tortured mental balances. When the worst that can be said about Volyen has been said—that there is unemployment, for instance, that the immigrant populations from other planets are not fully accepted as citizens, that the standard of living is falling because of the loss of Empire—when all this has been said, the lot of the poorest citizen on Volyen is better than that of the richest on Motz. As Stil expostulates, while he gloomily accompanies Grice everywhere in this task of his of "keeping an eye" on him, "You call this poverty? You tell me these people are rioting because they are poor? No, you'll have to explain to me, please! No, you just give me this poverty of yours, and let me take it back to my settlement. It would be riches for a year, what I can see wasted here, in just this one street."

Grice has succeeded in accommodating this, as he has everything else, as part of his grand "Indictment."

Grice could not find a lawyer to take his case, so he went to the Defender of the Public, a person specifically appointed to make sure legitimate grievances are heard. This gentleman leafed through the many hundreds of pages of the "Indictment" with the quizzical look which Grice was too much of an expert on his own kind not to understand. Before the Defender could throw him out, in the whimsical and charming way Grice himself had used often enough, Grice said, "Do you remember me, Spascock? We were at Infant School together in '53." The official admitted that, although he did not remember Grice, he had in fact been at that Infant School. "Do you remember Vera?" "Of course I remember Vera. One of the most fortunate influences on my life. My parents were more often than not on tours of duty on Volyenadna, and I am afraid I was rather starved of ordinary family affection." "You have never met Vera since then?" Grice continued excitedly. (I have a detailed account of this meeting from Incent, who was present: Incent and Grice have become great friends, not surprisingly.) Spascock was uncomfortable, and could not hide it. "Because I did meet Vera, much later, and her influence on *my* life was crucial."

Vera, charming and warmhearted girl, had gone for a holiday on Volyenadna, seen the suffering of the indigenous population under Volyen rule, and for the first time understood that the pleasant conditions on Volyen were not only not available to its colonies, but also that these conditions existed *because* of its colonies. Vera suffered an instant conversion to a belief in the Virtue of Sirius, and in short became an agent, but in the rather ambiguous way typical of the time. A few excited visits to a Sirian Embassy, some casual encounters at official receptions, an invitation to visit "Sirius"—in this case Alput, which most favourably impressed her—and then nothing happened. Quite soon she learned what a horrible tyranny Sirius was, and literally "forgot" her period of being an admirer of Sirius. But during this period she had been instrumental in introducing two ex-pupils, now grown up, to an admiration of Sirius. One of these was Grice, the other Spascock. She had in fact recruited them.

"In my view, people in our position should stand together," said Grice to Spascock.

Spascock, trying to smile, said he would look through the "Indictment" and let Grice know. "And who," he inquired, as Grice and Incent left, "is your friend?"

"He comes from far away, very far away indeed," said Grice, knowing how this must affect Spascock, who went straight back to his desk and began reading the "Indictment."

"Oh, no," he kept groaning, "oh, no, it really isn't on . . . but this is absolutely lunatic . . . it is utterly . . ." And then the telephone began ringing, with colleagues of all kinds, high and low—but some very high indeed—and Spascock found every one of these interesting conversations, all apparently about something else entirely, unmistakable reasons why he should in fact allow this case of Grice's to go forward.

"Yes, I am reading it," he spluttered and groaned to person after person, each of whom had remarked something to the effect that "Grice, you know, our colleague," had brought a copy of his Indictment. "Yes, but it may all be true, I am not saying it isn't, it's all very fascinating, I am sure, but, but . . . yes, very well. Very well. I hear you."

"But surely," Spascock moaned, as he sat alone in his office after about the twentieth telephone call, "we can't all be . . . ?" And of course they all weren't, but did wonder if anything they had ever done or said . . . ? Or were, but did not know to what an extent they were deemed to be "sleeping," or at least dozing, by Sirius; or were in fact actively engaged in undoing Volyen in any way that occurred to their ingenuity; or were in close contact with some secret Sirian taskmaster.

This case is going to take place. Grice is in a fever of pleasure. It is this relish of his that is perturbing his comrade and ally. That Volyen should be "exposed, once and for all," and "brought to the bar of history" seems to Incent only just, for while he is really very much better, certain sequences of words do still set him off easily; but his nature makes any form of pleasure suspect to him, except that which he experiences when contemplating his own deficiencies. In fact, his disapproval of Grice amounts to a form of envy. He has been heard to mutter, while Grice writhes with relish as he amends his Indictment to include yet another phrase that demolishes Volyen hypocrisy, "But Grice, I've been much worse than that, often, myself!"

A message from AM 5 on Motz begs that he be allowed to transfer here: he has developed, he says, a taste for the contemplation of farce. "Oh, Klorathy," he cried, "how can I bear these admirable Motzans! They never do anything that cannot be expected to result in a solid achievement of some kind. They never make a remark that isn't rooted 'in life itself.' Where are those famous 'contradictions' that I have come to enjoy now that Governor Grice has gone? There's only one now, and that is that these Motzans, whether they like it or not, are also Sirians. And they are saved by their total lack of imagination, for their minds work like this: We are good. We are Sirians. Therefore Sirians are good. They are preparing for the invasion of Volyen in the same spirit that is theirs when they take over a stretch of sand and turn it into a settlement. Because of Grice, they can see Volyen only as needing their guidance. When I suggest, in the slightly whimsical manner that I have perfected here to gain me immunity from their solemnities (and which, of course, rightly earns their mistrust), that perhaps not everyone on Volyen is like Grice, their eyes glaze over: they are all like one another, since they have been 'forged in the fire' (forgive me) of their common hardship, and so they cannot conceive of a planet full of diversity. Klorathy, rescue me, let me come to Volyen."

To which I answered: "You may not recognize this in yourself, but this 'whimsicality,' the deliberate half-concealed mockery, the 'enjoyment' is exactly the same indulgence in, the inner surrender to, the potentiality for anarchy in yourself, that caused a whole generation of upper-class Volyens to become agents (to one degree or another) of Sirius. Do you not recognize the atmosphere, the 'note'? I remember myself giving a series of classes, which I know you attended, on this particular period on Volyen, since it illustrated so well the laws of inner disaffection, of treachery. Do you not remember the lecture that was given under the title 'For If It Prosper, None Dare Call It Treason'? Obviously you do *not* remember. You are not an agent of Canopus in this (I admit) not very attractive little corner of the Galaxy in order to develop a taste for the study of historical anomaly. Which is nearly always rooted in *conceit*—it is no accident that it was the class on Volyen brought up to consider itself as natural rulers who were trained with that deep and pervasive frivolity—the pride of those who consider themselves better than others. The enjoyment of the anomalies that are always present when planets clash is from pride. Very well, I will admit that a little of this is allowable, even necessary, to save oneself from the depression and discouragement that lie in wait for us as we contemplate the wastefulness with which the Galaxy, or, as the Volyens put it, Nature, accomplishes its purpose. But one step beyond this small allowance, and you have taken off into contempt for those around you, and will soon be inflated by pleasure in your own cleverness. Agent AM 5 of *Canopus*—will you kindly do your work, as instructed, and moderate your enjoyment in it! As it happens, you are scheduled to come to Volyen with the invading Motzan armies, but do not imagine you will find much to *enjoy* in that."

In response to this rebuke, or, rather, reminder, I have received a sober acknowledgment that it was necessary.

The preliminary hearing has taken place. Spascock, in a last spasm of professional indignation, submitted formally that the case should be disallowed. This was in a small chamber off the regular court. Spascock, three Assessors, Grice, Incent, some court officials. The Assessors were all uncomfortable, and showed it.

"On what are you basing your Indictment?" asked the Chief Assessor.

"On this first clause of our Volyen Constitution," said Grice, who was standing there upright, burning-eyed, feeling himself the Judgment of History on Volyen personified.

"Read it."

" 'Volyen undertakes to protect and to provide for all its citizens in accordance with the development possible at a given time of its natural resources and with the evolution and growth of knowledge about the laws of Volyen nature and the laws of the dynamics of Volyen society.' "

Grice listened to this as if every word was an accusation no one could disagree with, and stood triumphant, waiting.

The three Assessors avoided one another's eyes.

Spascock said, "In my opinion, it is preposterous."

"Why, Spasky?" demanded Grice. "Sorry. I mean, Defender. Either Volyen means what it—she—he says, or does not. What is the point of having a Constitution when it is considered ridiculous even to ask if it is being honoured?"

Incent, who was looking very unhappy, said to Grice, "Well, yes, we all know that, but—"

"What do you know? This particular clause, the key clause of the whole Constitution, was put there because when the Constitution was reformed, it was discovered that the laws then had no relation at all with modern sociological and psychological knowledge. Then, and again now, the laws are an anomaly."

"Just a minute," said the Chief Assessor. "Who is *Volyen* in this context? Precisely who or what is it who 'undertakes'?"

"Obviously, the government."

"That isn't so easy, is it?" said Spascock. "Governments come and go. Is 'Volyen,' then, the Permanent Officials?"

"Of course not. It is obvious what Volyen is," said Grice. "It is the spirit of continuity. . . ." And, since Spascock and the Chief Assessor were about to challenge this rather tenuous concept, he said, "If 'Volyen' can 'undertake,' there has to be something permanent to do the undertaking, even if this something isn't easy to define."

"Logical enough," said Spascock, "but in my view, nonsense. For one thing, if 'Volyen' were to be continually reforming its own structures in accordance with the developments of scientific research, it would have to have some body or organ in existence to monitor these developments, and to incorporate them into the said structures."

"You have made my point, I think," said Grice.

"But," said Spascock, "it would have to agree about the results of modern research. And that is not so easy."

"Extremely easy," said Grice, "if it wanted to."

"It . . . ?" said the Chief Assessor. Normally he looks like one: judicious, cool, detached from pettiness. But he was uneasy and angry —and everyone knew why. Pressures from above.

"Look at it like this," said Incent, obviously making an effort to support Grice, though it was evident it *was* an effort. "If they felt it necessary to put that clause first, because our knowledge about ourselves had outgrown our legal and social structures, then there could not have been any agreement."

"*Our?*" inquired Spascock coldly of Incent, who is so obviously an alien and is known as coming "from far away" to everyone.

"I was identifying with Volyen," muttered Incent.

"With *what?*" inquired the Chief Assessor, with an attempt at humour.

A long unhappy silence at this point. It is not easy for professionals to go against their training. Ordinarily such a case would not even have reached this stage.

"I do not see how you can possibly deny," said Grice, with his manner of formalized contempt, "that there is a Constitution which makes certain promises."

"We do not deny it," said Spascock.

"And that these promises have not been kept."

"That is another matter."

"I propose to prove it."

"I have a suggestion. We should appoint a Select Committee—"

"Oh, no, you must be joking," said Grice.

"—to determine the exact meaning of Volyen, 'it' in this context, 'undertake,' 'provide for,' and particularly 'in accordance with.' "

"Agreed," said all three Assessors together.

"Very well," said Grice. "You are legally in the right. But I hereby demand the right to be heard by my Peers."

"Oh, Gricey," said the Defender, "do you have to?"

"Yes, Defender of the Public," said Grice, "I do."

Knowing that they were defeated, the Assessors and Spascock sat in angry resignation, while the court officials went out and brought into the chamber the first twelve individuals they could see.

The mood on Volyen is changing fast. Together with the unrest caused by the rumours of imminent invasion, there is also a rising elation and excitement. Everyone is restless, and they all run about looking for stimulation and events that will feed their need for it. The court officials' usual dignified and formal behaviour was modified almost into carelessness, something not far from contempt.

"You there, come along, you are wanted as a Peer for a real lulu of a court case. . . ." "You'd never believe what they have cooked up this time—you'll get a good laugh, if nothing else."

That was the spirit of the summons to the Peers. Seven soldiers, five civilians, crowded into the Peer-box, smiling and in the holiday mood that for some reason is evoked in Volyens by the approach of war. The Chief Assessor frowned at them, and they composed their faces, to hear: "Do you agree or not that Grice, Governor of Volyen-adna, has the right to cause trial to be made of Volyen for neglecting its duty to its citizens, as laid out in the Constitution?"

The Peers exchanged glances, only just suppressing smiles. "We agree, all right," they said. "Right on!" "Wow!" "Yes, we'd like a bit of that. . . ."

"Oh, very well," said Spascock, "very well. But let the Select Committee be summoned and set to work."

After this, Incent went to Grice and said that "objective conditions made this Trial a galactic anomaly." Grice is intrigued by the thoughts aroused in him by Incent, and words like "galactic" induce in him a condition whereby, as he says, he "feels as if his mind becomes filled with cool air." But on this occasion his view of Incent worked against Incent's intentions.

"You people from 'far away' can't understand our local conditions."

"But I am living here, aren't I?"

"It doesn't matter; you have to be born here too."

"You aren't much of an advertisement for it, then. Look at the mess you are all in."

"Yes, but this Trial will help, in a small and modest way to . . ."

"Grice, believe me, this Trial is simply—inappropriate."

"What a word to use, when things are so desperate! There you are, that's what I mean. You are cold, heartless!"

"Can't you see that—"

"Look, tell me truthfully, does Volyen do what its Constitution promises?"

"No, of course not. But, galactically speaking, one can say that happy is the planet which has no need of a Constitution."

"And you can *joke!*"

"I wasn't—but why not?"

"And in the meantime Justice is being . . ." The word *Justice*, on top of *galactic*, finally dissolved Grice. He sat with tears streaming, and turned his face so that Incent could see them.

"And anyway, it is quite wrong to say that you can understand local problems only when you are among them. On the contrary. And I am a proof of it. And so are you."

You will see that Incent is recovering fast.

But he has again been travelling over Volyen telling anyone who will listen about their animal brains and their higher brains. "You see," he exhorts earnestly, "when you are in a pack or a herd, then the instincts appropriate to these conditions rule you. When you are stampeding along a street in a herd, you have to let out rhythmic, repetitive cries, you have to burn and break and destroy, you have to kill. But when you are sitting quietly alone, as you are with me, then your higher brains rule you, and you are in that condition responsive to higher impulses, don't you see?"

Incent earns only agreement and intelligent comprehension from these Volyens when they are "sitting quietly"; but these same Volyens, when rushing about in their herds, seeing Incent exhorting them from the pavement, or from the lamppost he has climbed to be heard better, merely curse him or ignore him completely. "Don't you see," he has been heard to say afterwards to such a Volyen, who is shamefaced and embarrassed and saying, "I don't understand what got into me!," "the thing is, you must never, ever, allow yourself to become part of a mob, or you won't be able to help yourself."

"But that is all very well! We are always in groups of one kind or another, aren't we? Well, nearly always."

In such efforts Incent has been spending his time, and meanwhile Krolgul prowls, and watches for an opportunity to regain sway over him. But Incent, on seeing Krolgul, or even hearing that he is in the neighbourhood, runs away.

The following conversation has taken place between Incent and me.

"Incent, at some point you must face Krolgul."

"I can't. I'm afraid."

"But you are stronger now. You can stand up to him."

"I'm afraid of his words-of-power."

I am afraid too, for Incent, and, seeing this, Incent cried out: "Why did you put me in this position, this key position?"

"You volunteered, Incent."

"I did? I must have been mad. Why didn't you stop me?"

"I, as your tutor, encouraged you!"

"But it is too much for me."

"Others of our agents have volunteered to come to your aid, and have already arrived and are at work through the Volyen 'Empire,' and that is one reason why you are stronger. Instead of one 'conduit,' there are several."

"Well," he muttered, "I suppose it won't be long before they go bad too."

Johor, I really wish you could see our Incent at such moments of dramatic self-presentation. We know a modest, thoughtful individual, who even when in the garb of Volyen retained—on Canopus—these qualities. But here, imagine him as he flings himself into a reclining position, head on a long nervous hand, a black mane flowing over slender shoulders, and the vast black eyes of his (vanity-motivated, I am afraid) choice gazing at me. But really his look is inward, as it were in satisfied contemplation of an inner wound or shock. And then the lift of the eyes up and out, in a stare that proudly accepts infinite dolour.

"So far they are all doing nicely. Not one has gone bad. And for that we have partly to thank you, for standing firm. But really, Incent, you must see that it is time you came completely to yourself. It is really nonproductive, at this moment when all of Volyen is in the grip of mob emotion, to explain the mechanisms of mob emotion in this reasonable, low-voltage way of yours."

"But I can't bear it, I can't," he cried, "seeing them when they allow themselves to become . . . just animals. . . ." With his face in his hands, he wept.

"Incent. Be *yourself*."

"If I don't recover completely, then would you subject me to another dose of Total Immersion?"

"I certainly hadn't thought of it."

"But if you did, what would you choose to Immerse me in?"

You can imagine that I heard this with unease.

"I don't think anyone has ever been subjected twice to Total Immersion."

"Oh, don't tell me, it hasn't been necessary! Not everyone is as weak as I am!" This with satisfaction, and flinging out his arms as if to receive and accept blame.

"Only a strong person can withstand TI."

"Oh, really? And I did, didn't I? Well, tell me what other delights you have up your sleeve."

"Incent, it sounds to me as if you are enjoying your TI in retrospect, even if you didn't at the time."

At this he sobered up at once, and said, responsibly, "No, no, no, Klorathy. Never. I know painful experiences, in these latitudes, can acquire pleasurable associations, in memory—I remember your warning me. But no, never. Don't you see, I want you to—if you like—frighten me?"

"You are saying that you can't remain yourself, can't choose balance, when I say to you that it is of importance to Volyen, and to our Power here, that you do. But that you might be frightened into good sense and balance by what amounts to a threat!"

"Am I saying that? Well, if so, so be it! I can't help it. Then frighten me, Klorathy. I need it, obviously."

"Very well," I said, and Incent arranged himself, his hands already gripped together, his eyes with their characteristic look of being ready to listen, as if his ears were not enough. "It was on another planet, where a suddenly developing technology had enabled a war to impoverish large areas, to the extent that the inhabitants were desperate. Some people who saw themselves as being specially gifted for the manipulation of population, and whose first and strongest talent was the use of words, Rhetoric, used this desperation to instal themselves in power. Right from the very beginning, the announcement was, by the first leader of these tyrants, 'We stand for organized Terror,' a statement applauded and admired by his followers and by many people outside this particular—"

"I seem to sense a resemblance?" remarked Incent gloomily.

"Yes, I am describing the same planet as that I described in the 'court' on Volyenadna. It was not long after that other revolution, which so soon brought to birth compulsive murderers, and then a tyrant. The Rhetoricians, who at least had the clear sight to recognize the dangers to themselves, had studied the first revolution, whose excesses and brutalities they so much admired, and had agreed among themselves not to kill one another, but only the populations whom they intended to 'liberate,' if these resisted being liberated. Just as, in the first revolution, cries like 'We can be reborn only through blood' reached the primitive centres in every one of the more brutal, so in this second revolution 'the energy and mass nature of Terror must be encouraged' aroused frenzies of admiration. For these Rhetoricians knew they would only keep power if enemies, real or imagined, could be provided to keep the attention of the masses off their continued sufferings. The enslaved ones died in their millions, from starvation, from disease, and above all from the attentions of the Terror, now organized into a surveillance system that covered an empire the size of a sixth of the planet. And of course the Rhetoricians killed one another, just as if they had never made a pact among themselves not to. They saw themselves as in control of events, not as puppets of forces they had unleashed. And a new tyrant came, as has to happen when there is social chaos. And the populations went on dying or being murdered. But if nothing else, the inhabitants of that planet are fecund, and they soon replaced any losses of population from disease or catastrophe, even from their own machineries for murder."

I was watching Incent closely but could see little response in him. He continued to sit there quietly, attentively, but the tension in him had lessened. "What was perhaps more remarkable than anything else was that, while the mass murder, torture, and the most brutal methods of population control ever used anywhere before on that planet were well publicized, people in other, more favoured, parts of the planet, even parts that were well organized and pleasant, admired the tyranny. The fact is, there are always individuals who can respond only to violent and sensational descriptions of—" Here Incent looked embarrassed and made a gesture as if to say: Enough! "—They need the stimulus of violent words and violent thoughts. Very many, in all parts of that planet, secretly liked the idea of 'Terror,' of the torture and the organized brutality, enjoyed the idea of being the rulers of a population kept in conditions not far from slavery, thought with an arousal of their sensational apparatus of prison camps where millions of people died."

Incent was regarding me steadily, and into those expressive eyes had come a look not far from humour.

"Incent," I said, "it is not possible to find anything comic in this nasty little history."

"No, but perhaps I could be," said Incent, and flung himself down on his back, his limbs wide, in a posture of surrender. "Well—go on."

"But I have made my point. Which is not the slaughter of millions upon millions, either by negligence or intention; not the imposition of the machinery of Terror; not the enslavement of populations. But that all of these developments were *described* in words for purposes of enslavement, or manipulation, or concealment, or arousal; that tyrants were described as benefactors, butchers as social surgeons, sadists as saints, campaigns to wipe out whole nations as acts beneficial to these nations, war as peace, and a slow social degeneration, a descent into barbarism, as progress. Words, words, words, words . . . And when local diagnosticians told them of their condition, they cried enthusiastically, 'What wonderfully interesting *words!*' and went on as before."

"I am listening."

I did not go on, but contemplated my pupil, as I know you sometimes view me, Johor.

"Klorathy, if you had prescribed for me Total Immersion in this history, what would have been my role?"

"Can you ask? You would have been one of the instruments of the Terror. You would have murdered innumerable decent people by any means that you could devise, you would have been constantly developing ways to torture, to enslave through the skilled use of propaganda, and conditioning, and through the threat of death, torture, and prison. You would soon have been killed, according to the law that like attracts like, but I would have arranged for you at once to return and take a new place inside this machinery of brutality, where you would have continued to do all these things, while talking about comradeship, social responsibility, peace, friendship, and so on and so forth."

Again there was a long silence.

And then he slowly sat up. "I have never been more fascinated," he announced at length, with that relish in examination of his own processes that seems very far from lessening. "I know perfectly well that if I had experienced TI in this history, I would be grovelling here, crying and screaming, trying only to forget it. I'm glad to say I've already forgotten that other awful TI! I would be begging for you to expunge every thought of it from my mind. I'd be crying out to the Cosmos against its cruelties. But, you know, I can listen as much as I like, but I can't make it seem real. In fact, it all sounds rather—no, not attractive, not that—but interesting. . . . The fact is, Klorathy, *I don't believe it*. No, no, I don't mean it didn't happen, I don't mean it isn't still happening. I mean, I can't make it *seem* real. It is like a tale, an old tale, an old story of distant fighting somewhere, a long time ago."

"I'm not complaining, Incent! Surely this is a sign you are improving. Tell me, you didn't find any response in yourself to words like *blood, Terror*, and the rest?"

"No, only a sort of 'Oh, not *again*.' "

"Very good. Well, how about this: The tree of liberty must be refreshed from time to time with the blood of patriots and tyrants. It is its natural manure."

Incent shrugged and shook his head.

"We promise you we will purge from our midst every filthy traitor and all human scum and disgusting manifestations of outworn philosophy. We will fling all this outworn garbage onto the refuse tips of history."

At the word *history* Incent flinched, but smiled to himself.

"The worms and maggots that have crept into our healthy new society will be squeezed out and exposed before the bar of history for what they are—the squalid leftovers from an outmoded past."

Incent shook his head. He was looking rather pleased with himself.

"Do you think I am cured, Klorathy?"

"You certainly wouldn't have stood up to that even as recently as before your meeting with Grice."

"True enough. Grice has been a shock to me, I can tell you. I look at him and think, There but for the grace of . . ."

"You aren't safe yet, Incent."

"I do so want to be of use again. I can't bear to think how I've allowed myself to be used by Krolgul. Oh, Klorathy, how can I have done it?" And he jumped up, smiled tragically, and rushed out.

Have you guessed what I am going to say now? Yes, he succumbed, and almost at once, to Krolgul, who was lying in wait for him. Incent was running along the streets, elated and smiling. He saw coming towards him a crowd, and among them individuals he knew. They were not a shouting, screaming, destructive mob; they marched quietly, maintaining a decision made earlier at a public meeting place to proceed with discipline and responsibility. The leaders called out comradely greetings.

"Where are you going?" he called back.

"We are going to demand a general mobilization to defend Volyen against Sirius," was the reply. "Those traitors up there, they'll let us be overrun before they'll do anything; Sirian spies, all of them," was the reply.

By now Incent was walking beside the leaders in the opposite direction to the one he had been taking. "A very good idea," said Incent. "Though you'll be overrun anyway," he added, as if to himself, and saw the leaders look at one another and then draw away from him. "But never mind," he said cheerfully, still imbued with the perspectives of our recent lesson. "Their invasion won't last long. How can it? Sirius has so much overreached itself." He saw their angry, rejecting faces, and said: "Well, I don't see how you can get angry with *facts*."

"Facts, is it?" said one of the leaders. "Sounds more like treachery to me."

"Treachery?" gasped Incent, now running along beside them. "All Empires have a term, and often before they end they expand suddenly, as if they are crazed and fevered—"

"We are not interested in defeatist talk," shouted one of the leaders, and pushed Incent away. At this the crowd marching behind him let out an angry growl, then shouts of "Traitor!"

A leader said, "It's scum like you we are out to get—all that rotten lot up there. You are one of them, from the sound of it."

"I'm not," said Incent, still running beside them, even holding out a hand to someone he knew. And then, at this moment, he recognized who it was.

"Krolgul!" he said.

And it was in these circumstances that poor Incent underwent his test.

"Political innocent!" said Krolgul.

"*I* am?"

"*Revisionist*," hissed Krolgul.

"Oh, don't be silly," said Incent, but he was affected. "Can't you see, it doesn't mean anything?"

Krolgul had pulled him into the middle of the little group of leaders at the head of the mass, so that he was surrounded by threatening faces.

"So it doesn't mean anything? You are insulting the thoughts of the Sacred Leader, are you?"

"No, no, of course not, I'm not—"

"*Reactionary*," was the next word-of-power, stronger than the first, and Incent was weakened seriously by it.

But he was struggling still. "How can I be? What does it mean? What am I reacting to? from?" he demanded, while the people around him were cursing and growling like so many animals. Their independence of demeanour, their self-discipline, their determination not to be a mob—all this had gone, and it was Incent who had caused it; Incent under the smiling manipulation of Krolgul, who was the very image of a worthy, responsible revolutionary, his eyes alive with the determination to destroy everything in the path of historical inevitability, or whatever the formulation was, his face full of the vitality of triumphant cruelty.

"Bourgeois!" hissed Krolgul, and Incent nearly gave in.

But still Incent was himself. Just.

"Fascist," said Krolgul suddenly. And that was that. Incent shuddered to his depths. In a moment he was one of them, shouting and screaming: Death to . . . Down with . . . Blood . . .

And so on.

But do not be too concerned. I can *feel* that Incent is far from being in the pitiable state he was before; there is no great empty gap there where the substance of Volyen is sucked into the needs of Shammat. No, he is whole and strong. And he is in fact exerting a moderating influence on the committee of fanatics around him. When he says, "But surely that doesn't *mean* anything," as his response to some rousing bit of word-making, they often are checked and, though admittedly only temporarily, show disposition to *think*.

And Krolgul is beside himself with frustration. Our other agents stand firm. Incent is *not* his. Krolgul has used his strongest word-of-power, and there is nothing he can fall back on.

The next public excitement is Grice's Trial of Volyen, which I shall attend.

GRICE VS. VOLYEN

In his role of Defender of the Public, Spascock tried to get this Trial held in a small out-of-the-way court; as a possible agent of Sirius (Am I or am I not one? he has been groaning through sleepless nights) he has, because of the pressure from *his* Peers (all of them groaning, Am I? Am I not?), insisted on the main court of Volyen.

This is a large chamber, made sombre to impose respect, if not awe. Each wall is devoted to a different theme. "The limbs of our sacred body"—namely Volyenadna and Volyendesta, and Planets PE 70 (Maken) and PE 71 (Slovin)—each have their wall. Volyenadna, for instance, is represented by snowstorms and ice, as well as by happy miners led by Calder. Over all arches a ceiling painted to show benevolent scenes of Volyen personified as Donor, Provider, Adviser, with its "limbs" in grateful postures. But Maken and Slovin, having just thrown off the "yoke" of Volyen, sent delegations to paint over their respective walls, which was done hastily, leaving an unfinished, ugly effect. They also sprayed paint over the smiling faces of "Volyen" on the ceiling.

In this disturbing setting did the Trial start today.

Grice's Peers were raised up on a high box platform on one side. Taken together, they seemed even more in the ribald, reckless mood that often characterizes citizenry in periods just before a crisis, and were dressed fancifully and made an impression of jovial cynicism. When they were examined one by one, it was evident that not all were affected. Notably, a sensible and likable young woman was making attempts to take it all responsibly. Near them hovered Incent, trying to impress upon them with urgent looks and smiles that the occasion was serious. He was there officially as Grice's *Aide*. Near *him* lurked Krolgul, who, when his presence was objected to by the unfortunate Spascock, simply donned the robes of a court official, in a manner that insisted on Spascock's ridiculousness, while he directed towards the unfortunate man the single, almost tender query, "Spy?"

Grice, with Stil, was on the Prosecutor's dais.

A hundred or so citizens were in the public seats.

In the position of Judge was Spascock, who declared the Trial open in a perfunctory way, after a heavy-lidded, sarcastic inspection of the sullied ceiling and the two roughly painted-out walls of Volyen's former "limbs."

"Excuse me," demanded Grice, "but where is the Defendant?" For on the Defending side of the court was an empty platform and some empty chairs.

"Since it has proved impossible to decide *who* or *what* Volyen is . . ." drawled Spascock, and allowed himself a smile as Krolgul pointed up at the ceiling, where Volyen's faces had all been splodged out with white paint.

"Volyen is what has made promises to its citizens, in its Constitution," said Grice.

"That's it"—"That's right," came from the public benches, and the energy of this caused an increase of attention in everybody. As for the Peers, they surveyed their audience sombrely; they had come "for a laugh." One or two were heard to mutter, "Well, if it's going to be serious, what a drag. I'm off." And so on.

But they stayed, seemingly because of the influence of the young woman, whose position among them was then and there formalized by their electing her Chief Peer.

"Well, then, get on with it, Grice," said Spascock. "What is your first Indictment?"

"I accuse Volyen of not providing me—representing for the purpose of this Trial all Volyen's citizens—with real information as to our basic nature, thus enabling us to avoid certain traps into which we are likely to fall and . . ."

But I am enclosing herewith a copy of the Indictment.

Grice read this out—a not inconsiderable document, as you will agree—in a firm, strong voice, raising his eyes at key words to look at his Peers, who were silent, stilled by the prospect of a serious instead of a hilarious occasion.

The Chief Peer, Arithamea by name, had assumed a maternal look on her election, and now sat with a look of just-controlled exasperation.

Spascock inquired at last: "And that is your first Accusation, is it? Very well, where are your witnesses?"

At this Grice made a signal to Incent, who made another towards offstage, as it were, and an attendant wheeled in a trolley laden with about a hundred and fifty books.

"These are my witnesses."

A long gloomy silence. From his throne Spascock looked down at the heap of books, the Peers seemed incredulous, and the public benches let out a deep sigh.

"You are proposing that we should read all these books?" inquired Spascock, with the feeble sarcasm obligatory at such moments in Volyen's legal life.

"Not at all; I shall summarize."

Groans from one end of the court to the other.

"Order, order," admonished Spascock.

"In a few words," said Grice. "It is perfectly possible to do so. This is not a recondite or abstruse subject. . . . Shall I continue? Very well. The human animal, so recently evolved from a condition of living in groups, groups within herds, packs, flocks, troops, and clans, cannot exist now without them, and can be observed seeking out and joining groups of every conceivable kind because he—"

"And she," enjoined the Chief Peer.

"—and she have to be in a group. When the young animal—sorry, person—leaves the family group, he, she, has to seek another. But has not been told that this is what he, she, will do. She has not been informed, 'You will thrash about looking for a group, because without one you will be uncomfortable, because you are denying millions of V-years of evolution. You will do this blindly, and you will not have been informed that once in the group, you can no more refuse the ideas that the group will spin to make a whole than a fish can refuse to obey the movements of its shoal or a bird the patterns made by the flock it is part of.' This person is completely unarmoured, without protection against being swallowed whole by some set of ideas that need have no relevance to any real information that moves or drives the society. This person—"

Arithamea inquired, making it clear that she was only in search of exactness: "Just a minute, dear, but are you saying that young people like company of their own age?"

"Yes, if you want to put it like that," said Grice, for his part showing he thought that she was falling below an expected level.

"But everyone knows that, don't they, love?" said she, and started to knit.

"If *everyone* knows it, then *everyone* does not take it the necessary step further," said Grice firmly to her, raising his eyebrows at the flashing needles and directing urgent glances to the Judge. Spascock leaned forward, in turn raised his eyebrows, and remarked:

"Leader of the Peers, you really must not knit in this court; I am sorry."

"If you say so, Judge," said she equably, packing away vast quantities of wool, needles, and so forth in a hold-all, a process that engaged the eyes and attention of everyone in the court. "But it helps to keep my mind comfortable."

"But not ours," said Spascock. "Do you mind my remarking that this is a serious occasion?"

"Since you're Judge, you can say what you like, I suppose," she said. "But what I want to know is this—I mean, to put it in your kind of language, what I need is some clarification. And I am sure I speak for all of us—" Here she looked around and found that at least four of her Peers had dropped off, and others looked somnolent. "Wake up," she said.

"Yes, wake up," said Spascock, and the Peers roused themselves.

Incent came close to them to say, "Do you realize how important this is? This particular point? Do you *understand* how *vital*?"

Said the Chief Peer, "When I left home my mother said to me, 'Now, take care, and don't get into bad company.' Is that what all those tomes of yours are saying? Excuse me asking like that, I don't want to upset you at all," said she to Grice.

"Well, it's the gist of it, but the point is, were you told that you were a group animal and would have to absorb, whether you liked it or not, all the ideas of your group?"

"In so many words?" she inquired. "As it happened, I did meet up with some boys and girls, particularly boys of course"—here she offered and accepted tolerant smiles from everyone on the Peers' dais—"but I didn't go along with their ideas for long. They weren't up to much."

"Madam, how fortunate you are," remarked Spascock sombrely, and his tones made everyone in the court look up at him, where he sat isolated on his throne.

There was a long silence, into which was hissed, or breathed, the syllable *spies.* . . . But when we all looked towards Krolgul, the ventriloquist, he was standing there leaning sardonically against a wall, the folds of his black court dress hanging like limp wings. *Spies* . . . everyone was murmuring or thinking, and the hiss of it was in the air.

Spies are the subject of every other article, broadcast, broadsheet, popular song. Suddenly, the populations (not only of Volyen, but of the two "limbs" still remaining) look at Volyen's administrators and wonder what can have been the nature of that psychological epidemic that suborned, so it sometimes seems, a whole ruling class.

Arithamea, tactfully *not* looking at the Judge, remarked: "I am sure a lot of people in this country are wondering how they came to do the things they did. . . ."

"Precisely," said Grice sharply, causing everyone to look at him. "Exactly. *Why?* But if we, and others like us, had been told when we were at school, as part of our education, that our need to find acceptance within a group would make us helpless against its ideas—"

"Helpless, is it?" inquired another Peer, a solid young man dressed in a variety of red-and-green sportsgear and a funny hat. "Helpless? Some are and some are not."

"It's a question of people's characters," said the young woman. "People with some basic decency and common sense can stand firm against wrong notions."

And both Grice and Spascock let out at the same moment a groan, so desperate, so sad, that everyone again turned to look.

On reflex, Spascock hastily pulled out a pipe and lit it. So did Grice. The good citizens of Volyen do not know that their publicity experts (usually Krolgul) advised so many to smoke pipes as a sign of integrity

and moral balance, and most people in the court looked amazed.
Particularly since not merely the Judge and the Chief Accuser, but
others were pulling out pipes. Among the public on their benches,
among the court officials in their gloomy robes, and even among the
Peers, everywhere could be seen anxious and even trembling lips clos-
ing around the stems of pipes, and clouds of sweet moist smoke
dimmed the air. Spascock and Grice both leaned forward to examine
these unknown accomplices of theirs. On their faces could be read,
Don't tell me that *you* are another. . . .

"If you can smoke a pipe, then I shall knit," said the Chief Peer,
and pulled out her bundle again.

"No, no, certainly not. You are quite right. Smoking absolutely
forbidden!" And in a moment pipes were vanishing, hastily extin-
guished, all over the court.

Meanwhile, Stil, who had been sitting near Grice, correctly upright, arms folded, every inch of him under control, his face expressing
first incredulity, then shock, now remarked:

"If the courts on Volyen are so undisciplined, then what may we
expect of ordinary people?"

"And who are you, dear?" inquired the Chief Peer, who had not
put away her knitting, which lay on her lap.

"This is the Prosecution's Chief Witness for Indictment Two,"
said Spascock.

"Yes, I know that, but who is he?"

"I am from Motz."

"And where's that? Yes, we've heard of it, but it would be nice to
know—"

He's a Sirian spy was in the air—but of course Krolgul maintained
a smiling correctness.

"Are you a Sirian, love?" inquired the woman amiably, just as if
there were not talk of lynchings from one end of Volyen to the other.

"Yes, I am proud to call myself a Sirian."

"He is a Sirian as someone from Volyenadna is a Volyen," said
Grice.

"Or someone from Maken and Slovin," said Incent passionately,
not intending to evoke the sardonic laugh that swept the court. Everyone looked at the despoiled walls and the ceiling. A gale of laughter.

Stil said, "I am unable to see what is so humorous about the successful patriotic and revolutionary uprisings of downtrodden colonies."

"No, no, you are quite right, love," said the Chief Peer soothingly. "Don't mind us."

"Look, are you going to conduct this Trial properly or are you not, Spascock?" inquired Grice.

"If you can call it a Trial," said Spascock. "Right. Well, go on, then."

"I have already made my point."

"Not to my noticing," said Arithamea, and her associates agreed in chorus. "Just run over it again, will you? I don't seem to have got the point."

"Of course you've got the point," said Grice. "It's obvious, isn't it? We now know a great deal about the mechanisms that govern us, that make us dance like puppets. Some of the most powerful mechanisms are those that we can roughly describe as comprising the functioning of groups." Here he indicated the piles of red, green, blue, yellow books on the trolley below his little plinth. "There is no disagreement, not real disagreement, about these mechanisms. We know, within a certain group, the percentage of those who will not be able to disagree or dissent from the majority opinion of the group; we know the percentage of those who will carry out the orders of the leaders of the group, no matter how savage and how brutal; we know that such groups will fall into such-and-such patterns; we know that they will divide and subdivide in certain ways. We know they have lives that are organic."

"Like Empires, for instance," Incent could not stop himself from adding helpfully, and Krolgul again caused the word *spy* to appear in the minds of everyone.

"And who are *you*?" asked Arithamea. "No, I mean, where are you from?"

"He's a Sirian spy, of course," remarked one of the Peers. "They all are. They are everywhere."

"Oh come on, get on with it," said someone loudly from the public benches.

"Well, then, this is the point," Grice went on, trying to recover his momentum. "If we are governed by mechanisms, and we are, then we should be taught them. In school. At the age when one is taught how the body functions or how the state is run. We should be taught to understand these mechanisms so that we are not controlled by them."

"Just a minute, love," said Arithamea. "I know you mean well; I really do see what you are getting at. But don't tell me you believe that if you say to some young thing, all ready to take off for independence, and of course knowing much better than her elders—"

"Or *his* elders; fair's fair," said the colourful Peer beside her.

"His or her elders . . . you can't say to such as them, Keep a cool head and watch the mechanisms. That's the one thing they aren't capable of."

"That's right, she's right," from the public benches.

"I'll clear the court," threatened Spascock.

Silence.

Spascock: "Is your point made, then, Grice?"

"I don't agree with her. She's negative. She's pessimistic. Volyen can't jettison its responsibilities like that! Besides, Volyen has promised in the Constitution to—"

"Have you read Tatz and Palooza on Group Mechanisms?" inquired Krolgul.

"No, should I have?"

"They are in total disagreement with Quinck and Swaller," said Krolgul. "For instance, in the percentages of possible resistance to authority."

"Well," said Grice hotly, "I'm handicapped, aren't I? I've been in captivity on Motz, and I was in no position even to know if all the relevant literature was there. But it seems to me that this is evidence enough . . ." indicating the tomes.

"I'm just pointing out that the consensus is not a hundred percent," said Krolgul.

"Look, Judge," said Arithamea, "are you going to run this Trial, or are you not? This one here having his say as far as I can see is only an usher."

"Yes, yes, sorry," said Spascock. And to Grice: "Would you be kind enough to frame your request in adequate words?"

"Yes. I want this court to condemn Volyen utterly, root and

branch, for failing to instruct its young in the rules that its own psychologists and anthropologists have extracted from research and study; for failing to arm its youth with information that would enable it—the youth—to resist being swept away into any system of ideas that happens to be available. I want this court to say, clearly and loudly, that at least three generations of Volyen youth, and may I say at this point that I am one of the victims"—boos, cheers, hisses— "have been left unprotected because of the failure to provide knowledge that is readily available to any specialist in the field of group function. That Volyen has allowed, nay, connived at, a situation whereby its specialists acquire more and more expertise about groups, the primary unit of society, but where this information is never allowed to affect the actual institutions of society, which continue to be archaic, clumsy if not lethal, ridiculously inappropriate machineries. Our left hand does not know what our right hand does. On the one hand, ever-increasing facts, information, discovery. On the other, the lumbering stupidities of our culture. I want Volyen condemned."

A long silence. The citizens were, in fact, impressed. But the trouble was, in every mind was just one thought: It does look as if Sirius is about to invade—not that we shall let them get away with it—and we've got other things on our minds. . . .

Spascock turned to the Peers. "Well, do you want to retire?"

Arithamea consulted with her associates, those that were awake.

"No, Judge."

"Well, then, do you agree to call Volyen guilty, or not?"

Again she consulted—for no longer than it is taking me to write this sentence.

"Fair enough, Judge. Guilty. Of course, I'm taking Governor Grice's word for it that those books are what he says."

"Tatz and Palooza," murmured Krolgul.

"Oh, you keep out of it," she said. "I don't like the look of you at all. Volyen's guilty. Of course it is. We should have been told all that kind of thing. I'll be doing a bit of reading on my own account, now that I've had my attention drawn to it all. Yes. Guilty."

Spascock: "I hereby pronounce Volyen guilty on Indictment One. This is an intermediate judgment, which will come into force if and when the Select Committee has defined 'Volyen.' If and when Volyen is defined as an entity that can be sentenced, Volyen will duly be sentenced. Right. That's that. We shall now adjourn until tomorrow. We shall then take Indictment Two."

And Spascock went striding out, evidently in the last stages of emotional attrition. Grice and a gloomy and reluctant Stil went off together. Stil was heard to say, "If you can make this kind of criticism of your government, then how is this a tyranny? Explain, please." Incent was nearly captured by Krolgul, but came with me. Anyway, as will be obvious by now, Krolgul's work on this planet is done: total collapse and demoralization is his—Shammat's—meat and drink. Incent is coming out of the ordeal strengthened, and that is a good augury for the condition of Volyen during the Sirian occupation and the subsequent Sirian collapse. If he goes on like this, I propose leaving him here. If he can avoid getting strung up somewhere, I think he would be a beneficial influence.

It is now the end of the second day. When we assembled this morning, at least half of the Peers had not turned up; the Trial had not provided them with the entertainment they had expected. But a large number of a different kind of Volyens had arrived, hoping to take their places, hoping, indeed, for any kind of seat in the court. Word had gone about that attempts at serious criticism of Volyen's structure were being made. When the new Peers were accommodated there were strong contrasts between them and those of the festive ones who remained. Among them all sat the Chief Peer, at ease and ready.

As Spascock took his place with his attendants and sat down, Arithamea stood up and said, "Excuse me, Judge."

"What is it?"

"I have been awake all night," she said, not without dramatic effect.

"And so have a good many of us, I dare say," said Spascock, his pale and worried face attempting a smile.

A general silence. For the news today is that Sirian spaceships are poised to strike.

"No, I don't mean what you mean, Judge. Not that I am not bothered as much as the next person . . . But there is this business of the mechanisms of groups we were having us out yesterday."

"Oh, no," said Incent, his gracefully dramatic presence as it were infinitely at her service. "Oh, no, Chief Peer, that was a perfectly sound decision of yours yesterday. And it might have wonderful long-term results here in Volyen."

She looked him up and down. "Where else could it have a result? If it has results on Volyen, that's enough for me." Here a storm of cheers, boos, and general emotion. The mobs were out everywhere, and were asking every other person first, Were you born on Volyen? and then, finding that practically no one was, Are you a Volyen? and then, as the definitions of *Volyen* proliferated, simply beating up anyone they didn't like the look of. "And I don't want to add to all this mob stuff either," she announced. "Really, I don't know what has got into us all. I used to think of us on Volyen as fair and sensible people." Such was the force of this strong and competent presence that the crowd quietened and even looked ashamed. "No, it's this, Judge. I have been reading about the structure of groups all night, and it is obvious that yesterday I was authority in the group—because this is a *group* of Peers, isn't it? Right. I was a bit high-handed, it seems to me now. And I have to give notice that there's not going to be any nonsense about making snap decisions today in this court. We are all going to take our time about our decisions—"

"You're bossing us again, aren't you?" said one wag, a man from yesterday in bright colours, with a large button on his chest that read, "Volyen Rules: OK?"

"Well, if so, today I am within my rights. The rules allow for any member of the Peers, leader or not, to insist on a proper withdrawal to privacy."

Suddenly there was a stir on the Peers' bench. The half dozen or so that remained from yesterday were standing up and leaving. "Sorry," they were saying, and "All this is too much," and "We thought we were in for a bit of a laugh really," and went.

"Substitutes for the Peers," said Spascock, and in a moment the overcrowded public benches were providing serious-looking, responsible people.

And so, except for the Chief Peer, the citizens on the Peers' platform were different ones today from yesterday.

"May we begin?" inquired Spascock, his voice trembling with his attempts at the obligatory sarcasm.

"Yes, I think it's all right now, Judge," said Arithamea.

"Good. Then, with your permission, we shall start."

Grice stood up. He was as gloomy, dramatic, pale as Spascock. They are so obviously two of a kind, and could be used as an illustration of the type produced at the end of Empires.

Beside Grice, the admirable, the incomparable Stil seemed a living illustration of the subject of today's exchanges.

Grice said, "I wish to put my Chief Witness on the stand."

"Just a minute, Grice; what's your Indictment?"

"We all know what it is, Judge," said Arithamea. "It's written out on these programmes we've got. It's about us treating ourselves too well."

"Will you be good enough to let me conduct this Trial?" half screamed Spascock.

"Sorry."

"She has a point," said Grice.

Again these two thin, nervous, wan, quivering individuals confronted each other, each with the look of being about to attack the other, but at the same time showing every sign of the tenderest protective concern for the other, as if for himself.

"Yes, I dare say," said Spascock, "but it's not in order, and I simply cannot—"

"But if you could stretch a point. This Second Indictment will take half a day to read."

"I simply don't understand how no one is prepared to let me, the Judge, conduct this case in my own court. But if you insist . . ."

"It's not a question of insisting, but just listen to . . ."

Outside, the sounds of running, shouting mobs.

"Well, I suppose so, but it's really very—"

"Irregular, I know, but . . ." Grice motioned to Stil, who moved to the witness plinth and stood there waiting. There was another long silence. Volyen had not actually understood that they were about to be invaded by Motz: "Sirius" was still their word for what threatened. But what a contrast between this being and themselves, between this Motzan and anyone at this time in Volyen.

There he stood, this immensely strong man, all muscle and contained energy, with the exact and measured movements of those who use themselves to their limits. Stil is not taller than a Volyen. He is not any more intelligent. Not better endowed genetically. But as they looked at him, the Volyens let out a long sigh, and could be seen glancing at one another in disparagement.

Spy—released into the air by the ever-hovering Krolgul—could not survive; it was as if the atmosphere rejected it.

"I am not a spy," said Stil, in his sturdy, slow way. "I was invited here by this court, to assist in this Trial."

"All spies say that kind of thing," suggested Krolgul, and here Incent said, "Stop it, Shammat!" He had not meant to say "Shammat" but did, and then stood by it, for he turned himself around and confronted Krolgul, who lounged there, laughing in his hollow-cheeked, self-dramatizing way.

"Fascist," said Krolgul.

Incent did not collapse.

The Chief Peer said, her tolerance clearly leaking away, "Judge, do let's get on. I'm sure this gentleman means well, but that kind of talk used to get me irritated even when I was a girl."

"The Chief Peer is quite right," said Spascock. "Do let's get a move on."

"I want you to tell the story of your life, Stil," said Grice, and Stil did so. False modesty is not a convention among the Motzans, and his narrative, neither embellished nor played down, was impressive. If he seemed to forget something, Grice would interrupt: "But, Stil, you told me that when you were alone at that time, with no family, you earned your living digging up those plants and—"

"No, that was the second time I found myself alone. The first time, I found work stripping fish of its skin for use in the family of a fish merchant."

"What did you use the skin for?"

"For? What do *you* use it for?"

"We don't," said Grice.

"We don't need to use rubbish like that," came from the public benches.

"Rubbish?" said Stil, and took off a thick, sinuous belt, stuck full of knives, implements, needles, pouches. "Fish skin," he said.

"Very well. And when you could not find a family?"

"I earned my living thieving for a time, since I had to eat, and then I took to the moors and I dug up edible plants which I sold in the settlements. I lived like that for three M-years."

"And you were ten years old then?"

"Yes."

"And you were keeping your two siblings, a brother and a sister, and you all lived in a cave near a settlement where the two smaller children could get work as fish cleaners?"

"Yes."

"And then, as soon as your brother and sister were old enough, you three went off to an empty part of Motz and started your own settlement, draining marshes and digging dikes, and soon others came and joined you."

"Yes."

"Would you be good enough to tell the court what skills you have?"

Stil stood thinking for a moment before starting on a recital that lasted some minutes, beginning: "I understand all the processes to do with the catching, cleaning, curing of fish and its products, I can drain poor, sour land and clean it, I can plant and grow trees, and I can . . ." It ended with, "I know how to administer a settlement, and to use all the technical devices associated with that. Some of them we captured from you."

A long silence.

Spascock: "I gather that your point, Grice, is that Volyen, your motherland, has not provided you with an education as comprehensive as Stil's?"

"Exactly."

"I think his point is, Judge, that hardship has made Stil into what we see—and very admirable it is too," said the Chief Peer.

At this point there was a light hand-clapping from the public benches, and Spascock, scandalized, shouted: "This is not a public theatre!"

"I've never seen anything like him," went on Arithamea. "I'm sure we none of us have. But are you really complaining, Governor Grice, that Volyen hasn't treated you badly, half starved you, all that kind of thing?"

"Not exactly," said Grice, though his point was in fact not far from that. "All I know is this. I am fit for only one thing—if that. Governing a colony. Provided I have enough underlings to do the dirty work. Oh, *I* can't understand the technical devices used in administration. And all my life I have been soft, self-indulgent, weak. I cannot stand up to the slightest setback or hardship. I could not survive a day without the comforts and convenience I've known all my life. Compared with Stil here, compared with a Motzan, I am nothing."

Here we all examined Grice, we examined Spascock. Certainly there was nothing much there to admire. Meanwhile, the Motzan stood silent, his arms folded, looking ahead of him. A soldier, standing at ease: that was what he suggested, with his broad, healthy face, his great neck, his arms, his legs exposed under the short tunic in the Motzan fashion. Arithamea went on:

"I want to ask the witness a question."

"Certainly, if he agrees," said Spascock.

Stil nodded.

"How many Motzans died as children under such treatment?"

Stil looked uncomfortable for the first time. "A good many died. But we are talking of the past. You will remember, we developed a hostile planet from nothing, and it is only recently that—"

"But many died?"

"Yes."

"Not all have survived to tell the tale?"

"No."

"Are all the people of your planet as well equipped and strong and able as you?"

"Yes, I would say we all are," said Stil unexpectedly, for we had expected him in his honesty to admit less than that. But because of his honesty, we knew it was true. "Yes, we are all able to turn our hands to anything that comes up. We aren't afraid of hardship. We can eat anything."

"You all of you rise when your sun rises, and you work all day, you live on two small meals in the day, you drink very little intoxicating liquor, you sleep no more than three or four hours in the night."

Stil nodded. "That is so."

At this point an earnest, worried-looking man who had taken the place of the disappointed reveller on the seat next to Arithamea said, "It seems to me that what this Indictment is demanding is impossible."

"Not at all," said Grice. "It's perfectly obvious. It is generally known, everyone knows, that a population who are pampered, softened, allowed to go to flesh, become fit for nothing and degenerate. This is a law of nature. We observe it all the time, in plants, animals —and in people, though there seems to have arisen a convention with us on Volyen that people are exempt from these laws, and—"

"May I ask a question?" said the worried man.

"May he ask a question, Chief Peer?" asked Spascock.

"I didn't know I had to give him permission."

"He is being sarcastic," said Incent protectively, hovering about the group of Peers. "Take no notice."

"But we have to take notice of the Judge, dear, even if his manners aren't up to mine."

"Thank you, Chief Peer," said Spascock.

"This is my question, then. You say in your Second Indictment, which is what we are considering today, that Empires are like animal organisms: they have a curve of development and ultimately decay. All Empires show this. While they develop they are vigorous, admire simple virtues and capacities, teach their children discipline and how to devote themselves to duty. On the ascending curve they produce people like this Stil here, who are healthy and not neurotic, who admire forcefulness and determination and responsibility. But when they decline, they are like . . . like we are on Volyen. We are lazy and even proud of it. We teach our children that they are entitled to anything, without working for it. We are self-indulgent. We spend our time eating and drinking and sleeping. We dress as the fancy takes us. A lot of us take drugs and intoxicants."

"Speak for yourself," came from the public benches.

"If I am not speaking for most of us, where have I been living all my life?" said the worried man. "But the point is, if this is an organic process, and if an Empire, like a group, like a person, like an animal, has a time of growth, of flourishing, and then a descent, then how can you expect Volyen, which *is* this organism, to change its own laws? You haven't explained that. How? At what point should 'Volyen,' whatever that may be, and I'm told even this court hasn't made up its mind on the point, have said: 'Now, I am not going to let myself get decadent and soft, I'm going to contradict all the laws that I know operate'?"

Silence again.

"Well, Grice, that seems to be a reasonable question," said Spascock.

"Why do we have to take for granted that it can't be done? Pessimism again. Just like us, that is—pessimism and negativism."

"I agree with that," said Stil suddenly, "if I am entitled to say anything, as a witness. When we say we are going to do a thing, we do it. It's a question of will."

"Yes, but you are on the ascending curve, love," said Arithamea soothingly, "while we're going down. Judge, are we supposed to say that Volyen is guilty, or not guilty, of arresting some inevitable force or law of growth? Because I am with my fellow Peer here."

"Grice?" demanded Spascock.

"How is it that I've never heard Volyen, in the person of public body, teacher, court, President—not once has Volyen ever said to its citizens: 'We *were* energetic, self-disciplined, and dutiful; now we are softened and fit for nothing'?"

"I'm surprised at you, Governor Grice," said Krolgul. "How is it that you are not mentioning that while Volyen had all these noble qualities, Volyen was also conquering and grabbing and killing and imprisoning and taking over any little planet that took your fancy?"

"It is not my present point," said Grice, suffering.

"Well, love," inquired the Chief Peer of Stil, "do you Motzans conquer and steal and imprison and kill?"

He was silent, and then said: "No, no, I am sure not."

But he knew the Motzan fleets were poised waiting all around Volyen. He was more than uncomfortable, this Stil. He was suffering an assault on his entire emotional and intellectual apparatus. It had occurred to him for the very first time that the Virtue of Sirius was not to be embodied in one word and left undefined.

Krolgul said: "When Sirius invades, it will be the Motzan fleets who invade first." He said this quite lightly, even laughing. The information was too new, too raw to assimilate; and everyone looked doubtfully at this court official who was so saturnine and threatening, even though he was laughing.

"Do let's get on," said Spascock again. "You want a verdict passed, I take it, that 'Volyen' should have instructed us that these amenities

we have been taking for granted all our lives, our civilization, everything we have been proud of, our leisured lives, our ease, our plenty,
all this was quite simply decadence and would lead inevitably to our
defeat by stronger and more vigorous peoples?"

He was looking straight at Grice, with a grim, self-critical, angry
smile.

And Grice was looking at him, similarly. "Well, what do you think,
Spascock?"

"Well, yes . . . speaking personally," he said in a hurried, low voice,
and then loudly: "Very well, Peers, that's it. Will you retire and
consider your verdict."

The group of Peers looked at one another, consulted in low voices.

The court was in that restless, almost irritated atmosphere that
says people feel a thing has run its course. And when the Chief Peer
announced, "We are going to retire to consider our verdict," there
was even a groan.

Spascock: "I've already said this isn't a theatre."

"As good as one," shouted someone from the public benches. And
there was laughter as they all got up and jostled out, in a rough,
raucous, jeering mood that contrasted with the sober demeanour of
the retiring Peers.

The people who came in from the street to the Trial went through
three different moods. First, they hoped to be able to release in
laughter, because of the clumsy and ridiculous processes of the law,
their rage and frustration at everything that was happening around
them in Volyen. Then, finding something different, and that the
Peers after the first day were prepared to be serious, they became
attentive. Then, as they could be heard complaining on their way
out, "But there's nothing to take hold of, one way or the other,"
and so they again became derisive, ready to mock anything or anyone
in authority. At any rate, they left all together and as one, and from
then on the public benches were empty.

Spascock was looking in a hollow, appalled, incredulous way at
Grice, who was ruffling sheaves of papers as if some truth that lay
hidden there was escaping him.

"Grice," hissed Spascock, "you can't possibly want to go on with
this . . . this . . . ."

"Farce," offered Krolgul in a helpful way.

"Certainly I do," said Grice.

"Can't you see you are bringing the legal processes of Volyen into disrepute?"

"No, no, no," cried Incent, "on the contrary, he's asking questions that have to be asked!" And now he hovered about Grice, his big black eyes fervently offering total support.

"Yes, but not here," moaned Spascock.

"It's all *logical*," said Grice. "Tell me one thing I've said that isn't *logical*."

At this word, Incent did glance in doubt towards me, remembering how often I've told him that when that word appears in a situation, it is time to be on your guard. I shook my head at him, and Incent sank onto a near chair, his head in his hands.

Krolgul smiled at me. It is interesting that at such moments this old enemy of ours seems to regard himself almost as an ally.

"I see that number Three of the Indictment is a total condemnation, root and branch, of the entire Volyen system of education?" remarked Spascock.

"I suppose it amounts to that," agreed Grice. "You could perhaps tell them to bring in the relevant books?"

"Your next batch of witnesses, I suppose? But we haven't finished with your Second Indictment."

The two bickered on in the amiable, grumbling way that characterizes their relationship, until a group of serious, even suffering people entered the court. These were the Peers, and it was evident that their deliberations had united them: the way they stood so close, as if in support of one another, told us that any one of them could speak for the rest. But it was still Arithamea who spoke up, without stepping forward or separating herself from them.

"Judge," she said. "The little bit of talking we've done has made one thing clear: this is a very serious matter."

"Oh, is it?" groaned Spascock. "That's what you've decided, is it?"

"Yes, love, it is. And we want to criticize the conduct of this court from the start. It hasn't been treated seriously enough."

"Wha-a-at?" creaked Spascock. And to Grice: "You, as Accuser, are you complaining about the conduct of this case?"

"I'm glad," said Grice histrionically, "that my Peers recognize the importance of what I am saying."

"I didn't say we went all the way with you, Governor Grice. No, what we think is this. There's sense in what you say. We all think that—don't we?" And here she was supported, as she looked around at the others, by nods, smiles, and even touches and squeezes. "Yes. We do. We are shocked, Judge, because we haven't been told things we ought to know. And we are grateful to Governor Grice for bringing them up. But there's something we can't quite put our finger on, in a manner of speaking. . . ." And here she smiled in her helpful, motherly way around the court. "What we can't come to grips with is that, at the same time, there's something not right. How can we put it . . . ?"

"It's either right, or wrong," said Grice, standing up to them like a man before the firing squad, his whole being at stake. "Either good, or bad."

"Either with me or against me," suggested Krolgul.

"Logic," moaned poor Incent, who still huddled, stricken, on his seat.

"Well, there you are, love, that's it. There's something silly about it, but we can't put our finger on what. Because when we sit and think and remember what the Governor here said, we decide he's right. And then one of us says, But there's something silly, for all that. . . ."

Grice, with a gesture of long-suffering, turned away, as if from her, the Peers, the Judge—everyone.

"And so, what we ask is this, that you adjourn the court long enough for us to read these books, and then we'll give our verdict."

"My good woman, you can't possibly be serious!"

"Why not, Judge? Were these books brought into the court as evidence or were they not?"

"Logic," breathed Krolgul, smiling.

"Because if they were, and we have to make up our minds on evidence, we have the right to—"

"Oh, yes, yes, yes, very well," said Spascock. "Have the Peers taken to a private room, supply them with the books, feed them, and all that kind of thing."

"Thank you, Judge."

"Oh, don't mention it. We all have all the time in the world. You did actually hear the news this morning?" And he glared down at Arithamea.

"If you are saying that perhaps, at a time of National Emergency, such a case should have been put off to happier days, then we go along with that, but since you allowed the case to be brought, then you must allow it to be finished."

"Logic. *Since—then,*" remarked Krolgul, laughing.

"*Ergo,*" said Spascock. "And," he muttered, as if to himself, in real misery, "I suppose it has served its purpose."

"Which is?" demanded Grice, confronting him, full on.

"Which is to make this poor planet of ours look even more totally and absolutely and ridiculously *hopeless* than it does already. Or hasn't it occurred to you, Grice, that there are certain quarters who lose no opportunity to— Oh, what's the use! Case adjourned until these twenty or so assorted Peers have read—what is it? one hundred and fifty, at least—erudite volumes."

He swept out. The Peers left, followed by three court attendants trundling the trolley of books.

So ended the last court case to be heard on Volyen, the last under the old dispensation.

KLORATHY TO JOHOR.
FROM VOLYENDESTA.

Many events in a short time!

As the history books will put it, Sirius invaded Volyen, the day after the Trial was adjourned.

On Sirius the power struggle rages. The Questioners, recently repelled, made a comeback, and succeeded in dividing the Centre on the question of whether to invade Volyen or not. But this was part of the larger question: what the Questioners won the vote on was, "We propose that no further expansion of any kind takes place until we have learned from Canopus how to align ourselves with the Purpose; until we know what we are *for.*"

You will see that the silent influences of the Five have been potent indeed.

But the defeated faction sent a secret message to the Sirian armies to carry out existing plans; and by the time the Questioners knew about it, it was too late.

Motzans, in Sirian Centre spacecraft, landed all over Volyen, to be met by patchy resistance. Sirian "agents" everywhere saw to it that the defending armies were confused and got conflicting orders. The inverted commas are, of course, because many still had no idea to what extent they would be considered Sirian partisans. Most people allowed themselves to be motivated by patriotism, and so there were areas of Volyen where the fighting was bitter. The Motzan armies were in control in a few V-days.

Their demoralization began at once.

First, before they even landed, they heard rumours—contradicted at once—that the "Centre" had never ordered them to attack. These in any case unwilling soldiers were angry. And then, what they found when they landed . . . never had they imagined such plenty, such piles of everything. Men and women—Motzan females are willing and skilled soldiers—went about the streets of the Volyen cities, not believing what they saw. Volyen had been presented to them as a deprived and bitterly poor planet, needing Sirian assistance. In the shops and markets in every street, in every city, in every settlement, piles, wasteful rolling piles, of food: fruits and vegetables the frugal Motzans had never even heard of; meat and fish prepared in a thousand ways, clothes so fanciful and delicate and rare and delightful.

The Motzans, in the absence of clear orders from "the Centre itself," had instructed Volyen to establish normality at once. And so normality there was. And the Motzans could not believe it. At first they believed there was a gigantic conspiracy, cunningly organized, to present to them this vision of smiling plenty. And they went running around from street to street, looking for the horrible poverty and deprivation they had expected. But, like Stil on his first arrival, they said: We could feed one of our settlements on what they waste here in a day!

And, suddenly, they lost their discipline and became an invading army, and they ate, and they drank—particularly drank, for on Motz

152

there is very little strong liquor. Drunken, angry mobs of Motzans ravaged Volyen, and, when they came to their senses, were ashamed and frightened, even ascribing their behaviour to some sinister influence in the atmosphere of Volyen. At any rate, all they wanted was to get home. All, including the officers. From one end of Volyen to the other, Motzans were to be seen conferring in little groups, and then in larger ones, then forming into detachments, battalions, and going to the spaceports. Laden with Volyen's riches, they piled themselves into the spaceships. No order, not a word from Sirius, from the "Centre," where fighting was—and still is—going on. So they simply went home, and were no longer Sirian. These straightforward, single-minded people did not need more than to put the question to themselves: "Sirius has lied to us. Do we want to be considered Sirian?"

They dispatched a message to Sirius announcing that they were no longer to be counted as part of the Sirian Empire, and would repel any invasion. But their insubordination was hardly noticed. Meanwhile, the Motzan defection had been noted by their neighbour Alput, whose armies invaded Volyen at once.

I attach a letter from our AM 5. I am afraid it is characterized by the Elation that is the worst symptom of war fever.

Servus! (as I have *not* heard Krolgul say recently; where is he?) Klorathy, in such a situation do you expect me to be *sober?* No one else is, anywhere on Motz. Oh, these poor Embodiments, what a blow they have suffered, how the wings of their Virtue trail and drag. No, but seriously, it's serious, Klorathy. Before they went off to make Volyen as Virtuous as Motz, never once had any of them thought that their ways were not the best in the Galaxy. And those who went are not believed by those who stayed. "On Volyen, you'll see whole streets crammed with food and fruit and stuff, Volyens eat and drink what they fancy, stuff we've never dreamed of, and there's no limit to it. In the poorest Volyen household they live better than in our richest. . . ." But the reply is, "That's propaganda; you fell for it!" "No, it's the truth, believe us!" But they aren't believed, and so Motz is split, no longer has a single mind; Motzans are unsure of themselves, curse Sirius, and have thrown out everyone suspected of being Sirian, including me.

"You are a spy," they said to me.

"But not from Sirius. I am the agent of Canopus," said I, coming clean. "As you to Volyen," I said, "so Volyen to Canopus, but a thousand degrees of difference if you to Volyen are one degree. Do you understand?" I said. "You have been dazzled by a little fitful gleam, whereas if you imagine Canopus . . ." But they threw me out. They didn't kill me: Motz remains Motz, fair and decent, if not sober, for they have brought from Volyen knowledge of shops full of a hundred varieties of wines and spirits. They said, "Leave." So I went to Alput. No alien remains on Motz, not one.

Alput is not Motz! If Motz produces—*produced*—one type, the same all over Motz, the solid, hard-working, narrow, disciplined sort, then on Alput grow the representatives of a hundred planets; they are all aliens. As a result of Sirius's growing so Virtuous after the downfall of the Five, prisons proliferated, and Alput has been a prison planet, full of the best and the worst from everywhere. But their diversity means that the rigidities and conformities of the Virtue, with them, are cynicism, not, as it *was* with Motz, conviction. How clearly is exemplified our law that a state or Empire will be the more long-lived the more its propaganda is not believed in! Motz believed Sirius was perfect—and Motz is no longer Sirian! Alput believes everything and anything and is cruel and arbitrary—and will probably remain a Sirian outpost here, while all other colonies declare themselves free. Believe me, Klorathy, going with the Alputs into Volyen is not something I can *entertain* you with. They looked at the plenty and the amenities of Volyen, the many races and breeds that (on the whole) accommodated one another, they made speeches interminably, as conquerors do, extolling their superiorities, and the Virtue of Sirius did as well as anything else for this purpose, but no deep inner convictions were upset when they noted how fat and fair Volyen was and how—on the whole —tolerant and amiable its citizens. Alput is overpopulated. They see Volyen as a useful bit of property to expand into. They have been killing and killing and killing; I won't sicken you with it. As for the Sirian "agents" on Volyen, Alput knew no more about them than Motz did. From one end of "the Volyens" to the other, thousands of Volyens cowered and bit their nails and sweated at nights: "*How* will my treachery (or foresightedness?) be regarded by these Alputs, who call themselves Sirian, and who have never been to Sirius and know even less about it than we do?" Some presented themselves to these new and horrible conquerors with, "Excuse me, but I believe I am one of yours, I believe in Sirian Virtue . . ." and so on and so forth. "You do, do you?" came the reply. And "Well, what do you think now?" And hundreds of these sentimental agents found themselves in prison camps, where they were allowed to starve to death. A few have been employed by the Alputs as part of the Rule of Sirian Virtue (so they call their administration) in the role of overseers.

Spascock is one. I understand he refused our offer to take him to Volyendesta? That was brave of him, I suppose. He is running the law courts, and is (punishment fitting the crime) an expert on the Virtue as it affects the day-to-day life of the citizens.

And now a small tale, an incident, just a little light shining in all this darkness. While Motz came and went on Volyen, shut into a room in the court building were Arithamea and her associates, considering the Indictment of Volyen. Yes, they knew Motz had invaded; but had not Motz ordered "Business as usual"?

Some Motzan soldiers reeled drunkenly into the chamber where the Peers sat reading diligently, making notes and communicating to one another their thoughts; and, since they knew that books are Good, reeled out again.

Soon came the Alputs. Oh, Klorathy, imagine the scene, imagine it, allow me to indulge myself for just this one incident. . . .

A rather dusty room, with windows opening onto an inner court. None of the sights and sounds of invasion and sudden death. Twenty Peers sit together at one end of the room, among them Arithamea, and on a small dais an earnest, suffering soul, reading from a document. They are all much thinner, since supplies of food have been intermittent, all worried about their families, all concerned for the fate of Volyen. But this duty has been assigned to them, and this duty they will carry out. The document is a summing-up of Grice's complaint against Volyen.

The man who is reading has not yet heard that these Alputs are brutes likely to kill on a whim, and so, on seeing the five soldiers, of a type new to him—the Alputs have a varied genetic stock, but being Alputs gives them a characteristic easy, indulged, cynical good humour with which they conduct everything they do, with which they eat, drink, mate, kill, lie, cheat—he simply lifts a hand and says, "Just a minute, we are still considering our verdict," and goes on:

"These are my main points.

"One. You, Volyen, never gave me any obstacles to overcome. From cradle to grave, my paths have been made easy.

"Two. You have caused me to become soft and self-indulgent, unable to deny myself anything.

"Three. You taught me that what I wanted I could have, it was due to me because I had conceived the wish for it.

"Four. You inflicted on me a life of intolerable boredom, because you removed from me all risks and dangers, hid the face of death from me, behaved towards me like an overindulgent mother who believes that food and comfort can be equated with love—"

"Just a minute there," demands the captain of this little company of Alputs. "Just what do you think you are doing?"

"We are, as citizens of Volyen, doing our duty during the course of our turn of Peer service."

"Who told you to?"

"Judge Spascock."

The captain dispatches a soldier to find out who is currently in charge of the courts, and stands listening.

"Five. You never informed me that inherent in Volyen nature is the need to transcend ourselves, ever to step onwards and upwards on the corpses of our dead selves, achieve yet higher and higher steps on the ladder of evolution.

"Six. You taught me that to eat and drink and sleep and entertain myself was the object of life."

"Excuse me," says the captain, "*who* is complaining to *what?*"

"Well, actually, love," says Arithamea, "that hasn't been decided yet. There's a Select Committee sitting somewhere or other."

"Gawd," mutters the captain, "would you believe it."

"And as Leader of the Peers here, I really must ask you to let us proceed. It is our duty, do you see?"

"Seven. In other words, you have robbed me of my birthright, which is to struggle, to fight, to suffer, to overcome, to perform the impossible, to accomplish miracles, to—"

But at this point the messenger returns to say that one Spascock, a Volyen, had been nominated as Master, under Sirius, of the Courts.

"Well, I suppose we'll have to let you get on with it, won't we?" says the Alput, thoroughly bored with the whole thing, and disgusted too at the glimpse into Volyen "ordinary life," as he saw it.

"What a crew," one Alput mutters to another, as they march off down the corridors into the streets where they intend to resume the pleasures of looting and destroying. "Well, if what they want is a bit of rough treatment, I for one am going to give it to them!"

And so, Klorathy, here I am on Volyen with the Alput armies as interpreter. Do you want me to stay here? To go to Volyenadna? Volyendesta? I don't see that there is much to be done here. That is a way of saying I don't want to stay here. I do not see how Volyen can be any more than the fifth-rate colony of a disintegrating Empire.

And so, Johor, here *I* am, on Volyendesta.

I told AM 5 to stay on Volyen. I said that he was to make contact, and keep contact, with the Peers, who would continue to consider themselves a group, maintaining the knowledge of the laws of society gained by their period of enforced study, and would be sheltered by Spascock. Spascock is now *our* agent, this time without ambiguity. I said to him, "Stay alive. If you can manage that, it's a great deal. Shelter the Peer Group that originated from the Grice Trial. They will influence all Volyen, and when the Alputs depart as the Sirian Empire finally falls apart, there will grow a society based on a real knowledge of how things work, real socio-psychological laws. One day, from Volyen will come influences that will change all the planets in this part of the Galaxy. But in the meantime, this small group of vulnerable people must be sheltered. By you."

Before I come to affairs on Volyendesta—Volyenadna.

Except for the icecaps, all of this dour little planet now glows a soft red, as I saw when I directed the Space Traveller to fly over it. Calder caused the workers' organizations to start underground factories for the thousand products of Rocknosh. He has been so much admired for his foresight he is virtually boss of the planet. The factories are underground because they remembered what I said of the coming invasions. Sirius invaded, again on secret orders that were countermanded too late by the Questioners: the planet's minerals were of course the aim. But "Sirius" here was the wildest mix of peoples. The army that overran Volyenadna was composed of troops from land-hungry Alput, together with soldiers from several Sirian factory planets, all in desperate need of minerals as the Empire collapses. This army was really many armies, made up of peoples who disliked one another and were united by one thing, their hatred of this dour, chilly little planet, all tundra and rock, populated by dour, angry people. Alput is feeding off Volyen and has told its armies to fend for themselves. The factory colonies felt themselves abandoned by Sirius and have since announced their independence of the Sirian Empire, but in the meantime they had no food. Chaos—hunger—fighting between armies and factions of armies all over Volyenadna. Calder and his people watched all this, and no one told the invaders of the supplies of rich food that filled underground storehouses everywhere. And when these aliens saw that a reddish crust was being scraped off the rocks, and were told this was a lichen used for dyeing and as part of the processes of mining, they believed it. The invading armies had nothing to eat.

Calder and his people bribed them to go away, offering enough food to carry all these polyglot armies back home to their various planets.

"Food!" scoffed the Alputs and the starving armies of the factory planets. "What food? Where are you going to get it?"

"We'll give you all the food we have stored against bad years—for we have bad years, you know, when the snow falls through the growing months. We have to stockpile food."

"Show us!"

They were shown some underground storehouses specially prepared to contain only a few of the infinite variety of foods and products that Rocknosh can make. And these armies went away, the holds of their spaceships crammed with not very likable foodstuffs, pitying and despising the Volyenadnans, and never suspecting the crammed storehouses everywhere under the surface.

So Volyenadna is independent both of Volyen and of Sirius, its economy becomes daily more diversified, and its harsh climate is rapidly being modified by the influences of the new plant. Volyenadna, so recently the poorest and bleakest of the five planets that made the

Volyen "Empire," will have the easiest time of it and is in for at least four or five of their centuries of steady progress.

I see no need for our presence there, and with your agreement propose to withdraw all Agents except Agent AM 59, who will benefit by a period of Immersion in optimism and confidence. I have told her she is there for our benefit, but she is there for hers.

As I landed on Volyendesta, I saw Incent waiting for me. Behind him was Krolgul, who watched him anxiously, yearned at me while I walked towards them, again turned his attention on Incent, as if his eyes could swallow and digest him. This was Shammat, the poor animal whose roles and disguises had failed him. Incent stood smiling, proud of himself for having withstood Krolgul.

"We've done him," he said to me, as Krolgul capered about us, the monkeylike Krolgul, shrunken and lean-looking within his natty military-type uniform.

"For the time being," I said.

Krolgul was straining to hear what we said. I raised my voice. "I was saying, Krolgul, that it is only temporarily you have lost your conceit and your arrogance."

"Why do you Canopeans hate us so much?" he whined. "What have we done? Why are we worse than anyone else? All planets have their times and turns at taking what they can get. But Canopus is always there, helping them. Even at their worst. When Volyen was at the height of its Empire, did Canopus turn its back on the Volyens?" He was running along beside us, even dropped to all fours for a few moments—and then was up, was running along in front of us, backwards.

"Yes," I said, "but you've never been anything but a thieving, lying planet."

"But you say yourself," he yapped, "that Empires rise and fall— they have their laws, they can't help themselves."

"Yes, but you can help yourself, Shammat."

"What?" said Incent, indignant, stopping dead. "These animals better than—"

And Krolgul stopped and stood with one knuckle on the ground, so that he peered upwards, his eyes all hungry desperation.

"Why can we help ourselves? Why—what are you saying, Canopus?"

"You have put yourselves into opposition from the beginning of your history, Shammat. From your first moment as a planet, you looked at Canopus as the best and brightest—and decided to steal from everyone, but mostly from us. You have studied us, you have thought about us, you think about us Shammat-year in, Shammat-year out. You know a great deal about us. You know very well what you should do and what you should not. When you lie and steal and connive and intrigue, you know what you are doing."

There stopped Krolgul, still with one fist on the earth, peering up at me, his eyes wavering.

"Look here!" said Incent, all indignation. "You can't say that. They *don't* know. All their workings against us, their spitefulness during the fall of Volyen, was for nothing, came to nothing, because they *didn't* know, they had no idea how soon Sirius would invade, so that all their efforts would be wasted."

"No, no, no," said Krolgul hurriedly, anxious, avid. "No, we didn't. And you let us go on, you didn't warn . . ." And he began prancing and capering in frustrated rage.

"Listen to him," Incent jeered. " 'You let us go on,' he says, just as if he wasn't doing everything to undo us, doing everything to destroy us, using me as a sort of pump or siphon to steal Canopean power. 'You let us go on,' indeed!" And he kicked out at Krolgul, who yelped and stood rubbing the place where Incent's boot had landed.

Incent was astonished at himself, afraid to look at me, ashamed to look at Krolgul, who, mysteriously emboldened and encouraged, was giving him quick triumphant glances and edging closer, pushing out his backside as if to invite another kick.

"There's more than one way to feed Shammat on Canopus," I said.

"Oh, Klorathy, I am sorry, what can I do? There's no end to my foolishness." Incent was on the edge of tears.

Krolgul, seeing that this opportunity had passed, stood upright again, but seemed to wait for more.

"Krolgul," I said, "because you have thought of nothing but Canopus for so long, you have learned a good deal about the Purpose, the Law, the Alignments. Yet you never use them for anything but ill. Have you ever—has Shammat ever—asked what would happen if Shammat went to Canopus and said, 'Teach us, we are no longer thieves'?"

At this Shammat sidled and smirked and writhed and grinned, but at the same time he looked startled, and I knew that one day . . .

I said to him softly, "Shammat, it might surprise you to know that you understand more about us than any planet in the Galaxy; as much as the Five of Sirius who languish in their exile, waiting for their collapsing Empire to understand them. There are many ways to the path of the Purpose. When are you going to understand what it is you could be doing?"

"This animal," moaned Incent, "these horrible Shammats, oh, *no*, Klorathy, you can't possibly . . ."

And, indeed, Krolgul was dancing there in horrible triumph, looking like an ape or a spider, all limbs and eyes, and he was chanting: "Better than . . . better than . . . we're better than . . ."

"I didn't say that, or anything near it," I said. " 'Better' I didn't say."

But Krolgul, in a frenzy of self-congratulation, rushed off and away, yelping and squealing, "Better . . . best . . ."

Incent was silent for a while. "Klorathy, tell me, what good could that have done him—done them?"

"He'll remember it," I said. "He'll think about it when he's by himself."

Incent, as he walked quietly there beside me towards Ormarin, was far from the cocky, delighted person who had stood waiting for my spacecraft to land. He looked sober, even tired.

"I wish I didn't know that," he said. "It's hard to bear, having to think of Shammat like that. Bad enough to learn to be on one's guard every minute of the day and night, let alone having to remember that animal is . . . that animal is . . ."

"That animal is?"

A silence, a long one. We were in sight of Ormarin's house before Incent said, "I've been his prey. What does that make me?"

You will see that Incent is what I had hoped he would become; his lessons here, on and through Volyen, have achieved what we planned when we discussed his future. Frail, he is—very; vulnerable, unstable, far from being immune to what Krolgul will try to trick him into. But he will never again writhe around in ecstasies of enjoyable suffering, never again be the eager victim of words. And I can report that all our agents have come through this ordeal well, strengthened and tempered, and can take on greater responsibilities.

But I have yet to report on Volyendesta itself.

Sirius, when it was functioning as an Empire, had different plans for each of the Volyen's parts. PE 70 and 71 were destined to supply armies for the invasion of Volyenadna, and afterwards for the invasion of further parts of the Galaxy. These planets will certainly follow paths of conquest, but on their own account. Volyenadna's fate had been planned for it to remain as an occupied planet indefinitely, to ensure the supply of minerals. Sirius did not expect Volyen to put up much resistance, either to invasion or to occupation, because of the number of Sirian agents, and because of the degree to which the general population was softened by admiration for the Sirian Virtue. Besides, Sirius thought little of the Volyen people, believed them to be weakened beyond redemption by easy living.

Volyendesta was where their greatest efforts were concentrated. They had planned to establish an HQ here, to govern the planets that were once "Volyen" and to undertake further Empire-building.

All over this planet they built roads, bases, whole towns that would be Sirian. Everywhere are camps and settlements where suffer the slaves who have built the roads, the bases, the towns. They come from many different planets and are at different levels of evolution, but during this period of their shared suffering they have developed networks that ignore their differences and which are used to plan their deliverance, plan uprisings and revolutions—against Sirius. But Sirius is not yet here.

Volyendesta is from end to end in a condition of waiting, for the Sirian invasion. It is also full of refugees from Volyen, who are occupying the towns and bases planned for the Sirians.

In other words, unlike PE 70 and 71 (Maken and Slovin), unlike Volyenadna, like Volyen—but much more than Volyen—this planet is full, crammed, with differing races, kinds, types, nations, classes, sorts, genders, breeds, strains, tribes, clans, sects, castes, varieties, grades, even species; all of them united by *waiting*.

On the Mother Planet of Sirius the factions wage war by every means. They fight one another in the streets, they argue interminably in council chambers and parliaments and hidden rooms, they intrigue, change sides, promise eternal brotherhood, kill one another. The Questioners are indisputably on top, looked at from a formal, legal point of view, but the possessors of the "Virtue" simply issue orders and commands, according to how things strike the leaders and commanders at any given moment. The Sirian Empire disintegrates. An outlying planet of the Empire is instructed to invade another, which is rebelling, but before it can invade, a different order is issued. Planets simply announce their secession, their independence. Within each planet rages war, actual or verbal, as the former administrations that took orders from Sirius fight the new rulers, who despise them as stooges and cowards. Planets announce independence under one government, which can be overthrown the next day, and continue independent but with different aims, such as that they plan, or do not plan, to invade a richer neighbour or to invite co-operation. There are as many new alliances between planets only just released from Sirian bondage as there are invasions, as many treaties as there are ultimatums—Sirius is dead, submit to us!—while they struggle and fight and make war. Change is the rule of the moment: everything shifts and changes as you look. And everywhere is Shammat, is Puttiora, at work by every means, stirring up disagreement, strife, war, feeding off the effluvia of disintegration.

It is known that the invasion of Volyendesta has been imminent several times, but by different planets.

Ormarin has come into his own. All his manifold qualities are being put into use . . . *"at last,"* as he himself quietly exults. For one thing, the contradiction he has never been able to resolve, which has always tormented him: events have healed it. He speaks now for the millions of the slaves, is invited to their secret meetings, unites the Volyen refugees in plans to withstand and survive invasion, is everywhere . . . and was away when Incent and I arrived at his headquarters.

We decided to go to the Hospital for Rhetorical Diseases to visit Grice, who is a patient in Rhetorical Logic. I confess I was nervous about Incent, and told him so. He was full of confidence, and even insisted on being taken at once to Basic Rhetoric, where we watched through the observation glass some sufferers in the grip of the same symptoms that had afflicted him such a short time ago. Mostly refugees from Volyen, about twenty or so young males and females, in a variety of clothing that looked like attempts at uniforms, sat in a huddle on the floor, swaying back and forth and from side to side chanting a lament, or dirge, of the most dispiriting sort, that had the words:

We shall overcome
We shall overcome
We shall overcome one day
Deep in our hearts
We do believe
We shall overcome one day.

The tune of this dirge originated V-millenniums ago on Volyen during its time as a Volyenadnan colony, to express the hopelessness of slaves.

"A strange thing," I said to Incent, "that *words* of an energetic kind should be thought to outweigh such a dismal chant."

He was silent, his whole person expressing certain only-too-familiar emotions.

The poor sufferers, still re-enacting that moment when their amateur defences were smashed by the invading Motzans, were intoning:

We shall not be moved
They shall not pass!
We shall not be moved
They shall not pass!

Incent was weeping. "Oh, have you ever seen anything so *moving?*" he demanded.

"Incent, stop it at once. Do you want to have to go through that whole course of treatment again?"

"No, no, of course not. I'm sorry." And he pulled himself together.

"Do you think I can trust you in Logic?" I inquired.

"Yes, yes, of course you can."

"And it is hardly so *moving* as Basic. . . . Well, let's see."

Before the Motzans invaded Volyen, we had offered a lift to anyone who would leave. Grice was hanging around the courts, a lean, green, cadaverous figure with rapt eyes, who muttered incessantly phrases like: "If a equals b, then c must equal d. If you take a pound of pickled peppers then it follows as the night the day that . . . Let A stand for Truth, and B for Lies, then C is . . ."

We took him, Incent and I, by the arms so that he would be conscious of our being there, and said, "Grice, you are ill. Come with us."

"Ill? I'm Governor Grice, and I'm suing Volyen for . . . Who's that? Oh, it's you, Incent. Did the Trial go against us? It's you, Klorathy? But I'm in the right, aren't I? Just look at me, Klorathy; look, Incent. What a mess! It's all their fault. If just once in my life I'd been taken in hand and made to face up to anything . . ."

"We'll take you in hand, Grice, don't worry," said Incent, nearly succumbing to his emotions because of Grice's state.

"After all, there's nothing wrong with my genetic codes! I had them checked! So why does *everything* I touch go wrong?"

"Not everything, Gricey," said Incent, stroking and patting him. "You may think that was a bit of a farce in there, but—"

"A farce, you say? It was the only constructive thing I've ever done in my life."

"Yes, yes, and one of these V-years, but that will be long after we both are dead—"

"And the sooner the soil of Volyen is rid of my useless weight . . ."

"Yes, yes, yes," said Incent. "But I was going to say that all that nonsense in there, it will one day lead to those Peers of yours' establishing a new way of—"

"Nonsense, yes, that's it. I'm the stuff that nonsense is made of."

I arranged for his transportation to Volyendesta and had him taken to the Hospital for Rhetorical Diseases.

In a large white room, with a plain black floor, and no furnishings but some simple chairs, and of course our Logics, we found Grice sitting all by himself. Clearly he was already much improved, and absorbed in his therapy:

PATTERNS OF SOCIO-LOGIC

I   If a certain ruler is by definition in the right, because he incarnates the forward thrust of History, then a failure in an assignment set by him, or his ministers, by definition is an act of hostility to History itself. Using socio-rhetorical measurements, calculate what punishments are appropriate.

    1) Death.   2) Severe torture.   3) Imprisonment.

II Since none of us know the results of our actions, calculate the penalties appropriate for doing anything at all.

    1) Death.   (Obviously there can be only one answer to this question.)

III In the Shikastan Northwest fringes, there was a period when females were deemed to be wicked according to criteria (verbal formulae) arbitrarily established by a male religious ruling class, tortured to make them confess, and then burned to death. Their families, if any, or what possessions they might have had, were made to pay for, or sold to pay for, the cost of the firewood used to burn them with, as well as the time and efforts of the interrogators and the executioners.

This beautiful, matchless example of Logic only gives up its treasures to an effort of real contemplation. Contemplate it and then discuss.

IV Read *The Thoughts of President Motz*. Then, extending Sirian "Virtue" in its various dimensions, assess the degree of Subjective and Objective Guilt in the following story:

A devoted supporter of the Party of Virtue makes an error of judgment that causes several million people to die from starvation, his or her stated objective and intention being to establish a Rule of Virtue designed to better the lot of these same millions.

V Calculate how many moves on the Logistic Spiral it needs to get from "This person is an embodiment of the finest flower of the class of Virtue" to "Look at what has just crawled out of the woodwork!"

VI Calculate on the Logistic Spiral the parameters of: "He who is not with us is against us." Discuss.

VII Draw, paint, sculpt, or in some other way portray your conception of the Logic of History.

VIII Thesis: Sirian Virtue by definition must improve whichever parts of the Galaxy it reaches.

Antithesis: But in fact it spreads tyranny, misery, enslavement and deprivation.

Synthesis: ?

Grice looked very much better. He was sallow and hollow-faced still, but knew at once who we were, and greeted us cheerfully.

"This planet is about to be invaded," I said.

"Wouldn't you know it," he moaned, relapsing. "Of course, as soon as I get here, where I can feel it's doing me good, then naturally Sirius is going to invade. What else could you expect?"

"I'm afraid you are far from cured," I said. "But it isn't going to be Sirius. So cheer up."

"Oh, you mean about my being a spy!" he said, sulking. "Well, I've been thinking quite a bit about it. If a spy is one who betrays his country's interests, and if it turns out that actually, by some quirk or other of history—sorry, I mean dynamic of history—or by the logic of events, the said country is in the long run benefited by his actions . . ."

"You could feed the question into your Rhetorical Computers," I said.

But he will be all right.

The planet Motz, demoralized, confused, unable to prescribe remedies for itself, remembers Grice, who sat in the stolen library reading, Grice talking of socio-economic laws, Grice, who they thought was a madman.

They want to invite him back as an adviser on Comparative Planetology. I shall advise him to accept.

Since Ormarin is still away, I am taking the opportunity to "dry out." It is no good pretending that I have been unaffected by the plu-super-emotionality of recent events. Incent too feels in need of a respite. We shall become voluntary patients in Basic Rhetoric, Withdrawal-of-All-Stimuli Department. The tall, dim, silent, isolated room in the hotel on Volyen is inspired by it.

ORMARIN TO KLORATHY.

My information is that you are on Volyendesta. I received this news with considerable lightening of my spirits. It is no use disguising from you that I am deeply perturbed by certain rumours of which I am sure you must have cognizance. I refer, of course, to those concerning a possible invasion of this planet. I acknowledge freely that you have been warning me of this eventuality, and I and my colleagues have been taking every step within our power to make our defences viable. But recently our agents have been sending in reports of advance formations of skyborne troops which have been seen more than once over the Inland Desert Area. That is to say, formations of *individual* soldiers who, if the reports can be credited, arrive by sky-freighter and subsequently are released to become airborne *under their own power*. I would very much value your galactic advice. I was under the impression I knew all the different species under the Sirian hegemony—which I understand in any case is not what it was?—yet neither I nor any of my colleagues have heard of a species with wings.

KLORATHY TO JOHOR,
ENCLOSING THE ABOVE.

This letter showed me that, no matter how much Ormarin had changed while becoming—in fact, if not in name—ruler of the planet, he had not become any less of an official.

It showed me too that I have been careless, have not taken the trouble to reflect on how the PE 70 (Maken) armies must be experienced here. In what is for us such a short time, for them such a long one, PE 70 have made a change in their functioning which amounts to a social, if not a genetic, leap forward in evolution. A species of flying creature, hardy and adaptable, and widespread all over PE 70, have been taken by them into a partnership or social osmosis. PE 70 is poor in transport and working animals. They lack a species that can be deliberately evolved in this direction. The flying Pipisaurus supplies this lack, carrying loads over long distances, supplying them with skins, which they use for clothing and for a variety of domestic products, and with a glandular secretion that has extended the not-very-prolific foods of the planet, so that you may find in some areas that they eat and drink nothing but this secretion, prepared in various ways. So close and so harmonious is the partnership between the two species that an infant of the superior species is given his or her own pipisaur at birth, and the two grow up together, sharing sleeping and living space, though not often food. The Pipisaurus is by nature a bird- and insect-eater, and therefore these animals cannot be allowed to breed unchecked: there was a time when Maken had almost no birds or insects left, because of the great flocks of pipisaurs. The practice of supplying each infant with an infant pipisaur, but allowing no more, serves as a check on numbers. You will easily imagine the closeness of the bond, and, if one or the other of the partner dies, how great is the loss; often the survivor will languish and die, or kill itself.

Under Volyen, Maken was regarded mainly as a supplier of pipisaurian products for the elites of the Volyen "Empire." It was also a favourite holiday place, being regarded as backward and primitive: the effete ruling classes of Volyen enjoyed visiting planets whose inhabitants could be seen in close relation to primary physical mechanisms, and stories and pictures of the "barbarians" and their flocks were of great sentimental interest.

Under Volyen, the planet was not allowed an army. The truth is, Volyen was afraid of soldiers who can operate on land and in the air with equal ease. Secretly, however, an army was trained. The practice that each pipisaur had its place beside its mistress or master, living in the same dwelling, meant that the training and the arming of guerrilla troops was almost invisible to the Volyen overlords.

It was Maken that first overthrew Volyen, and did it easily, because of the effectiveness of its armies. Maken assisted Slovin to expel Volyen, and then, you will not be surprised to hear, stayed on Slovin to "assist": in other words, Maken is now the effective ruler of Slovin. Maken is at the beginning of its career as an Empire, an Empire that will conquer the near planets, now in a state of chaos and civil war, that were so recently subjects of Sirius. But Maken does not know this, has no such plans. Maken sees itself as virtuous, as indeed an embodiment of Virtue, the heir of Sirian Virtue.

The faction on Maken that overthrew the Volyen forces there called itself "Sirius." Maken has no knowledge at all of the ruthlessness of Sirius, of the arbitrary, capricious cruelty that characterizes its last days. Maken's idealistic young had heard tales of this "Virtue," had been captivated by the language of nobility, by the rumours of a golden age, by Justice, by Liberty, by Freedom, by—of course—the Logics of History, and the rest. It was with songs of Sirian Virtue that Maken freed, and then captured Slovin. As the armies of Maken train in the skies over Maken and over Slovin—and recently, daringly, in the deserts of Volyendesta—they sing of Virtue, and their war cries promise Peace and Plenty.

But I had not given myself time to think of how all this must strike poor Ormarin, who had never seen flying animals larger than his hand or his head, has never imagined animals as colleagues—more, friends, blood friends, for when an infant is given his or her pipisaur, and this before either can properly walk, the adults cut a vein on both, so that the blood may flow between them.

I went to meet Ormarin in a slave camp, on a plain between mountains where grew plantations of a certain berry that they use as a stimulating beverage. The slaves provide the labour for the plantations. The camp, consisting of identical rows of small single-room dwellings, each with a boxlike outbuilding for the disposal of bodily wastes, stretched out of sight in every direction. I stood there in its centre, waiting. The slaves, or ex-slaves, were all from Sirian Planet 181, and have never bred with any but their own kind, so that in the camps you see only these very tall, lithe, long-limbed creatures, of a uniform pale yellow: their height and their immensely long arms are of use in picking the berries. S 181 is a planet that has not been invaded, and its inhabitants have evolved uniformly. Standing there, I felt an unfamiliar sensation that I diagnosed as the dullness resulting from lack of variety or stimulus. Everywhere around me these tall, yellow, spindly people with their black eyes, so alike. As I waited for Ormarin to come to me, I reflected that in the streets of this planet's cities you may watch its people passing for hours, and never see a face repeated or a bodily shape the same as another. So long has Volyendesta been invaded, settled, "protected," so long has it invaded other planets, so long and thoroughly have the genes been stirred and mingled and added to and inspired and excited by new material, that the natives have no general type or sort; they are tall and thin and blue-eyed and fair-haired, they are short and fat and dark-haired and black-eyed, they are of every skin colour from creamy white to glossy black, they are of every conceivable mix of these characteristics. I never tire of sitting in a Volyendestan public place and watching the infinite inventiveness of our galaxy. And it is not only the natives: Volyen's settlers are just as varied, because Volyen itself has been conquered and invaded, has invaded and conquered. The Volyen settlers and the natives have bred together for fifteen V-centuries. These two planets, Volyen and Volyendesta, have as variegated inhabitants as any I have encountered anywhere in the Galaxy. An inhabitant of Volyendesta will take it for granted that he will never, or hardly ever, see two individuals who resemble each other; if two are alike, then it is a matter for comment.

The slaves from S 181, the other slaves imported by Volyen, the slaves used by Sirius on road-building and spacecraft landing places, are kept in camps by themselves and are hardly seen by ordinary people.

And I began to understand, standing there, the unease, even the repugnance, often expressed by the Volyendestans. "They are as if stamped out of the same material by the same mould," is the complaint.

But what of the Makens? What were the Volyendestans going to see when they invaded?

Ormarin came to meet me through the huts of the camp, by himself. I knew that these days he was seldom without a group of "colleagues," his entourage, so I knew that he was still afraid I might be taken for a Sirian spy.

He was smoking his pipe and had on his face a friendly comradely grin.

This business of the pipe: admiration for Ormarin has spread the practice of pipe-smoking. From end to end of this planet, the inhabitants have had small stiff wooden objects in their mouths that emit smoke. Volyendesta has not as many forests as it would like; as wood became short, other substances have been used. An outward sign of inner calm, solidity, and sense ceases to be of use when an entire population employs it, so a law has been passed that only officials above a certain rank may smoke pipes. So now you may pick out the higher-ranking officials in any crowd by the pipes they smoke. Smoking has become, you will not be surprised to hear, a secret ritual in the camps of the slaves. All kinds of statements are made by the way a pipe is lit, held, filled with weed; the way the smoke is allowed to emerge from the bowl of the pipe. A superior will show his good will or benevolence by inviting an inferior to join in a ritual of smoking on a special occasion.

"Will you smoke?" was the first thing Ormarin asked me, and we stood there together, surrounded by the ugly little dwellings of the S 181 slaves, he smoking, I not.

This large bluff personage, when examined, showed only signs of unease.

"Ormarin," I said, "I will now describe your situation to you. Stop me if I go wrong. . . . You have been travelling all over your planet, uniting slaves and citizens, Volyendestans and former Volyens, refugees and Sirian officials who have settled here—you have united the planet in a single-minded, passionate determination to defend yourselves against invasion."

"Right!" he said, standing foursquare, his grey eyes full on mine, his mouth gripped tight over his jetting pipe-stem, while the embers in it glowed red and then faded, glowed, and faded.

"You are about to defend yourselves against Sirius—"

"It was you who said Sirius would invade."

"In the name of Sirius you will be invaded, by troops who will use nothing that Sirius made to facilitate invasion—they will not use roads, or even spaceports."

He nodded. "You made a mistake, then?"

"If I had known exactly which planet was going to invade you, then there is no preparation I could have advised that could help you except a psychological one."

As he stood thinking soberly, his pipe, which he did not actually enjoy, dangled from his hand at his side.

"Well, at least we've united the planet," he said, "if nothing else."

"And you are going to fight to the last drop of everybody's blood?"

"What else?" he demanded, again puffing furiously so that he stood in a swirling cloud. "I suppose whichever planet it is this time is just as bad as the Sirians? Don't tell me we've got to put up with all that guff about the Virtue again?"

"I'm afraid so."

"Do you know, I think I'd settle for a boss planet that described itself as bloody-minded, ruthless, and only out for what it could get. I think one more dose of all that Virtue will do me in."

"What's in a word?" I asked, not without a certain moral weariness.

"At any rate, we won't have to learn a new vocabulary for the new rulers."

"Why do you take it for granted you will be defeated?" I asked.

"I don't know—it's because of the reports of those, *what are they,*

Klorathy? Half man, half bird? I've never even imagined . . . I can tell you, I'm scared stiff! I'll admit it to you, though I wouldn't to my mates, of course. . . ." And he looked quite exhausted with terror, shrunken with it. "I know we inhabitants of the Galaxy run to some pretty queer shapes and sizes. I mean, it took me a while to get used to this lot. . . ." And we looked, together, at people from S 181 standing all around us, watching curiously but with that passive, withdrawn, waiting look that marks a subordinate population biding its time. The tall, immensely thin creatures, with this dull yellow skin, their round black glistening eyes . . . "Compared with bird-men, this lot here are our twins!"

"Ormarin, they aren't bird-men. . . ." And I explained about the relationship the Makens have with their beasts. I saw Ormarin's face twist up in disgust, and then with fear. "You tell me that these people have animals in their homes with them?"

"A Maken will sleep with his head on the side of his pipisaur."

"And they eat these animals' secretions?"

"Sometimes nothing else. Can you imagine the closeness of the bond?"

"I don't want to," said Ormarin, looking sick. "I simply don't want to think about it."

"Very well. But what you have to think about is this—how to limit their influence here, their power. And you can."

"If one planet invades another, it is not for anything but the loot!"

"There is very little you have that will interest them. If it had been Sirius, yes. Your plantations here; they planned to make on Volyendesta vast plantations of the berry. They were going to use you too, because of your extraordinarily varied genetic mix, for all kinds of social experiments. But Maken is millenniums away from an interest in social thought. They are not yet conscious of themselves in that way. Their strength, the Pipisaurus, is their weakness. They can only function now within this bond. They see themselves only in relation to their beasts. They will invade other planets and take only what will benefit Maken from this point of view."

"And what will?"

"Very little. They are looking for birds and insects to take back and try out on Maken so that they may allow themselves to breed more pipisaurs. They see this animal as their wealth, their only wealth. And as they are now, this animal *is* their wealth, their strength, their centre of affection, of emotion."

"And their weakness!"

"Yes, because they will find all kinds of new birds, new flying things, even small mammals they will introduce to their beasts' diet. Their flocks will increase—no longer will the ratio of one Maken to one beast be observed—there will soon be vast herds or flocks of pipisaurs who have no ties of affection with the Makens, and they will declare themselves independent, for they are intelligent and in rapid evolution, and there will be the most terrible civil war on Maken. But all that is a long way in the future, in your time scale. It will not concern you, that time when the Maken Empire will be a rule not of Makens as we know them, but of pipisaurs. That will be a terrible rule indeed. . . . Your immediate problem is how to allow the Makens to land, how to welcome them, how to *invite* some of them to stay as your guests, how to give them what they want without depleting yourselves, how to change those that stay, for some will want to stay, so that they become as flexible and open-minded as in fact you are, how to wait until they go, or, rather, until one day you realize you have not been visited for a long time by the Maken forces, and that those of them that are here are like you, that you have so absorbed them, that Volyendesta is in fact independent, though nominally a part of the Maken Empire. . . ."

"Are we never to be independent?" he groaned.

"Yes, as good as. And quite soon."

"They'll never stand for it," he objected. He was thinking of his long travels over the planet, talking of defence, bloodshed, willing martyrdom.

"Yes, they will. You try it."

And so Incent and I will be travelling with Ormarin and his colleagues all over Volyendesta, to prepare the Volyendestans for a sight, for an experience, which without preparation they could only find appalling, horrifying, even to the point of total inner collapse.

THE HISTORY OF THE VOLYEN EMPIRE,
VOLUME 97, PART III:
THE INVASION OF VOLYENDESTA BY
MAKEN. (WRITTEN BY KLORATHY.)

The inhabitants of Volyendesta waited for the Makens calmly, having been well prepared by Ormarin. Agents gave them warning of the approach of the spaceships. These vast structures, each designed to hold a thousand Makens with their beasts, lay in the atmosphere above the planet for some time, looking like solid silvery clouds. All over Volyendesta, well-organized and self-disciplined crowds stood looking up, anxious to see what had been described to them, though even at this last moment they found it hard to believe.

Small black apertures appeared in the bodies of the carriers, and from each dropped out small black dots that formed themselves into blocks of a hundred each. They were too high to be seen as more than dots, but soon these blocks, or companies, dropped swiftly down, and what came into sight were the "bird-men" of the rumours. This was the moment when panic might have—but did not—set in. Lower and lower they fell, and the sky was regularly patterned with the flying horrors. . . . The Pipisaurus is like a furred lizard, but with a heavy, blunt beak, and on each, as close as if growing from it, was a Maken dressed in pipisaurian fur, his head inside a cap that was the head of a pipisaur, ears, beak, complete: the savage, heavy heads of the beasts, and above them the same beaked heads, as if each beast had two heads. Down, down they came, thousands upon thousands, all over the planet, and the sound of the wings, which were black membranes stiffened with slender rods of bones, was a beating, fluttering, drumming that disturbed the air, that hurt the hearing, so that everywhere could be seen people with hands over their ears, trying to shut out the sound even while they peered and strained to see.

When the Makens were a few measures above the surface, they hovered there so that everyone could see them very clearly. The Makens had learned, to their surprise and pleasure, how terrifying their opponents found the appearance they made.

Close to, these double-headed bird-animals, with their terrible weapons of beaks, their hard glittering eyes, their thick black fur, their clapping thunderous wings, their claws, were even more awful than the Volyendestans had been warned they would be. Yet they stood their ground, did not allow panic to show, remained quiet and undisturbed in outward demeanour.

Before the Makens could land on the earth, Ormarin came forward —just as representatives were doing all over the planet—and began on a speech of welcome.

"Fellow victims of Volyen! Fellow Colonials! We, the second colonized planet of Volyen, welcome you, the third planet to be Volyen's victim, on our soil. Please land, please come forward, and allow us to extend to you our sincere greetings . . ." and so on.

In the midst of these speeches, the bird-men alighted, folded their wings, and waited. Each company had a leader, who jumped off his beast and stood beside it. There was a moment of indecision. On the back of each beast were tied weapons of all kinds, for the Maken spy system was as yet very poorly developed and they had believed that as soon as they landed they would have to fight for their existence. But they were faced with quiet and even friendly crowds, and speeches of welcome.

The weapons were taken off the backs of the beasts, but were held loosely, not aggressively. Meanwhile, the Volyendestans were observing this development: by each beast now stood the beast's other half, an upright two-legged creature, in shape and structure not unlike the other inhabitants of the Galaxy, not unlike the Volyendestans. But it was too soon, with the Makens still inside the tight furred singlets and trousers, inside the great headpieces, for the Volyendestans to see—and this was what the Volyendestans really could not understand, what they were always to remain uneasy about—how absolutely like each other they are.

At last, the Maken company commanders conferred, decided to send back to Maken for orders, allowed themselves to play the part of welcomed guests, left their weapons to sit loosely in the crooks of their arms—and took off their headpieces. The Volyendestans were dismayed by these short, rather lumpy, furred creatures, with round, smooth, yellow, bare heads—they shaved them—and smooth, round, yellowish faces, in which were slantingly set small black eyes that had no eyebrows or lashes. Smooth, dark, furred animals with maggot-like heads, and they were all alike. Although they had been told, had been prepared for uniformity by observation of the slaves from S 181, Volyendestans could not take it in, were uncomfortable, did not know where to look; and then did look, with relief and appreciation, at themselves, at one another, resting their eyes and their understandings on their own infinite variety, on hair yellow and brown and red and silver and black, on skins that were white and cream and grey and pink and yellow and brown and black; they could not get enough of gazing at one another, and marvelling at the infinite ranges of shape and size and texture, and at the surprises and amazingness of what they were. And then looked again at the Makens, who, having taken off their tight, smooth fur bodysuits, showed themselves as roundish, sturdy, smooth-yellow-skinned people, with their roundish, slit-eyed yellowish faces. All alike. All, all, absolutely alike. There might be a minimal difference in height, in thickness, and if their faces were examined hopefully for variegation, for a slight difference in the set of a feature, a mouth, then minor differences could in fact be seen.

Never had Volyendesta been so united, and it was by their own appreciation of themselves, the richnesses of their heritage.

Meanwhile, festivities, speeches: and when the Makens were tired, they were led to recently constructed barracks, most thoughtfully designed to accommodate soldiers with their beasts, though food for the beasts had indeed proved a problem. And this led at once to discussions—suggested by Ormarin, whose large, solid, bluff, sensible presence was everywhere—on how to supply the Makens' need, of which this planet had heard long ago and which the Volyendestans wanted only to accommodate, out of the sympathy one colonized planet must feel for another, on new strains of animals and birds and insects that could be adapted for the pipisaurs.

The Makens did not know how to take it all. Not the most sophisticated, the most agile-minded of peoples, they had expected a sharp and unpleasant war of conquest, which they meant to win, and then . . . but then what? On Slovin they had landed as allies, and then had taken over. They had not fought there either. Secretly they longed for war, wanted to see if their horrid appearance—as they now knew it was—would indeed stun terrified opponents. But having conquered a new planet, what then? The Makens were every bit as uneasy as their "hosts." They spent all their waking moments on their beasts. They woke beside their friends, embraced them, exchanged licks and kisses; then the Makens were on their beasts' backs and off into the air, until enough birds had been caught and eaten (on the wing) to satisfy the pipisaurs, or they ran everywhere over the ground, the great clawed legs bounding and leaping, until the strong beaks had speared up enough insects (on Maken, often the size of a Maken infant) to fill them. And then the day was spent, most often, in the air: all kinds of games and tournaments and sports went on up there. And, on the ground, races and sports again. Twice in the day a brief meal was taken, sometimes drunk straight from the glands of the pipisaurs, sometimes eaten on the beasts' backs.

On this planet, Volyendesta, halfhearted attempts were made to live as on Maken. But it was not the same. For one thing, the atmosphere was not identical, and the Makens felt lethargic. And then, while the Makens enjoyed the idea that other planets thought them terrifying, they did not seem to themselves terrifying, and it was awkward to try to enjoy themselves with so many Volyendestans gawking and staring: not with terror, it was true, but, rather, as if they found them, the Makens, repulsive or in some way unlikable. And then, the Makens felt the obverse for the Volyendestans of what the Volyendestans felt for them: at first they could not believe, and then they could not become used to crowds of people who were all so different from one another. Wasn't there something off-putting . . . no, unpleasant, even *wrong* about it? How could there be any fellow-feeling, any real togetherness, among people who, when they looked at one another must see something so different from themselves that surely they must carry around mirrors to look in so as to reassure themselves that their own appearances were as valid, as good, as *right* as what they saw? How awful—thought the Makens—it must be to belong to a planet so constituted that there was no pleasant, easy-going, *natural*, and *right* similarity of appearance. How awful it must be always to be adjusting yourselves to differences, instead of reposing comfortably in the knowledge that everyone was of the same kind. And some Makens even took to sneaking off to the slave camps, to rest their sight on masses of people who looked like one another. And again there was this business of having these satisfactory, right people shut away together in camps as slaves, as if they were worse than the so wildly various and differentiated ones.

When asked, Ormarin said it was not so, they were no longer slaves now that Volyen had gone, now that the Mother Planet of Sirius— yes, yes, we know you have inherited the mantle of the Virtue, but Sirius brought in these slaves, they were not our invention—now we are ourselves again, and independent, slavery will not be tolerated.

At this information, that the—surely?—conquered planet of Volyendesta considered itself independent, the conquerors again applied to Maken itself for instructions, and were told to establish an occupying force, to liberate any species that might prove useful, and to return home. Only too thankfully, the Maken armies did this. Speeches, celebrations, even a few embraces. Not all Volyendestans found all Makens repulsive. There would soon be a strain of Maken in the planet's genetic inheritance; a pleasant thought for them all, and even more pleasant now that they had learned how sad a state of affairs it is when a planet's inhabitants can all look alike.

And the spaceships came and stood everywhere over Volyendesta, and the Makens put on their fur suits and their beaked headdresses and leaped onto their animals' backs, and again the sky was filled with the terrible double-headed beasts whose wings made the air flutter and beat and vibrate so that the ears hurt, and up they flew in their hundreds to the spaceships, and small black dots could be seen vanishing one after another into the black holes in the bellies of the craft. And then the spaceships were gone, the skies of Volyendesta were empty.

The "occupying force," not at all pleased at being left here in this polyglot, overfriendly, difficult little planet, nevertheless soon made comfortable circumstances for themselves, slept and ate with (and off) their beasts, continued their games and sports and entertainments, and soon found the place not so bad after all. Yes, perhaps it had been a bit limiting never to see anyone but people exactly like yourself, always to be part of a symbiosis with pipisaurs.

Quite soon, Maken more or less forgot about Volyendesta. The Makens on Volyendesta ceased to be Makens.

The roads, the spaceports, all the amenities created by Sirius for its own use, made Volyendesta rich and prosperous. Of the four colonized planets of Volyen, this was the planet that enjoyed the longest period of peace, independence, and prosperity before—as always happened during that phase of galactic history—it lost its independence to a stronger planet. But that is not part of this history.

KLORATHY TO JOHOR,
FROM HIS SPACE TRAVELLER,
EN ROUTE TO SHAMMAT.

Unfortunately I was overoptimistic about poor Incent, who has had a relapse. Convinced that it is his mission to reform Krolgul, he . . .